Relentless

Books by Brian Garfield

Fiction

RELENTLESS

DEEP COVER

WHAT OF TERRY CONNISTON?

THE VILLIERS TOUCH

GUN DOWN

SWEENY'S HONOR

THE HIT

SLIPHAMMER

VALLEY OF THE SHADOW

THE LAST BRIDGE

THE VANQUISHED

TRAIL DRIVE

APACHE CANYON

THE LAST OUTLAW

HIGH STORM
(with Theodore V. Olsen)

VULTURES IN THE SUN

SEVEN BRAVE MEN

THE LAWBRINGERS

THE ARIZONANS

RANGE JUSTICE

Nonfiction

THE THOUSAND-MILE WAR:
World War II in Alaska and the Aleutians

Relentless

Brian Garfield

C. 1

WORLD PUBLISHING
TIMES MIRROR
NEW YORK

Published by The World Publishing Company
Published simultaneously in Canada
by Nelson, Foster & Scott Ltd.

First printing—1972

Copyright © 1972 by Brian Garfield
All rights reserved
ISBN 0-529-04549-4
Library of Congress catalog card number: 71-159586
Printed in the United States of America
Designed by Jacques Chazaud

WORLD PUBLISHING
TIMES MIRROR

For Jim and Linda
—May your house be free
of Kavanagh's displeasure.

Relentless

CHAPTER

1

This stretch always tempted the drivers who had Le Mans fixations: it came down off the mountain like a ski slope and two-laned straight out across the twenty-mile flat below.

It was a Friday forenoon at the dying end of October. The aspen forest had turned gold. Watchman and Stevens lay in wait in the Roadside Rest Area, parked under the trees. There wasn't a billboard to hide behind but the ritual was the same. Under the molten brass sun the shadows were black and had sharp edges; drivers barreling down the highway wouldn't spot the cruiser until it had them nailed.

Downstate on more populous roads you could poke along five miles under the limit and gather a clot of traffic tamed and intimidated by the presence of your Highway Patrol car, and it would create a chain wave of caution that would slow them down for miles ahead and behind. But up in this corner

1

of Arizona you seldom got more than one car in half an hour and the strategy of Visible Presence didn't work. They had put Watchman and the rookie on this beat four months ago and it had been easy to size up: State Highway 793 was the only through route in the district but it was wide open for a hundred and fifty miles. Watchman had planted the word with gas stations and cafés from the mountains to the Nevada line and now the tourists were getting the warnings: *You want to watch out, there's a cop car posted somewheres between here and the Nevada border—speed trap, watch your step.* Up here they didn't assign a ticket quota and Watchman didn't care about writing up violations but back in August a Cadillac going down this stretch at a hundred and five had dropped a tie rod and they had spent two hours with a blowtorch scraping the remains of the five passengers out of the wreckage. Now the word had spread and the road had been tamed, except for the occasional drunk and a few hot-rod tourists on their way to Las Vegas who hadn't got the word.

Trooper Stevens shook up his bottle of root beer and spouted foam into his mouth from six inches away. "This sucks. I've had more fun watching TV test patterns."

"Possibly you'd rather work for a living?"

"Typical lazy Inyun remark."

Watchman gave him a pained look. "For you I pay taxes?"

"Join the Highway Patrol, see the world. Glamour, excitement, thrills!"

Sam Watchman slid down in the driver's seat until he was sitting on the back of his neck and his knees butted the steering column. He cupped a brown hand around the back of his neck and reared his head back lazily. He hadn't expected to like working with the rookie—he'd never had a partner before —but it was working out. What Buck Stevens didn't know about the job could fill a thick manual but he was good-humored and he was flexible and in the end, when push came to shove, that was what counted: flexibility.

"Just about time to break for lunch," Stevens said. "Oh joy. Another vulcanized steak sandwich at Holcombe's."

"No. We'll go into town today. I've got to pick up something at the jeweler's."

Lisa . . .

There was a radio call, description of stolen car; Stevens wrote it down at the bottom of the week's list. The speaker sputtered out, "Ten Four," and Watchman straightened up and reached for the ignition key. "Okay, lunch." The Fury's starter popped and the engine began to hum.

That was when the speeder shot past: a baroque old oil burner of a Buick, chromium-laden, overstuffed, covered with stickers—*It's Your Flag Love It Or Leave It; These Colors Do Not Run; Grand Canyon National Park*—traveling at relentless speed, swaying across the white line, the bored driver's left hand hooked outside against the vent window in the slipstream.

"Jesus," Buck Stevens said. "Craig Breedlove trying for the land speed record again."

Watchman slid the Fury out onto the highway and gave chase. He pushed it up to ninety-five and Stevens said, "We're not gaining on him."

Watchman drawled gently. "Might be a good idea to clock him first, don't you think?"

A crimson flush suffused the rookie's face up to the blond hairline.

"Plenty of time. Get on the mileposts, I've got the speedometer."

Stevens got out the clipboard. "Christ, I'm sorry, Sam."

"No charge."

"All right. Mile zero."

The road had a high crown and blacktop patches where road crews had filled in last winter's chuckholes. Watchman had both hands full keeping the cruiser on the road and he was a graduate of the California pursuit driving course, and that clown up ahead was driving one-handed.

"Mile One. Shee-yit." Stevens checked his watch and scribbled a calculation on the clipboard pad. "Ninety-seven and a fraction."

"Confirmed," Watchman said, and flicked his eyes up from the speedometer. "Hold your hat."

He floored the pedal and switched on the rooftop dome flasher. No point turning on the siren because at this speed the Buick wouldn't hear it. The wind was a blast in his left ear, bouncing off the foothills and buffeting the road across the gaps. At a hundred and ten he was gaining on the Buick, not rapidly, but there wasn't a crossroad in thirteen miles and there was plenty of time. The Buick had got a jump on them and it took four or five minutes to get up close but evidently the driver of the Buick had no use for his rear view mirror and Watchman had to pull out alongside and blow the horn at him. When he saw the thin shoulders jerk and the narrow face shift toward him he dropped back quickly because the fool was likely to panic and he didn't want to be in the way if the Buick slewed across the road.

But the Buick slowed well, with just a touch of brakes, and when Watchman parked on the shoulder behind it Stevens said, "I'll give him credit. He's good."

"Good and dead if he hit anything bigger than a jack rabbit at that speed."

"Can I tag this one, kemo sabe?"

"Go ahead, paleface."

Stevens' face was still a little red. He reached for the door handle. Up front the driver had got out of the Buick and was standing with his hands in his pockets and his face wreathed in saturnine disgust.

"Give him the cheesecake," Watchman said. He slipped one of the three-by-five glossies out of the envelope. It was a good sharp photo of the remains they had torched out of the Cadillac. He had bought six dozen copies from the police lab. "Don't let him rile you."

"I'll tell him if he don't behave I got a wild-eyed partner who'd just as soon lift his scalp." Stevens left the door open and walked over with his clipboard. Watchman saw the way the driver sized up the rookie—thinking about asking if twenty dollars cash would take care of it, and rejecting the thought at close sight of Stevens' earnest young varsity pass-receiver's face.

A few years back Watchman had been a rookie himself, partnering in a cruiser with a veteran hairbags trooper named Custis, and when they had pulled over a stop-sign runner and Watchman had started to make out the first moving-violation ticket of his career the driver had shown the edge of a twenty-dollar bill and lifted his eyebrows inquiringly. Watchman had gone back to the cruiser full of excitement and told Custis about it: "We can arrest the son of a bitch for attempted bribery, Fred."

"You crazy? I'll handle it." Custis had left him behind and gone over to talk to the man and Watchman had seen the money change hands. When Custis had returned he'd offered to split the money with Watchman. Watchman had refused and Custis had said, "Gee, thanks, Sam, that's white of you," and launched into a hard-luck story about his wife and kids and how much he needed the money.

Now Fred Custis was a Captain in Phoenix and Sam Watchman was a line trooper overdue for promotion and assigned to the dullest hick bailiwick in the state, and there was a connection between those two facts. Fred Custis handled beat assignments and Fred Custis didn't like Watchman. It had something to do with the fact that Watchman was a fullblood Navajo. Something. Well that was all right too. Watchman didn't itch to set the world on fire. You just did your job and went through each day at a steady pace. In the end it would take you longer than it would take a white man but if you did the job well enough you'd get the promotions sooner or later and that would be good for Sam Watchman and good for The People too. And in the meantime you'd get married and move into the cute little two-bedroom in Flagstaff and maybe have a kid or two, with your black-olive eyes and Lisa's blinding smile.

The rusty wreckage of a pickup truck came rattling up the road from the direction of San Miguel and the cowboy driver gave Watchman a cold look on his way past. Watchman wrote up the time and milepost location in his daybook and checked down the stolen-car list but the old Buick wasn't on it. The car had local plates and he had a feeling he'd seen it, maybe parked up in Fredonia or Marble Canyon. He'd never seen the driver. The man was rawboned, dressed in khaki trousers and a thin windbreaker with sleeves six inches too short for him. He had a sardonic look and he wasn't arguing, just standing there waiting for Stevens to finish writing up the ticket. Once the man turned his wrist over to look at his watch and Watchman saw a large pale weal of hairless flesh running up the wrist and forearm—the scar of a bad burn. It was instantly noticeable, the kind of "Identifying Marks or Scars" you loved to be able to put out on a fugitive description, but by the same token you wouldn't forget a feature that striking and Watchman knew he had never come across it in a mug book. He played this game with himself to test his own diligence, studying faces everywhere he went; once in Holbrook he had spotted a wanted man walking across a gas station apron and had arrested the man on the spot. It had earned him a citation but no promotion.

Stevens tore out the ticket and handed it to the man, gave back the driver's license and registration, and stepped back while the driver got into the Buick and drove away sedately.

When Stevens got into the cruiser he said, "He didn't even bother with a preamble. Just asked me, 'How much was I doing?' I told him ninety-seven and he just shook his head and smiled with half his mouth. Oddball kind of character. He must've had something on his mind."

"Any reason for the big hurry?"

"Said he had to get to the bank in San Miguel before closing time. Hell, he's got three hours yet." Stevens was writing up the tag. "Name of Baraclough. The car's registered to somebody named Sweeney in Fredonia. Baraclough's brother-in-law, he says."

"You have any reason to disbelieve him?"

Stevens looked up. The pencil paused. "I guess not."

"Only?"

"Only—I don't know. You can lose a lot of money playing hunches."

"You didn't push it, then?"

"How could I?"

"Never mind, then. Let's go on into town and eat."

2

They drove into San Miguel past the strip signs: MODERN CABINS—EAT—BAR & GRILL—AIR CONDITIONED —SALES AND SERVICE—ALL CARDS HONORED— REASONABLE RATES. It was a company town and it was the only town of any size on the plateau. The interstate highways had bypassed the region and it was untouched by mushrooming population because few living things could survive in it: in winter the snow drifted deep and in summer the heat could reach 135 degrees, and so the twenty-five thousand square miles were mostly uninhabited except for ranches, filling stations, crossroad bars, campgrounds, and the town here that had grown up around the big open-pit diggings of the San Miguel Copper Company. Most of the surrounding land was Federal—Reservations, National Forests. For active men and women San Miguel was a dead dull town; the mine and smelter employed 12,400 workers and a good many of them spent their weekends in Las Vegas, which was one hundred fifty miles away but the nearest entertainment available to them.

The main street was nine blocks of parking meters and facelifted chain stores, a grain warehouse, used-car lots with flapping pennants, three gas stations, the company-owned San Miguel Bank & Trust, the Hollywood Beauty Salon ("What Price Beauty? Free Estimate!"). Rusty pickup trucks and muddy Chryslers were parked on the slant at a few meters and the clinging film of red dust coated everything—the display windows, the beer joints, the hamburger drive-in, the laundromat and the baroque old Paramount movie show with its Moorish marquee.

Watchman parked in front of the Copper King Café and plugged a nickel into the meter. "I'll meet you inside." He walked on past Woolworth's to the corner, turned by the bank entrance and went into Zane's Jewelers next door. Behind the glass counter the old man looked up from his watch-repair bench, jeweler's glass perched on top of his spectacles.

"So. You've come to ransom the ring? I thought it was about time." The old man got it out of the safe and Watchman bent over the countertop on his elbows, laboriously scrawling out the check in his crabbed hand. When he looked up the old man had placed the pale blue velvety case by his elbow.

The old man picked up the check and examined it as if he suspected its worth; held it up against the light, flapped it back and forth and blew on it, although Watchman's pen was a ballpoint.

Watchman popped the velvet lid open and the ring winked at him with all its facets.

"You gotch self a beauty there."

"I guess so," Watchman said. "It sure cost enough."

"Hell, I give it to you cheap. Anybody else had to pay a hundred more. Some of us appreciate what you people do for us." The old man said it accusingly. He filled out a receipt and pushed it across the counter.

Watchman gave it a wooden look. "At least us redskins only scalp enemies. You always skin your friends like this?"

The old man was hurt. "Sam—Sam!" He spread his hands wide in the Old World gesture of helplessness, head cocked to one side. "You can afford it, you've got a steady job."

"Aeah. The pay's bad, but the work's terrible." He snapped the little box shut and put it in his pocket. "Thanks." And went outside with his hand in the pocket touching the velvet-covered hardness of the ring case. Going around the corner he was picturing Lisa, her lovely eyes, the surprise of delight that would shine in them; he almost crashed into old Jasper Simalie on the bank steps.

"Jesus, Tsosie, you want to look out where you are going." Old Jasper was grinning.

"Yah'a'teh, Jasper?"

Jasper Simalie still had a full bush of hair, grayshot and thick but very short; he had a big round Navajo face, deep

square brackets creasing it right down past the mouth into the
big dependable jaw. He had put on a few pounds since they
had measured him for his guard's uniform and he was beginning to look a little like W. C. Fields as the Bank Dick, with
the grey seams straining around his shoulders and paunch. He
had a big forty-five in the black Army holster at his waist and
the policeman's cap was tipped far back on his head.

Watchman grinned and poked his jaw toward the café.
"Buy you a lunch."

"Naw. I got to es-stick close to the bank." Jasper indicated
the green armored truck parked across the street in the shade.
"It's the fourth Friday."

Every second and fourth Friday of the month the company-
owned bank had a heavy load of cash brought in from Salt
Lake to meet the payroll needs of the mine and smelter. On
weekends the casinos over in Vegas wouldn't accept out-of-
state payroll checks and San Miguel accommodated its employees by cashing their checks before they set out for the
Nevada weekend.

It was one of the regional facts of life they had impressed on
Watchman when they had assigned him to the district. At
first he hadn't believed the size of the sums involved but when
you worked it out it added up. You had more than twelve
thousand workers drawing down an average wage of two
hundred dollars a week. With a biweekly payroll that added
up to five million dollars every two weeks. If five thousand of
those men drew half their pay in cash that came to a round
million dollars, part of which made a one-way trip to Las
Vegas. Usually it didn't come to that much but the bank had
to prepare for the maximum and so every other Friday morning the armored truck brought in one million dollars in tens,
twenties, fifties and hundreds: largely hundreds, because the
big bills were popular with weekend gamblers. The truck
waited all day and after closing it would transport whatever

was left back to the head office in Salt Lake City. It was a long day's run and the Utah office provided maximum security: the armored truck carried four guards and was convoyed by two cars, one in front and one behind, each containing two armed men. The run itself was judged to be that risky. But once the money reached the San Miguel bank it appeared to be safe enough, partly because the eight armed guards and the driver hung around the bank all day but mostly because the single highway through town could be stoppered at both ends on five minutes' notice to prevent getaways. There were no other roads out. Not even dirt tracks. And the buckled terrain around the flats was impassable to anything but goats.

Even so, these Fridays were tense for old Jasper. He was the head guard: the safety of all that cash was his responsibility.

Jasper took it very seriously because it had taken him thirty-five years to work his way up to this job from a sheep-flock beginning in a hardscrabble back-country hogan forty miles from Kiacochomovi village on the Window Rock Reservation. Jasper and Sam Watchman's father had been Agency Policemen at Canyon de Chelly together; Jasper was like an uncle to Watchman and he still called Watchman by his Navajo name, which was Tsosie Duggai, and Watchman loved the fat old man with deep fond warmth.

Jasper flapped a hand toward the bank door. "I keep telling Mr. Whipple we ought to put in some of them bank protection devices. We going to get hit one day."

"I doubt it. More likely they'd go for the truck out on the highway someplace. Up in Utah."

"With all that armor plate and all them guards?"

"If they hit the bank how are they going to get out of here? You want to relax, Jasper."

"Maybe. I es-still think we ought to put in some cameras and bulletproof plexiglass panes for them tellers to work behind."

"You've got a good alarm system and a big gun on your belt. But I'll tell you what, Jasper, if you really want to keep the bad guys scared off maybe you ought to get yourself a feathered headdress and a tomahawk."

3

He stopped just outside the café and looked at the sky: he could smell a change in weather coming, a thin scent of winter in the air. The sky was clear cobalt, only a few cloud banks to the west, but there was a sharp chill to it and those clouds were advancing fast. Snowstorms sometimes hit the high plateau as early as the end of September and here it was the fourth Friday in October. It was a sudden country.

He went inside. The café was filled with the bass thumpings of Johnny Cash on the jukebox. "Custer's Last Fight" on the wall and denim buttocks arrayed in a row along the counter stools; high-top boots and cowboy hats. Ranch fresh eggs and chicken-fried steaks and the smell of fried grease. Over in a booth Buck Stevens was consuming a hamburger with lots of raw onions. Stevens was a wholesome kid with a square sturdy face and bright china-blue eyes that had an antic way of bobbing about, seldom missing much. He was going to make a good cop.

Jace Cunningham was there in the same booth, wolfing a sandwich, keeping his hat on while he ate. When Watchman reached the table Cunningham slid over into the corner without missing a mouthful and said something muffled that Watchman took to be an invitation to sit.

"How's it going, Jace?" He sat down and planted his elbows on the plastic table top.

Cunningham wore a business suit with an elaborate brazen badge pinned to the lapel. It looked like the kind of badge you could buy in the toy department at Woolworth's; it said "City Constable." Cunningham had a long spare body and a solemn little face. His skin was as freckled as knockwurst. He had been born fifty-three years old—dependable, proper, sober, deliberate. He was employed by the copper company as chief of police in San Miguel and he was one-fourth of its manpower.

The buxom blonde waitress came over and propped her left elbow into her waist to write in her pad. "Looks like a policemen's convention here. What'll it be, Trooper?"

Watchman studied the chalked menu on the blackboard above the counter. "How's the chili today?"

"I don't know. I ain't tried it."

Stevens was watching her and she was aware of his attention; she cocked her hip slightly.

"Maybe you ought to try it," Stevens said. "Might put hair on your chest."

"In a minute," she said in a tone laced with scorn, "I'm leaving. I can't take this police brutality."

Watchman said chili and coffee. When the girl went away, with a little extra swing in her walk because she knew Stevens was watching, Cunningham said, "They got snow over to Nevada last night. Like as not we'll catch some tonight. You two planning to stay up here or go on down to Flag?"

"Hadn't thought about it," Watchman said.

"Maybe you ought to. You don't want to get caught up in them high passes."

The diamond ring in its little box made a hard knot in his pocket and he said, "I guess we'll start back for Flag, then. All right with you, Buck?"

There was a rowdy flavor to the rookie's grin. "Snow hell. You just want to get back to Lisa and cozy up in Flag till it blows over. Snowstorm? Hah—red man speak with forked tongue."

Cunningham, with his mouth full, rolled his eyes from face

to face to see how Watchman would take that. Cunningham had always been a little uneasy with him: Cunningham was an old wrangler from Texas. Watchman had been down in West Texas once years ago and he hadn't stayed any longer than he'd had to: in the filling station they'd had three sets of toilets—*Whites, Colored, Mexicans*—and evidently if you were a native American you had to practice extreme continence in those parts.

Watchman slid the ring case out of his pocket and pushed it across the table. Stevens clicked it open and his mouth formed a circle. "Jesus. I've seen Eskimos living on smaller rocks than this. What'd you pay for it—twenty-four dollars in glass beads and red cloth?"

Cunningham squirmed and addressed himself to the remains of his sandwich.

Watchman laughed softly and retrieved the ring and Stevens said, "You figure to give it to her tonight?"

"I had it in mind." All the months of counting up the back pay he'd saved: this night was going to be sweet. He could picture the soft shine of joy on her face.

The waitress delivered Watchman's chili and when she turned away Stevens reached for her wrist. "Honey, what's your name?"

"Francine. What's yours?"

"Buck. Buck Stevens." He said it with an aw-shucks tilt of his head and the blond cowlick fell over his eyebrow and Watchman tried to repress a grin. "You weren't by any chance looking for a lift into Flagstaff this afternoon, Francine?"

"Now if I was, what makes you think I'd go with you?"

Stevens brightened. "How about it, then?"

"Nuts." She reached over to pick up Cunningham's plate and the white dress stretched tight over her ample breasts. "I've got work to do." She straightened and gave him an arch look. "But come back when you're big enough." She even looked like Mae West.

"Big enough where?" Stevens riposted softly; his eyes began to flash with lecherous hilarity.

When Francine laughed her eyes wrinkled up until they were almost shut. "Y'all come back, hear? I'll be around." And flounced away.

Watchman laughed till his stomach hurt. It was a good day for laughter. A fine day, with Lisa waiting at the end of it.

Cunningham got up awkwardly and Watchman let him out. "You boys look out for that snow, now," the constable said, and went tottering over to the cashier's register on his cowboy boots. He hadn't even cracked a smile the whole time. You could always depend on white men to be inscrutable.

"Sour old fart," Stevens observed.

"I'll tell you, son, comes the red revolution and there'll be some changes made. We're going to guide the white man in the proper enjoyment of life. We're going to educate his funny bone so he can rise up to our level of civilization from his unhappy savage state. And when that's done the Bureau of White Folks' Affairs will sign over full citizenship rights to the white man for as long as the sun shall rise and the rivers flow to the sea."

"You tell 'em, *kemo sabe.*"

4

The clouds to the west didn't look sinister yet but up here it could hit very fast. They cleared the edge of town and Watchman put the cruiser up to sixty on the road heading east toward the mountains. A light plane went by overhead at four or five thousand feet with a buzzing sound that irritated

Watchman: there were several fly-by-night outfits over on the Utah and Nevada slopes which made a business out of taking rich poachers into the Arizona high country at night to hunt antelope and whitetail from slow, low-flying planes equipped with enormous floodlamps that could pin an animal, dazzle it, paralyze it until the arrogant "sportsmen" had made their kill. Then the guide outfit would send in a flunky in a pickup truck to collect the carcass and if the pickup got intercepted the driver would claim he had collided with the animal and killed it by accident. Game wardens seldom had time or facilities to perform autopsies and most of the time the flying poachers got away with it.

This plane didn't look like a hunter; more like a business executive's charter job. One of those Twin Apaches that seated seven or eight. It went over with a harsh drone, flying west toward the clouds, probably headed for Las Vegas or Reno.

"They're likely to run into some turbulence, heading that way," Stevens observed.

"Those guys usually know what they're doing." Watchman had a secret admiration for pilots. He'd only been up in airplanes a few times, mostly in big liners, but every time he happened to drive past a private airport he would run his eyes over the little planes and start to think about maybe investing a little money in flying lessons and getting himself a license. The Highway Patrol had a few planes and maybe...

It was idle fantasy; nothing was likely to come of it but daydreams. Basically he was a groundling, rooted in the earth. In the Army after high school he'd been MOS Infantry all the way—that had been in 'fifty-seven and 'fifty-eight—and they'd flown him all the way from Fort Bliss to West Berlin during the crisis but there'd been no action and when he had returned to the States they had refused his application for transfer into the Military Police, so he'd let his enlistment expire and come back to school on the GI Bill—two years at the State College in Flagstaff and then a rookie beat with the Highway Patrol. At thirty-three he had been a cop almost exactly one-third of his lifetime. To show for it, he had three commendations, two citations for bravery, and five written reprimands.

Just the same it was a long way up for a *Diné*, which was the Navajo word for *Navajo* (*Navajo* being an Apache word that meant "enemy"). He had been born in 1938 in one of four mud-brush hogans that belonged to the cluster of his grandmother's family—grandmother and married daughters and their children—just about dead center on the sixteen-million-acre Window Rock Reservation. When he was a kid they'd had to carry water up to the hogan in a bucket from a well a quarter mile away and it was a twenty-five-mile walk to the trading post where his father worked as an Agency cop. You never got out of debt to the white trader. But you were taught never to complain. In those days there hadn't been any Red Power movements but Watchman's father had been a man of strength who had refused to be degraded by charity or the patronizing paternalism of the Bureau of Indian Affairs. The old man had had one thing nobody had ever taken away from him and that was his sense of humor; and that was Sam Watchman's legacy. No point in fighting the Indian wars all over again; the thing to do was get along with folks, have a few laughs, love a good woman and take pride in the dignity of your work. On the college psychological tests there had been a question, "How would you characterize yourself?" and of the five choices for answers Watchman had picked "Easygoing." He just didn't understand folks who made one big crisis out of life.

They passed Holcombe's roadside oasis—half a dozen sycamores, a dusty trailer park, a decrepit old motel with five "modern cabins" and Holcombe's store and filling station with its untrue sign, "Last Gas Before Desert." Watchman got comfortable in the seat for the long afternoon's drive ahead, with his wrist hooked over the top of the steering wheel and his left elbow poking out the window, and then the radio coughed and sputtered and Buck Stevens reached down to turn up the volume against the noise of the wind.

". . . Repeat, we have a Code Ten Thirteen from San Miguel. Car Niner Zero, acknowledge. Car Niner Zero."

Watchman plucked the mike off its sprocket and took his foot off the gas while he talked into the microphone. "Niner Zero to Dispatch, Niner Zero to Dispatch. Go ahead—what's the ruckus?"

"We have a Ten Thirteen from San Miguel, Officer Needs Assistance. Robbery in progress—repeat, robbery in progress. That you, Sam?"

"Aeah, Ernie, go ahead." He had the brakes on now to swing wide for a U-turn.

Buck Stevens sat up higher in his seat. "What the fuck? . . ." The shape of his blue eyes was changing.

The rear wheels slewed in the gravel as Watchman hung the end-for-end turn on the shoulders and started back the way they had come. The radio kept coughing: "It looks like the San Miguel bank, Sam."

Watchman's eye flicked the passing milepost—twenty-three more miles into town. Stevens was switching on the flasher. Watchman cranked his window closed to hear the two-way's speaker. The needle climbed up past the eighty m.p.h. mark.

". . . coming in on the emergency shortwave band. Their teletype lines must be down and we can't get through on the phone. It could be some ham operator pulling a hoax but they've got the right signal codes. It keeps fading in and out—pretty weak. Something about robbery in progress, officer needs assistance, maybe the bank. It's coming in garbled— possibly one of Cunningham's company cops on the key."

"We're on our way."

"How far out are you?"

"Be there in fourteer minutes." Watchman saw Buck Stevens' hand reach the jolting dashboard and grip its edge. "We're east of town. You'd better put a stopper on the road west."

"Affirmative, Niner Zero. Two Nevada patrol cars coming east from the state line. They'll cross the line in seven minutes."

They worked like that up here, operating vaguely under interstate "hot pursuit" statutes; in fact a Utah sheriff's office regularly covered the northwest corner of Arizona's Mohave County. It had to be done that way. Watchman's was the only Arizona police car in fifteen thousand square miles.

Even so it would take the two Nevada cars an hour to reach San Miguel.

Watchman reached up for the siren switch. "God knows what we'll run into—better get armed."

Buck Stevens was pale. He twisted in the seat to get at the rack inside the back door that held the riot shotgun and rifle; dragged both weapons over the back of the seat and held them across his knees. In the corner of his vision Watchman saw the rookie's Adam's apple shift up and down.

They whipped past the city-limit sign and several cars and pickups crowded over close to the curb to let them by. Watchman brought the speed down and came into the last bend at forty; the cruiser swayed on its springs, tires wailing, the ten-foot spring-mounted radio antenna lashing violently from its mountings on the rear bumper.

A small crowd stood gaping outside the bank and Watchman slid in at the curb, switched off the siren but left the flasher on. "Never mind the guns." People in crowds could be stupid but not that stupid; if there was any chance of shooting here these people would have been behind cover. Conclusion: if the bank had been robbed, the robbers had already fled.

The crowd was a tight knot around the door and when Watchman and Stevens came across the curb the crowd parted like the waters of the Red Sea. A barefoot kid in frayed jeans stood open-mouthed with his nose pressed to the window. Watchman went inside.

People were clustered inside the bank. Most of the men had no trousers on.

There was a little group crouched around an object on the floor by the rear teller's cage.

There was a lot of talking, everybody shouting at one another and at Watchman. He lifted his voice: "All right, let's hold it down."

The racket subsided from clamor to mutter. A thin shape straightened and detached itself from the knot of people by the teller's cage—Jace Cunningham, looking greenish and soft around the mouth. He came forward quickly and showed his consternation by shaking his head grievously and letting his hand dangle limply at the wrist, shaking it back and forth as if wearily drying his fingertips. "Jesus H. Christ." He had his pants on.

"What happened, Jace?"

"I ain't sure. I wasn't here—I just got here. But somebody hit the bank, a bunch of them. They got the cash, pretty close to a million. And that over there . . ."

Past the crowded people Watchman could see a pair of boots protruding and he heard Cunningham say, "They killed Jasper Simalie, Sam."

5

Watchman gripped Buck Stevens by the arm. "They didn't pass by us going out so they've gone out the other way—west on 793. Get on the radio and report. Tell those Nevada patrol cars to stop and search anything that moves on that road. On the run, now."

When Stevens sprinted past him he pushed Jace Cunningham aside with the heel of his hand and shoved into the crowd around Jasper Simalie. He recognized Doctor Jamieson —a gaunt man with a hollow-cheeked death's head and big yellow teeth, sparrow-chested and frail. The doctor was breathing like a teakettle. He looked up at Watchman and shook his head.

Jasper lay on his face. There was a great deal of blood on the floor.

"Shotguns," the doctor said through his teeth. "They weren't pistols, they were shotguns. The poor son of a bitch never had a prayer."

A pudgy man with pink hands was waiting, licking his lips with a pink tongue, when Watchman straightened and turned. Cunningham said, "This here's Mr. Whipple. He owns the bank."

"Not really," the pudgy man said. "I'm the manager—I work for the San Miguel Copper Company and I'm supposed to—"

"Were you here?"

"What's that?" Whipple's eyelids fluttered like semaphores.

"When this happened. Were you here? Can you tell me what happened?"

"I suppose so. It's all so unreal, you know?"

The doctor came by, lugging his bag. "I've got to have a

look at those armored-car guards. You coming, Jace?"

Watchman turned with an abrupt snap of his wide shoulders. "What about the guards?"

Cunningham flapped a bony hand reassuringly. "Don't worry about it. They're okay. They got sprayed with something and need gettin' their eyes washed out, that's all."

The doctor said, "I think it was chemical Mace," and went.

6

It was the biggest bank haul in the history of Arizona.

Watchman absorbed the facts quickly, piecing them together from the disjointed reportage of Whipple and Cunningham and two of the tellers he questioned. The tellers stood awkwardly, trying to ignore the fact that they were standing there in shirts, neckties, and underdrawers.

That was because the bandits had relieved them not only of the better part of a million in cash—Terrell, the head cashier, estimated $930,000—but of their pants as well, to discourage them from venturing out in pursuit.

It wasn't clear whether there had been four men or five. The company guards who rode the armored truck and its two convoy cars had instructions to stay near the bank in case of trouble and they had developed the habit of playing dime-quarter poker in the mud room in the back of the bank where employees hung their coats and boots on winter days. The bandits had known that; at least two of them had rushed in through the back door and squirted a chemical from spray cans—probably Mace, a disabling gas. It had affected the guards' vision, disoriented them, made them violently nauseous. Whatever it was, it had taken the eight guards out immediately and silently and none of them was able to give more than a sketchy description of their attackers. The bandits had relieved them of their side arms and locked them in the mud room. When Watchman talked to them the Tally Ho cards and coins were still scattered all over the room.

One man had entered the bank proper from the rear and two others had walked in the front door. They wore stocking masks and carried two double shotguns and an automatic pistol. About eight customers had been in the bank along with Whipple and seven employees. Another robber had waited outside at the wheel of the car. It was possible a fifth man had remained posted by the mud room to make sure the guards didn't break through the locked door.

In the bank the robbers had told everybody to remove their trousers and get down on the floor. Two of them had leaped over the low fence and gone into the vault, carrying military duffel bags which they stuffed with loot. The third man, with a shotgun, had waited just inside the front door. The bank guard, Jasper Simalie, had sneezed and stirred or had not stirred—there were conflicting eyewitness reports—and in either case the nervous bandit had fired. The shotgun charge had blasted Jasper Simalie back against the tellers' counter and he had slid down and fallen over on his face, leaving behind a red smear on the face of the counter.

The head cashier, Terrell, had pressed the alarm button under the lip of his desk very shortly after the bandits had entered the place, and the alarm had sounded in the police shack four blocks away. Jace Cunningham had been in the office with one of his patrolmen and he had told the patrolman to get through to the Sheriff and the Highway Patrol; Cunningham himself had grabbed a rifle off the rack and sprinted for the bank. But by the time Cunningham arrived the bandits had fled; he got a glimpse of their car speeding by, heading west.

The entire operation had taken no more than four minutes.

7

"They must have cut the phone and telegraph wires at both ends of town," Cunningham said. "Everything's dead except the radio. They had everything figured out—it took a lot of planning. This was no amateur job."

"But they're on the main highway," Buck Stevens said. "They're on the main road because there aren't any secondary roads. We can nail them easy. Maybe those Nevada cars have got them by now."

Watchman looked at his watch. They had been here twelve or fifteen minutes. He said to Cunningham, "Did you get a make on the car?"

"Not really. The play went around the other end. It was an old car—maybe an Olds, Buick, something like that."

"Anybody get a look at the driver?"

No answer.

Whipple said nervously, "I did notice one thing. One of them had an ugly scar on his wrist—here, like this."

Watchman's eyes locked on Stevens' and Stevens nodded emphatically.

Watchman took Cunningham by the arm and walked him toward the front door, talking while he moved. "They'd have known what the highway situation is around here. They must have allowed for it. I wouldn't be surprised if they hadn't doubled back and taken cover somewhere right here in town. You'd better get all your men looking for them."

"What about you two?"

"We'll head west, try to catch them in a pincer between us and those Nevada cruisers. If we don't find them we'll have to assume they doubled back. I'll get on the radio and have another Highway Patrol car dispatched from Fredonia to block off the road west of here—we didn't pass them coming in but they may have tried to get back that way while we've been inside here jawing. Now get moving, Jace."

Cunningham stiffened a little: he didn't like taking orders from Sam Watchman and in fact he was under no obligation to do so but it was obvious that Watchman was right and Cunningham was enough of a cop to know that. In the end he nodded and swung away and Watchman got into the car and reached for the radio mike.

8

The cruiser surged along the highway. Beyond the San Miguel hills there was a long stretch of level flat pavement, thirty-seven miles without a single turning. Watchman was brisk: he had the situation securely in his mind and he barked terse commentary into the transmitter, sealing the net. The last thing the dispatcher said to him in reply was, somewhat drily, "Looks like we've got some federal stuff horning in, Sam —FBI special agent heading up your way by Lear jet. I guess the G-men want to hog some credit."

He was doing eighty but he had his eyes alertly on the road and he saw the pinpoint glitters in the road just ahead: he hit the brakes hard but he saw he didn't have room to stop so he released the brake and steered off the highway, bumping violently across the shoulder and crashing through the bits and pieces of sagebrush and stunt growth. Stevens was holding on tight: "What the fuck?"

"Guerrilla spikes on the road."

There was a hundred-foot patch of them—twisted nails welded into little grappling-hook shapes to impale tires and blow them out.

Watchman got out and walked over to the road. He didn't waste time looking at the spikes; what he was looking for was tracks in the dirt alongside the road. He didn't find any. He walked back to the car, got in and started forward, pulling back onto the pavement beyond the patch of spikes.

Stevens said, "What was that all about?"

"They went by here fast and they dropped those things behind them to slow down anybody coming after them. So they wanted to buy a little time—what for?"

"I don't get it."

"And they didn't come back this way. There's no sign of the car detouring around that patch. The only tracks were the ones we left. They're still out ahead of us."

"Then they've run into those Nevada cars by now." Stevens looked at his watch. "In fact we ought to intercept them ourselves any time now."

Way out ahead, several miles, the sun winked on something that might be an approaching car. Watchman swept both sides of the unrolling highway with close attention. His knuckles on the steering wheel began to ache: he was thinking of Jasper Simalie—upright, forthright, downright, a sweet old man and no gunslinger; Jasper would have had trouble hitting the ground with his hat and Jasper hadn't been one for empty heroics. It was impossible to believe he had been trying to get to his gun when the bandit had shotgunned him. No; it had been cold-blooded, casual, unnecessary murder.

Stevens was talking into the radio: "Driver's license in the name of Steven D. Baraclough, Seven-Niner-Niner South Steward Avenue, Tucson. Vehicle is yellow and green nine-

teen fifty-seven Buick fordor, Arizona license plates Bravo
X ray One Four One Three Five Charlie. Registered to John P.
Sweeney, Fredonia. Repeat, Steven D. Baraclough, B-a-r-a-
c-l-o-u-g-h . . . "

The money was of no special concern to Watchman but
because of Jasper Simalie he had a personal stake in this. They
were going to pay for that.

*Hold on now. Let's just don't fill the air with bullets,
Tsosie. Sure, a little good old-fashioned Innun-style retribution—let's start a massacre, folks.*

His knuckles eased on the wheel and he made a face.

Stevens was still on the radio: " . . . patch of nails on the
highway eight miles west of San Miguel. Better send somebody out there with a broom and get it swept off."

The approaching vehicle winked in the distant sunlight and
Watchman's eyes kept scanning both sides of the road. When
he saw the downed phone cables he pulled over and stopped.
The roof-top flasher was still revolving like a red lighthouse
beacon and he left it on when he got out of the car.

The telephone-telegraph poles ran along quite close beside
the road here and that must have been why they had chosen
this spot to cut the wires. Stevens said, "Piece of rope over
there, see it?"

Watchman walked over and got down on one knee to
examine it. Stevens came crunching along and Watchman
said, "They slung one end of the rope over the wires and tied
both ends of the rope to the back bumper of the car. Pulled
the cables down. They must have done the same thing beyond
the other end of town."

"Cute," Stevens said with a sour downturn of his mouth.

Watchman stood up and turned a slow circle on his heels.
His eyes were narrowed in a thoughtful squint. The wind
rubbed itself against him, cool and thin, and the clouds were

building and darkening over the western quarter of the sky. About two hundred yards off the road to the right stood a clump of stunt growth—withered trees, bushes nourished by some fitfully intermittent underground stream. Up ahead by the roadside several sections of barbwire fence were down. Watchman walked back to the car and started it up and when Stevens got in, asking questions, he rolled the car forward to the break in the fence. Several sets of tire tracks went off the road here and rutted across the flats to the clump of scrub-oak and sycamore. Nothing but sagebrush flats surrounded the grove, miles of open ground beaten into pale colors out to the horizons, here and there a weathered bush.

Stevens said, "Jesus, you don't think they're trying to *hide* in there?"

The approaching car was slowing down—the Nevada cruiser. When it pulled over by Watchman the visiting trooper stuck his head out the window. "What's happening?"

"Let's have a look and find out."

The Nevada cop got out of his car and Watchman said, "I guess you didn't pass anybody."

"A couple of pickups and a Jeep. I checked them out and let them go."

Buck Stevens said, "Where's your partner? They said two cars."

"He's back by the state line. Waiting to bottle up anybody who happened to get past me. What the hell, you mean nobody passed you guys either?"

Watchman just pointed at the tire tracks leading off toward the grove.

The Nevada cop's face changed and he pushbuttoned his clamshell holster. When it popped open on its spring catch he lifted the service revolver out and turned to stand squarely facing the grove. "Do we go in after them or wait for rein-forcements?"

Watchman suppressed a smile. "Let's go in and have a look before we call out the troops."

"Radio said there was four, five of them."

"All right. But I doubt they're in those trees." Watchman was studying the black-rubber dashes on the road pavement—smears a car might have left if it locked its brakes trying to stop suddenly. Maybe somebody'd had a blowout; there was no telling how long that had been there; but it was all piecing together in Watchman's mind and he didn't bother taking out his gun when he began to walk toward the grove.

The other two trailed along gingerly and began to spread out to either side as they approached the trees. Watchman said, "Don't get too jumpy." The way he had it figured, all they were likely to find was an empty 'fifty-seven Buick.

9

He went in straight up because there was no point crouching and dodging. If there was anybody waiting inside those trees with a bead on him they'd nail him either way. He had a theory and he was sure enough of it to be confident he wasn't going to draw any fire. Two of the sets of tire tracks were wide-set with narrow tread; there was a single track running down the middle, like a motorcycle spoor, and then there were three sets of tracks left by the Buick—it had come in, gone out, and come in again: therefore it was still here.

From boyhood his eyes had been trained to read signs left in the earth's surface. You learned these things quickly when you grew up hunting strayed sheep across the broken badlands of the Window Rock country. For Buck Stevens and the Nevada trooper it wasn't all that easy—the tire markings were a jumble of intertwining grooves, disorderly and blurred and often superimposed—but Stevens did say, "Is that a motorbike track?"

"I doubt it." Watchman was about forty yards out now and the Nevada cop was bouncing his revolver nervously in his fist, eyes darting, trying to keep every inch of the grove covered.

The patch of scrub was crescent-shaped, perhaps eighty feet wide, with its convex face toward the road. No doubt it followed the course of an underground stream that came close enough to the surface, under artesian pressure, to support the root systems of the growth at this point. The tracks didn't go straight into it; they went past the left-hand end and curled out of sight behind the scrub.

Watchman walked in the tracks, going around the end of the patch and sighting the gleam of sunlight reflected on metal. When he got past the obscuring branches he saw it was the chrome bumper of the Buick. They had parked it back here hard against the inside of the bend so it wouldn't be spotted from the road.

Stevens was coming along behind him, gun lifted, and the Nevada cop had spread out to go around the far side of the grove; now he appeared beyond the Buick, face screwed up in bafflement.

Watchman walked over to the Buick and looked inside. The back seat was littered with what looked like a spilled pile of dirty laundry: nearly a dozen pairs of men's trousers. There were five nylon stockings and four small gray-painted spray canisters, about the size of spray cans of shaving foam. The canisters had military markings in stencil.

The Nevada cop came up holstering his gun and peered inside over Watchman's shoulder. "I just don't get this."

"They took everybody's pants when they held up the bank. To keep people from following them outside."

"To hell with that. What I mean, they can't have just disappeared into thin air."

"That's exactly what they did."

Buck Stevens reached in through the open window and picked up one of the spray canisters. "Mace chemical, all right. Army issue—riot control. Maybe they got it out of an armory someplace."

"Or maybe they had a source handy to them," Watchman replied. "This whole thing feels like a military operation."

The Nevada cop said, "I don't get it. I don't get any one bit of it."

Watchman started to walk away. "Let's get on that radio."

"And tell them what?" the Nevada cop insisted, hurrying to catch up because Watchman had long legs and was using them.

Buck Stevens was hanging back to give the Buick a last glance. Soon enough there would be a crowd of technicians out here to go over it for microscopic clues but Watchman had seen all he needed to see. Mainly what had cinched it was those black dashes on the highway.

The Nevada cop said, "Maybe you ought to spell it out for us country boys."

Buck Stevens caught up, dogtrotting, and Watchman said, "They broke a hole in the fence and hid it over there behind the brush. Baraclough came along in the Buick and picked them up, and they went into town and hit the bank, and I guess they had it all timed down to seconds. They must have worked it out how much time they needed—that's why they scattered those guerrilla spikes on the road, to buy enough time to get back here and transfer everything out of the Buick."

"What are you talking about? Motorcycles?"

Watchman made a face. They went through the hole in the fence and he pointed at the black dashes on the pavement. "Ever looked at the surface of an airport runway? Those are the marks a plane leaves when it lands. You've got thirty-seven miles of straight and level road here. It makes a good runway. They used an airplane."

Buck Stevens said, "Smartass Inyun."

CHAPTER

1

"We've got to go around it," Keith Walker said.

The Major beside him said, "Negative."

"We haven't got oxygen. I can't get above it—hell, it goes up forty thousand feet anyway."

He was scowling at the wall of tumbling storm clouds dead ahead. "We can cut around north of it."

"We haven't got time."

"Nuts. You're a long time dead."

"You can cut it," the Major said. "It might do you some good—prove something to yourself."

After the number of missions Walker had flown he did not need to prove anything to anybody. What he said was, "Up yours, Major." But he was thinking, *I guess I could cut it.* And then: *Of course pilots always have to believe that. Christ don't let him talk you into this one.* And so he said, "Just this once we're going to do things my way, Major."

He gave it a little aileron and a little rudder—gingerly, because he was flying on the deck, holding less than two hundred feet above the hilltops. The mountain range ran along to starboard, parallel to his course, and he was staying below it because of the radar at Nellis Air Force Base just outside Las Vegas.

He came around to a heading of Three Zero Five magnetic, vectoring north of Las Vegas VOR. The storm ahead of him was a black cascade, wall-to-wall violence. Under him cool air settled into gully shadows and hot air came rising explosively from the sunwhacked hilltops, and the ground turbulence kept the twin Apache bouncing around.

He had a broad-band receiver mounted below the dashboard, designed to detect radar transmissions, and he was picking up the jiggles of the flicking Nellis scanner circuit. But the mountains above him to starboard would absorb the signals and hide him in the scanner's ground-return. They hadn't picked him up; if they had, he would have seen a change in the interval of the signal—it would have gone to a quicker pattern, a fast localized sweep, but it wasn't doing that. The radar didn't worry him. The weather did. He had never been a white-knuckle flier but he had a survivor's respect for enemy weather and he wasn't confident of the aging Piper's capacity for punishment.

The Major was watching him and when Walker looked at him the Major smiled very slightly with his mouth. The opaque eyes blocked all argument and inquiry, turned all objections back, as effectively as if they had been the eyes of a dead man.

The Major said, "We don't have enough gas to go around it."

Walker considered that. His eyes swept the panel. The quivering flow meters, manifold pressures, temperatures. The gauges stood half-full; there had been no place to refuel since take-off this morning. With the weight of five passengers and the money she was running on rich mixtures and she didn't have another four hundred miles in her tanks; they had the Beechcraft waiting on a dirt landing strip northwest of Reno and that was something more than three hundred miles from here in a straight line. To go around the storm would eat up another hundred and twenty miles and they just didn't have it. The Major's eyes didn't miss a thing.

Walker said, "Then we won't make it anyway. You know how much gas you eat up bucking a storm."

"The winds are counterclockwise. Stay on the north side of the storm and you'll have a tail wind."

"More like a sixty-mile gale. It'll shake this crate to pieces."

The Major's eyes just stood against him, like a knife blade —motionless but prepared to cut.

He had to think. Behind him in the passenger seats the others were talking loudly, keyed up, nervy. Eddie Burt was making exultant noises and Baraclough was saying in his flat nasal voice, "No need to smack your lips so loud," but laughing off-key with excitement. The Piper 235 had seats for six, including pilot, and there were five men in it; the sixth seat held the duffel bags. Too cramped in here to count it but Baraclough had a good eye and had estimated it at a minimum of nine hundred thousand dollars. About ten cubic feet of tens, twenties, fifties and hundreds. Walker had hefted the four duffel bags when they'd put them aboard and the things weighed maybe sixty pounds each.

Baraclough was saying in a travelogue-narrator voice, "And now, happier but wearier, we bid a warm farewell to the home of the jolly green swag. . . ."

"Jesus, will you please shut up?" Jack Hanratty was in a fever of terror. He couldn't take heights, airplanes terrified him, and the Major was angry with him—back there in the car for a minute Walker had thought the Major was going to kill Hanratty for shotgunning the fat old Indian bank guard. The Major could have done it without working up a sweat; the Major was versed in a dozen methods of killing a man bare-handed and silently and very quickly.

When somebody got killed during the commission of a felony all parties to the felony were automatically and equally guilty of first-degree murder. That was the felony-murder statute. Hanratty and his shotgun. The son of a bitch just had to carry that shotgun. Walker hadn't even had a gun but Hanratty had made a murderer out of him. It was no wonder Hanratty was shaking: all five of them had got sucked into this mess by his nervous trigger finger.

The Major had drummed it into them time and time again while they were setting up the score. *Arizona still has the death penalty. I don't want anybody killed. I don't even want anybody bruised. They'll forget the money but there's no statute of limitations on murder.*

Hanratty and his fucking shotgun.

The fat old Indian guard had sneezed.

Sneezed.

It was the stupid little things that got you every time.

2

Walker had a tooth with a hole in it. Food got stuck there and made him suck on the tooth. He should have gone to a dentist weeks ago.

He glanced at the ASI and saw the airspeed was down to 140 in the thinning dead air ahead of the storm front. He gave the throttles a boost, up to seventy percent of power, got the engines in synch and adjusted the trim tabs. "Look, we can turn north, go up to Ely or Elko and set down. We could steal another plane there or maybe even a car."

"No."

"Why the hell not? They'll get it figured out we used a plane. They'll start an air search. If we switch to a car they won't be looking for us. Why the hell not?"

"Because I'm telling you. Because it's all worked out down to the button. We're not going to start changing the plan now," the Major said.

The engines made a harsh drone and there was a loose rivet somewhere, rattling. Walker pointed at the blackness ahead of them. It ran right up out of sight above them. The mountain peaks, running alongside their course on the right-hand side, disappeared right into the opacity of weather. The Nevada state line was somewhere under all that. "Look, we've got four or five minutes to make a turn and get out of the way of it, that's all. That thing's no autumn shower, Major, that's a fucking blizzard. You saw the weather map."

He had picked up the map overlay this morning at five o'clock at the Reno tower, when he'd filed the phony VFR flight plan for Salt Lake City. That had been the midnight weather report. At that time the storm had been crossing the California–Nevada line somewhere south of Reno and the projections indicated it would hit Vegas around midmorning and keep moving east toward Kingman at about twenty-five or thirty knots. But obviously it had gathered speed and shifted course since then. Now it was getting sawed up by the mountaintops northeast of Vegas and that meant it was dumping moisture.

He said, "There's snow and hail in there."

The Major glanced at the quivering needle of the outside-temperature gauge. It stood at 43 degrees, but Walker shook his head. "You don't get this. We haven't crossed the front yet. Inside there you'll get a ten- or fifteen-degree drop. You get a hailstone driven by a sixty-knot wind and you can get bullet holes in the wings of a light plane. This is no Air Force cargo job, Major."

In back the others had stopped talking: they could see the storm for themselves and it was beginning to penetrate past their other fears and past the excitement the money had generated.

Now Baraclough leaned forward and Walker could feel the man's menthol-cigarette breath on his neck. "Listen, Major, I think he's right. That's no monsoon rainstorm."

"Ice," said Eddie Burt. "We don't want to go into that."

"Now you're getting the idea," Walker said. His mouth felt powder dry. He locked both fists on the split wheel and toed the rudder pedal with his right foot. "I'm turning."

The Major stiffened to speak but then they hit the front and the plane stuttered. The blast of the wind hit the underbelly of the banking plane and skidded it back, and Walker, feeling her begin to slide, had to give her a heavy left aileron. It leveled her off and he let the wind push her around and complete the turn for him, sideslipping rather than banking. But now the mountains were dead ahead and he had to put on full power and lift the nose into a climb, and in the low air pressure she responded only sluggishly. Half a minute of this and he could see it was no good.

"We're not going to make it," he said. "We've got to turn around and get some altitude."

The Major didn't say anything. Walker didn't have time to look at him, to measure his expression, but he knew what the Major's face would be showing: irritation, not fear.

At least the Major wasn't arguing with him.

He completed the ninety-degree turn and now he was headed east again, the way they had come, and the winds of the storm's leading edge were pushing him forward while he climbed. He would have to pick up at least five or six thousand feet of additional altitude before he could think about turning north again and crossing over the mountains; in fact it would be better to climb 7,500 feet higher because you never knew what kind of downdrafts you might hit over those canyons. And with the low pressure of the air and the heavy load inside the plane she wasn't going to climb that high very fast. It was going to take a while.

When he had a chance he glanced at the Major and saw the thoughtful squint on the Major's cold hawked features. In back the rest of them began to talk again in harsh snappish voices—they had the sweats, all of them—but the Major held his tongue, squinted forward, worked his jaw from side to side. The Major was thinking, hatching a plan. It would probably be a good one.

3

In the old days he had known Major Leo Hargit at Tan Son Nhut and Da Nang but they hadn't been close or anything near it, and when Walker had come back to the States he'd never given the Major another thought until the night the Major had looked him up in Tucson.

The breaks had passed Walker by. He'd been good at war, not so good at much of anything else. In Vietnam the Army had trusted him with a plane worth half a million dollars and ten men's lives but now, since the Portland accident, it appeared nobody would trust him with a cropduster.

The Army—not the Air Force—had recruited him to fly and he'd flown Med-Evac planes up and down the Indochina peninsula for three years, saving up his back pay and re-upping twice to get the combat bonuses. A few times he'd been shot up by ground fire but he'd never been shot down; he was twenty-nine now and he'd been flying since he was seventeen, he had eleven thousand hours behind him and until Portland he had been rated and certified for instrument flying in anything from single-engine to multiple jet.

When he had enough money saved he had come back to his home town, Sacramento, and bought into a third-level carrier outfit that did air cargo and taxi and business-commuter charter work up and down the west coast, covering all the small towns in northern California and southern Oregon that the scheduled feeder lines missed. Or-Cal Coast Airways had a Lear, two twin Apaches, a Convair and a DC–6B, and when Walker had bought in they had used his capital to pick up an almost new British Dart 500 twin turboprop which carried fifty-six passengers or a prodigious tonnage of cargo. It gave him a one-fifth ownership in a working airline and that was what he had always wanted; that first year was the best year of his life but it was the last good one.

It had started to fall apart when one of the pilots broke his leg in a bowling accident and they had had to hire a temporary replacement on a half-hour's notice to fly a four-passenger taxi charter to Eugene. The stupid pilot had forgotten to put down his gear at Eugene, gone in with the wheels retracted and ground-looped on his belly, totaled the Apache and killed himself and all four passengers.

That had brought the National Transportation Safety Board down on them and their certifications had been yanked for two weeks, after which they had gone on probationary status with Government snoops hanging around doing constant checks on their safety standards.

They were limping but they were still on their feet, and

they might have overcome that, but Walker was having private trouble then.

He had met Carla at a TWA pilot's party in San Francisco less than a week after he'd become a full partner in Or-Cal; he'd been flushed with success and he'd infected her with it. She had been a stew on Northwest Orient but she hadn't liked it much—"I'm sort of a cozy quiet girl, Keith, I just didn't like living in hotel rooms." When Walker met her she'd been working four months in an airline ticket office in the St. Francis and she admitted frankly she was anxious to settle down and make a home, be a mother, be a wife.

It suited him. She wasn't gorgeous but she had a cute little face, a triangle of good bones with enormous soft onyx eyes. A small soft cuddly girl, nervously vivacious, with a quick flashing smile and a healthy frank body. He had felt good with her, right from the start.

He hadn't thought much about whether he loved her; he had never actually seen any love lying around. His romantic dreams had been focused on airplanes from the time he'd built his first model kit plane at the age of nine. But in the Army he'd worked it all out for himself, how he was going to save money and buy into an airline and get married and have kids. That way he'd have the best of both worlds—the kind of success everybody admired, the solid-citizen home and family and free-enterprise ownership of his own business; and at the same time an airplane to fly. The only real freedom was being in motion, piloting yourself across the sky.

Five weeks after he had met Carla he had married her. That had been part of the good year too. It had been a sybaritic year, a lot of drinking and a lot of laughs and a lot of sex. Carla knew airplanes and pilots and she was part of the whole thing, not an outsider.

But she hadn't got pregnant.

They went to doctors. She took hormones. They had tests. Jesus, the money it all cost. But it didn't solve anything and finally after a year of specialists and lab analyses the pussyfooting doctor had screwed up courage enough to tell him. "I'm sorry, Mr. Walker. You might try artificial insemination—have you thought of it? It's probably the only answer if you're still adamant about not adopting children. You're sterile, you see. No, don't worry about your potency, it's nothing to do with that. But some men have natural antibodies. Something in the chemical make-up of the body—a genetic incompatibility between the genes of your mother and father. The spermatozoa simply don't function properly, and therefore you can't impregnate your wife—or any other woman for that matter, it's not merely a matter of individual sexual partners." And the sly wink: "In a way you know it gives you a kind of freedom some men would give their right arms for."

At first it didn't seem to matter to him all that much. There were plenty of kids around for adoption. But Carla wasn't having any of that.

She became gloomy, depressed. And his own uncertainty had begun to feed on her despondency. Somehow his manhood had been challenged, denied.

She had turned chilly and sarcastic—angry and moody by turns; he had to tiptoe around her.

Finally the plane had crashed in Eugene and he had had a lot to drink that night when he'd heard about it. The next day she had collapsed in tears: "I just don't want you near me."

And she had moved out the same day. Packed all her clothes and left.

In time a lawyer served the divorce notice on him—she'd gone to Reno for six weeks. He had to hock some of his Or-Cal stock to make the settlement. By then he had gone into a kind of emotional anaesthesia and it didn't seem to matter very much but gradually it had begun to tear at him: grief, the sense of stinging loss. For the first time he realized it: he had loved her.

But she was married again. Another pilot, a United Air Lines captain, twenty years older than she was. And he heard from the airport grapevine that she was pregnant and glowing.

All right; people got along without an arm, without an eye, without their hearing, without both legs. You could get along without love. He had plunged himself into the business; he had flown the maximum number of hours every month that the CAA would permit, and some they didn't permit. He had gone out on the stump to drum up business, talking up air-freight contracts with coastal fishing outfits and printers and gimcrack cottage industries up in the mountain towns with their ragged-windsock dirt runways.

Then the Post Office Department had started awarding contracts on a low-bid basis to private air-taxi carriers to try for one-day delivery of first class mail in the hick towns. It meant a lot of night flying and a lot of instrument flying because you had to live up to the stupid tradition about the dangers of snow and rain and gloom of night. Walker had sweated blood to get the contract and had started flying the route himself in the Lear—an overnight round-trip from Sacramento to Eureka every twenty-four hours with four stops between, each way— half the time flying blind in bad weather, relying on cockpit instruments and radio ranges. The postal contract left it up to the pilot whether to fly in questionable weather but the point was, if you didn't fly you didn't get paid.

It was a grueling grind and you couldn't keep it up forever, six nights a week. You started taking a harmless-looking little heart-shaped amphetamine tablet now and then, just to give yourself a bit of an edge. Then you took two and three and four and after a while you had a pocket full of them on every flight, and your nerves drew up like bowstrings and your judgment began to play tricks on you: you'd come in too long, overshoot, tear rubber off the tires braking too hard; you'd overestimate your altitude and come down so hard you bent the landing-gear bracings; you'd be flying through a clear night sky and you'd start to hallucinate, you'd see Carla's face winking sleepily at you from a cloud, you'd see a North Vietnamese MIG–21 diving at you with tracers winking silently out of its wing guns and you'd take violent evasive action and barely miss clipping a mountaintop.

He began to recognize that he was falling apart and he resolved to steady himself. He took two weeks off and spent the time at Tahoe in a motel just off the lake shore. It took a few days to withdraw from the pills and that was sheer hell but he knew what he was doing. He spent the days around the swimming pool soaking up the mountain sun—this was last June—and evenings he'd go out and gamble a little, taking it easy, just playing a bit of dollar roulette and two-dollar black-jack and not losing more than he could handle. He could feel the tension draining out of him as if a drainplug had been pulled. He started going over to the Nevada side and casually dating the recently freed divorcees who were always in the casinos dying for a man, any man, with no promises demanded and no questions asked.

But he was still putting Carla's face on every woman he slept with. There was no cure for that malaise.

He'd gone back to work toward the end of June and he'd been flying the old DC–6B up to Portland on a cargo job for a paper mill when he'd flown into a high-tension cable.

There was no excuse for it. The day had been a little misty with drizzling rain but he was flying into a first-class airport on the beams and the visibility was good enough to see the ground from seven or eight hundred feet. The aircraft was in good working order and the copilot had gone through the landing checklist with him without a hitch. But the voice of the girl on the headset, giving him his landing instructions, had reminded him of Carla's voice and he was seeing Carla's face in his mind when he should have been watching the earth come up, and the copilot had been working flaps and under-carriage instead of watching the runway, and Walker had lost too much altitude too fast and clipped the power line with the starboard wheel. It had thrown the plane around through a ten-degree arc and she had hit the ground on the port wingtip and spun as if the wingtip were a pivot. The gear had col-lapsed under her, the props had broken against the concrete, the fuselage had spun with the port wing snapping off at its root and the plane ending up on the grass in half a dozen pieces.

He'd sat in the overturned pilot's seat, hanging by his seat belt, not feeling a thing, hearing the meatwagon sirens and the wail of tires and the spouting foam of the fire hoses, and then the crash crews had pried the plane open and climbed inside to drag him and the copilot outside. In the ambulance they'd tested him for breaks and concussion but all he had was a few cuts and bruises. The copilot had a gash on his head from the control wheel and for twelve hours he'd been on the critical list, and Walker had waited in the hospital; but the copilot had pulled through, so there was no manslaughter charge against him.

The downed power line had cut electricity in two factories and four hundred houses and a shopping center. The commu-nity was incensed, the insurance company was outraged, and when the government had pulled Walker's license Or-Cal had kicked him out of the firm. They agreed to charge off the demolished airplane against Walker's invested capital. They lost money on it but they were willing to do that to get rid of him.

It put him on the street without even a tin cup. He had no money and no pilot's license; anyhow the wreck had made it impossible for him to get a job anywhere in the country in any company that had anything to do with airplanes. They didn't even want him around airports selling tickets.

The fraternity of airmen had a primitive pride. They didn't want him around because he was a reminder: *It could happen to any of us.* Walker's crash had cost Or-Cal half its contracts and the fraternity couldn't afford even a hint that this kind of man might be tolerated by them: pilots were always suspect, and partly because of their arrogance they were watched eagerly by groundlings for evidence of recklessness. If it had been only hard luck he might have been protected and supported by his own kind—you rarely heard of a pilot on welfare—but when it was more than hard luck, when it was your own inexcusable stupid failure, there was no room for you because you had disgraced the fraternity.

He was bitter, there was no way not to be. But he couldn't blame them. He had been one of them and he understood.

And now at twenty-nine he was burnt out. Washed up.

He'd been in Tucson two months, pumping Texaco gas and drinking up his wages, when the Major had found him.

4

"You may not remember me. Hargit, Leo Hargit."

"I remember you, Major."

The Major had driven into the gas station in a four-year-old Lincoln Continental. It suited him; he had the carriage to bring it off. Steel gray hair close-cropped against a well-shaped skull. Near six feet tall, long-boned, a straight taut body in superb condition. In mufti now, a cool light grey suit that had not come from stock. When Walker had last seen him at Hué the Major had been wearing a Green Beret uniform.

Hargit had a flashing grin, the teeth as white and even as a military cemetery. He was powerfully handsome with that larger-than-life magnetism which was, in certain men, a force of leadership. His face was big and square and all straight lines.

He had got out of the car and shaken hands with Walker. He wasn't a bone crusher but you could feel the power in his grip; he had muscles he hadn't even used yet.

"They tell me you've had it a little rough, Captain."

"I haven't exactly been sweating the income tax."

"Someplace we can talk?"

Then it wasn't just an accidental meeting.

"I've got the place to myself till three o'clock or so."

The Major glanced at his watch and shot his cuff. "That ought to be time enough."

"You want gas in that thing?"

"Let it wait." The Major had thrown his big arm across Walker's shoulders and walked him inside the filling station. There was only one chair, by the telephone desk with its credit-card machines and free roadmap stand. The place was a litter of tools and old batteries and cans of oil; it smelled of lubricants. The Major swept a patch of workbench clear of tools, cocked himself on it hipshot with one foot on the floor, and waved Walker into the chair. It gave Hargit the position of command.

The doors were open but it was hot and close. The desert sun shot painful reflections off passing cars and the store windows across the boulevard. Traffic was a steady noise.

"I might have a job for you."

"Doing what? Back in the Army?"

"No. Something else. Flying a plane."

Walker's laugh was more of a snarl. "I haven't got a license."

"I'll get you one."

"It's not that easy. They took it away from me and they're not likely to give it back before World War Five."

"I'll get you a license. Hell, a piece of paper?"

"It's not that easy," Walker said again, keeping his face blank, trying not to show the bitterness. His overalls were black and filthy with grease and he found himself wiping his hands on the bib front. His fingernails were inky.

"It might not be in your own name," the Major said, watching him unblinkingly.

Walker's face shifted. "Just what kind of flying did you have in mind?"

"Twin-engine. Mostly daylight flying, mostly on radio ranges. You could do it with your eyes shut."

"Not according to the FAA." But he leaned forward, bracing a hand on his knee. "Unless you're talking about flying somewhere outside of the country?"

"Partly in, partly out."

"Look, Major, I don't like fencing. The last time I saw you, you had a couple of Special Forces A-Teams working the back hills in Cambodia and Laos. All right, I read the newspapers, I saw where they were recalling the Green Berets and cutting them back."

Hargit said drily, "A few lard-ass Pentagon generals decided there wasn't room in the United States Army for an elite corps. Which was pretty funny coming from charter members of the West Point Protective Association."

"Okay, they did you out of a job. But I hear the CIA's hiring hundreds of former Green Berets to serve in Laos.

That's just what I read in the papers. I don't know anything. But if you're traveling around signing up recruits to fight some ass-hole war out in Laos you can count me out. I've had my ass shot at enough."

The Major laughed, his eyes closing up to slits. "It's got nothing to do with Laos."

"Or the CIA?"

"Or the CIA." The Major pulled a flat billfold out of his inside pocket and extracted a folded newspaper clipping. "Evidently you didn't read all the papers."

It was eight or nine months old, starting to yellow and get brittle at the folds. It had a one-column head shot of Hargit in his beret at the top. The caption spelled his name and the headline beneath it said: BERET MAJOR DISCHARGED AFTER VIET COURT-MARTIAL.

Hargit took it back before he'd had time to read more than a paragraph. He folded it carefully and put it back in the billfold. "Some South Vietnamese civilians got killed and they needed a scapegoat. The details don't matter, it's all politics. The gooks were VC at night and law-abiding citizens during the day—you know the drill. But it was supposed to be a pacified hamlet and Saigon raised hell."

Walker stared at him. "I'll be damned. So they threw you out."

"Seventeen years in uniform," the Major said in a dull low voice. "If I hadn't had a friend or two they'd have put me in the stockade for murder. Murder, for God's sake—there's a war going on." The Major slipped the billfold into his pocket and adjusted the hang of his jacket. "So you see we've got something in common, Captain."

"You don't look like you're hurting." He couldn't help it. The big car and the three-hundred-dollar suit didn't stimulate his sympathies.

If it angered Hargit he didn't show it. "Money? I had a little saved up. It doesn't amount to anything." He stood up and turned to stare out the plate-glass front window, talking over his shoulder. "I could have hired out to half a dozen armies. South America, Africa—plenty of work around for a mercenary who knows guerrilla work."

"You were damn good," Walker agreed. "Why didn't you do that?"

"I'm going to. But on my terms, not theirs. It's always a mistake to get into a position where you've got responsibility but not authority. From here on in I don't take orders from anybody but Leo Hargit."

"Easy to say. You going to hire yourself?"

"Yes." Hargit turned to face him. There was no reading the expression but the eyes were hard as glass. "There are countries around willing to hire whole armies at a clip."

Now it really began to frighten him. "And you're going to raise an army?"

"I figure to put together the best mobile force of crack guerrilla mercenaries anybody ever saw. And then I figure to hire out to the high bidder and run his war the right way—my way, with no interference from anybody and no Pentagon to court-martial me."

It took time to absorb. After a while Walker said, "And you don't care who you fight for. Which side, I mean."

"Sides don't mean anything below the Equator."

"Well I know that. I hate to sound like a hick but I meant what about right and wrong?"

"Virtues make sense when you can afford them, I suppose. I can't. Anyhow, morality's a pen for sheep, built by wolves. Take what you want and don't look back, that's all that matters."

Walker blinked. "Why'd you come to me?"

"I told you. I want a pilot."

"I never flew a combat plane in my life."

"I wouldn't ask you to."

It wasn't making any sense. All he knew was that Hargit was playing him, enjoying the game; and Hargit wasn't about to spell it out until he was good and ready. So Walker tried another tack. "How'd you find me?"

"Does it matter? I traced you through some old contacts." Then the billfold came out again and Walker was staring at a multi-engine commercial instrument-rated FAA pilot's license, complete with seals and stamps and a description: *Kendall Williams, date of birth 10/27/41, place of birth Albuquerque, N. Mex., ht 5' 11", wt 160 lbs, hair brown, eyes gray.* Everything had been filled in except the bearer's signature.

Walker's hand, holding it, was not steady; the document fluttered with vibration.

"Where'd you get this?"

"It's a forgery but nobody has to know that."

"It's a damned good phony."

"Of course it is. What do you take me for, an amateur?"

"Okay, Major, you're a professional." He stood up and thrust the pilot's license back at him. "The question is, a professional what?"

"Let's say a professional thief."

5

"Captain, you've got your tit in a wringer. I'm offering you a way out—enough money to go to Canada or Brazil and start your own bush airline. There'll be a minimum of fifty thousand in it for you and it may come to more. All you've got to do is fly a couple of airplanes and drive a car twenty miles."

"It's too risky."

"Nothing's risky if the stakes are high enough."

"What the hell do you want with all that money anyway?"

"It takes a lot of money to raise an army, Captain. Recruiting, training, equipping."

"Jesus, the kind of money you're talking about you could forget all that and just retire on it."

"Some men could."

It was terrifying to see a Green Beret type go bad. For all those years, in line of duty, he'd been breaking all the rules of civilized conduct, and it gave him a feeling of untouchable immunity from all those rules.

"Do you want me to go over it again, Captain?"

"No. I get the pitch. You're going to rob a bank."

"Not just any bank. A million-dollar cash bank."

"And if we get caught?"

"This is a military operation, Captain. We'll be prepared for every possibility. We're not going to get caught."

"Jesus, I don't know. I never stole anything bigger than a pack of chewing gum."

"Captain, it may be the last chance you'll ever get at owning your own airline and flying your own plane." Hargit was an astute and clever judge of weakness and of a man's needs.

"I'm not asking you to turn to a life of crime," he added. "We pull off one score and that's all. It's the habituals who get caught—the odds catch up to them." And the Major unfolded the unsigned pilot's license, put it on the desk in front of Walker, took a fountain pen out of his pocket, uncapped it, and handed it to him.

After a while Walker took the pen and signed at the tip of the Major's finger.

6

"But why me?"

They were riding north in the Lincoln on Interstate 10. The speedometer hovered at seventy but it was cool and quiet inside the air-conditioned sedan. The Major drove the way he did most things—with casual and unflappable efficiency. Walker repeated, "Why pick me?"

"Because it's always better to deal with a known quantity. You were a good officer. You know how to take orders, you're accustomed to military operations. There were half a dozen uniformed pilots I could have brought into this thing, but they'd have had to go AWOL and it would have made a fuss. Nobody's going to miss you."

He didn't think the Major meant anything by that remark but it chilled him, made the little hairs stand up on the back of his neck. He fought the feeling and changed the subject. "Who else is in this?"

"Three others. You may have known two of them."

"Baraclough?"

"Yes."

Baraclough had been mentioned in the clipping. He'd been an Army captain, Hargit's second-in-command. He'd been drummed out of the Army by the same court-martial board. He remembered Baraclough vaguely: a thin sardonic opportunist with a napalm scar on one arm.

"Who else?"

"Eddie Burt."

"I don't think I remember him."

"He was a sergeant under my command."

"They court-martial him too?"

"No. They thought about it but they had to draw the line someplace—on those charges you could cashier every other

American soldier out there."

"But this fellow Burt stayed with you."

"He's a loyal man." You couldn't picture the Major smirking but there was considerable satisfaction in his little smile.

"Who's the fifth man?"

The Major's face changed abruptly. "You've never met him. An ex-convict named Hanratty." He didn't bother to conceal the contempt in his voice.

7

Baraclough was waiting at The Sands in Phoenix. The three of them had dinner there and talked about old times in Saigon as if they had nothing else on their minds. Baraclough was dressed in casual weekend slacks and sport shirt but both garments, and his shoes, had the look of money. Obviously the operation wasn't being financed on a shoestring.

Baraclough was gaunt, dour, with a twisted sense of humor and curious areas of indifference and sensitivity. He paid great attention to such things as good manners and good diction, and his humor was the self-deprecating kind that often went with a high order of intelligence. He was also capable of gratuitous cruelties: he treated the cocktail waitress like a lower form of life—"Have you thought of having that moustache removed, dear?"—but he left her a lavish tip.

After a while it occurred to Walker that the two men worked well together because they complemented each other: each filled gaps in the other's capacities. They were both cruel men but their brutalities were of different kinds.

Baraclough's sadistic streak was deliberate and malicious and he enjoyed exercising it, but he only did it when the circumstances gave him the edge so that there was no likelihood of retaliation against him.

Hargit's cruelty was that of the predatory carnivore. A matter of indifference. It never occurred to him to be concerned about other people's feelings. Hawked, lithe, violent, charismatic—he had the roughshod instincts of a jungle cat, and the grace.

They drove to Reno with only two gas stops and a half-hour in Las Vegas for lunch. Baraclough did most of the talking, filling Walker in; Baraclough was the one who handled details. He was a superb driver: he kept the needle right on the speed limit and when he had to pass on narrow roads he did it smoothly with no great bursts of power and no sudden braking.

Burt was waiting for them in Reno. Walker remembered him now that he saw him. Burt had a shaven head and a waxy, slightly concave face and the build of an oil drum. He had the stolid unimaginative personality of a career master sergeant, which he had been; the threads on the sleeve of his khaki shirt showed where he had carried nine reenlistment hashmarks.

The house Burt had rented was one of those week-by-week rentals Reno served up to people who set up "permanent" Nevada residences for six weeks to get their divorces. It was six miles out of town, a thirty-year-old hunting cabin set back a mile off the highway in scrub timber, out of sight of neighbors. It had two bedrooms and a large paneled front room with stone fireplace and exposed rafters that gave it the look of a hunting lodge. Hanratty, the fifth man, had arrived a day earlier by plane from Los Angeles and Burt had picked him up at the airport. They had two cars among them—Hargit's Lincoln Continental and a Plymouth that Burt had rented from a Reno agency.

Hanratty was a narrow lizard of a man who had been up the river more times than an anxious salmon—a three time ex-con. It turned out he was Eddie Burt's ex-brother-in-law: Burt's sister had divorced him during his second prison term. Hanratty had a narrow face, rough, pitted all over, the hue of veal. His nose was a teapot snout and he looked as if he had been assembled out of leftover mismatched parts—fat legs and hips, a short torso, matchstick arms and a small nervous face. He talked with his teeth together as ex-convicts invariably do, speaking out of the corner of his mouth like a ventriloquist. He was never without a large revolver.

The reason for Hanratty's presence became gradually clear: he was the one who had proposed the operation.

They had released him from the Florence penitentiary eight months ago and the parole department had helped get him a job in the San Miguel smelter. The company bank's Friday afternoon ritual had drawn his attention from the start. He had begun to think about getting in touch with some of the professionals he'd met in stir but in the meantime he'd run into his former brother-in-law in a Las Vegas casino and somehow the conversation had worked its way around to the San Miguel bank—Hanratty had a habit, he kept talking until he found something to say—and Burt had introduced him to the Major. After that it had been inevitable that the Major would take over.

The others had already been over the ground. Baraclough had Polaroid photographs of the bank and the street. That first night in Reno they sat around the kitchen table and the Major filled in the details of the plan, using a No. 2 pencil as a pointer, outlining the campaign like a field general giving instructions to his battalion commanders.

The next day Baraclough had driven him to the airport to show him one of the planes they were going to use. "We'll use

two planes because they may get a fix on the first one.
Anybody could spot us—there's always that vulnerable moment just after you take off. Once they know we're using a
plane they'll figure we're heading for Mexico. That's where
we'll have the edge on them. We'll change planes here—we'll
have to set up a second plane, something with enough range to
get us up into Canada across the Idaho border. We've already
set up a landing strip in British Columbia."

"How long?"

"The strip? Four thousand feet. One of the lumber outfits
used to use it. It's on the weedy side but it'll do, I checked it
out myself last week." They were sitting in the Plymouth
beside the runway; Baraclough had his arm across the back of
the seat. "I thought I'd leave the choice of the second plane
up to you."

The plane beside the hangar was a Piper twin Apache.
"Where'd you get the money to buy that one?"

"Who bought it? I rented it in Pasadena under a phony
name. We hired a pilot to fly it up here for us and I told him
we'd get in touch with him when we needed him again. He
thinks it's something to do with a rich man's divorce case.
They do that all the time around here, people hiring private
planes to sneak in and out of the state while they're supposed-
ly living here establishing six weeks' residence." Baraclough
took the key out of the ignition and opened the door. "You'll
want to have a look at her."

Walker went over to the plane with him. A mechanic
working on a Cessna gave them an incurious glance and went
back to work, standing on a ladder propped against the cowl-
ing.

It looked all right but appearances didn't mean anything.
You couldn't tell much about an airplane by kicking the tires.
"You got a key to it?"

Baraclough supplied one and Walker climbed inside, unlocked the glove box on the inside door panel and had a look at the logbooks: three of them—one for the airframe, one for each engine. The plane had quite a few hours on it since its last overhaul. One explosion per cylinder for every two rpm's —after 460 hours, how many explosions? The plane had something like fifteen thousand parts. Walker shook his head. "I'd like to take her up and try her out."

"Tomorrow. We'll get your documentation fixed up and you can tell the tower you're a Los Angeles pilot we hired. Now what about the other plane? What'll we need?"

They discussed it and settled on a twin Beech. "If we can find one for rent."

"If we can't," Baraclough said, "we'll just have to steal one, won't we."

8

The Major and Baraclough obtained hand grenades and the Mace chemical spray cans from a Guard Armory near Sacramento. They drove over by way of Tahoe and pulled the Inspecting Officer bit. The National Guard sergeant on duty had been conditioned to demand identifications and passes from everyone who tried to get in but the Army had started earlier and spent longer conditioning him to salivate properly to the sound of a high-ranking officer's voice, and Hargit's bluff carried them through. He brought out three grenades and four cans of the chemical in a canvas AWOL bag and the sergeant gave him a smart salute as he left.

There was a suitable Beech for rent in Salt Lake and Burt drove Walker up there to pick it up. Walker was nervous around airports—there were bound to be people around who would recognize him—but he kept his head down and let Burt take care of the paperwork. They brought the Beech back and set it down on a meadow near the rented cabin. Burt went into town, rented a tank truck and brought aviation fuel out to the meadow to fill up the Beech's tanks.

Wednesday afternoon—D-day minus two—Baraclough left Reno alone, driving the Lincoln. They were going to use it for their getaway car and abandon it afterward. Walker was surprised by that until Baraclough explained they had stolen it in the first place. They had cruised a rich El Paso residential neighborhood one evening until they'd found a house where there was a big party. People often left keys in their cars at parties because they didn't want their cars to block the driveway. Hargit had picked out the big new Lincoln and they had driven it to Las Cruces, repainted it, and put a pair of Arizona plates on it that had come off a one hundred fifty dollar flivver Burt had bought in Willcox under a fake name. It seemed a lot of money to spend on a pair of plates but this way the license number wouldn't be listed on any police blotter of stolen car numbers. They parked the flivver in a pay lot in Tucson and threw away the ticket.

Ultimately the cops would trace the Lincoln and find out that it belonged to some rich doctor in El Paso. It seemed to amuse Baraclough.

After Baraclough left Reno to drive to Arizona the rest of them had nothing to do but wait thirty-six hours. It wasn't a good time for Walker. Up to now he hadn't had much time for reflection. It had taken all his concentration to get the plan straight in his head and to account for the tedious details that were going to be his responsibility. He had his courses plotted on sectional air charts and it took a while to get the radio ranges worked out on Jeppesen charts; he had to figure fuel-consumption versus weight, possible wind directions and velocities, take-off and landing time schedules, and a low-altitude route that would keep them out of the Nellis radar picture and at the same time take them as far as possible from any highways and towns where people on the ground might notice the plane. There was no point giving the cops a chance to get a fix on their course.

But when all that was done and they had gone over the last verbal runthrough there was nothing left to think about but the risk of failure, and nothing left to do but think about it.

It had a complete unreality about it. You heard about such crimes, you read about them. You saw a dapper, good-humored, aging fellow being interviewed on a late TV talk show and you were enormously amused to realize that this engaging little old man was Willie Sutton, giving his classic answer to the interviewer's straight-man question: *But what made you decide to rob banks, Mr. Sutton? Well, Dick, y'know, it's because that's where the money is, see?* And as audience to a trivial television entertainment you were amused by Willie Sutton's quiet sparkling understatements about how he'd broken out of Sing Sing—he made it sound absurdly casual—how he'd disguised himself as a bank guard one time, a cop another, an armored-car guard yet another. But when you turned the set off and thought about it you saw that Willie Sutton didn't have all that much to laugh about. He'd spent two-thirds of his life in prison.

It was depressing to think about. Walker wondered why he'd let them talk him into this. He went through Wednesday night and all day Thursday with a hard knot in his throat and a dry coppery taste on his tongue. On the face of it the whole caper was absurd. None of them knew anything about banks and the only one with any criminal experience was Hanratty —and Hanratty's batting average was a lot worse than Willie Sutton's. Hanratty had never tried anything above the level of petty crime before but just the same they'd nailed him three times running and he'd spent fifteen of the last twenty-three years of his miserable life behind bars. Here they were, a grounded pilot, three ex-soldiers, and a petty thief, hoping to bring off a million-dollar score without a ruffle. It just didn't make sense. The percentages were wildly wrong.

Three things kept him from clearing out. One: Hargit, and Baraclough in his erratic way, appeared to know what they were doing. The plan seemed workable, the escape system was ingenious, and the Major had a self-confidence that was infectious. When he told you it was going to work you believed him, partly because of his personality and partly because you knew his record in the Army. Hargit knew guerrilla operations as well as any man alive. Two: if Walker tried to bug out now they'd probably kill him; they couldn't let him walk around loose knowing what he knew about them. Nobody had uttered any threats but it was too obvious to ignore. The risk of quitting was at least as volatile as the risk of carrying it through.

And Three: There wasn't anything else Walker wanted to do. He wanted the money—he had 10 percent of the take coming, and it looked now as if that would be closer to one hundred thousand dollars than to the fifty thousand that the Major had mentioned in the beginning. With that kind of money in the right South American country you could buy a lot of silence, you could buy all the licenses and certifications you wanted, you could pick up two or three serviceable airplanes and build the beginnings of a workable international airline. In a way he realized his ambitions weren't all that much at odds with the Major's. They each wanted the money not for itself but for the jobs it could buy for them.

In the end he knew it was the only chance he was going to have—one last grab at the brass ring before they shut down the merry-go-round. And so after all the panic and all the considerations of what might go wrong, he stayed with it.

9

Thursday night—H-hour minus eighteen—the Major gathered them together in the log-paneled front room for a precombat pep talk. Walker, who was scared but had made a kind of peace with himself, sat in one of the leather captain's chairs and lifted his pack of cigarettes out of the bicep pocket of his leather flight jacket. His chin stung a little—a tiny nick from a nervous morning razor—and the tooth cavity was giving him trouble, but he felt surprisingly good: alert, anxious to start; confident and balanced like a halfback who, expecting to be rammed, intended to stay on his feet regardless.

He lit the cigarette and watched the Major open the long brown case and display the guns they would use.

"The shotguns will make them nervous. We want them scared. Baraclough and Hanratty carry these because they're the two who'll be in front holding everybody still. Burt and I will take out the armored-car guards; we'll need our hands free for the spray cans so we'll carry these revolvers. Walker stays with the car, he won't need a weapon. Burt will stay with the guards in back until he gets my signal, and then he'll come around the side of the building to the car. As soon as we've taken out the guards I'll go into the bank and Steve Baraclough will come across the tellers' fence with the duffel bags. The two of us will stuff the bags while Hanratty stays by the door and keeps the room covered with his shotgun. Any questions?"

They had been over it a dozen times; nobody spoke. Walker saw how cleverly the Major had worked out the assignments.

The Major figured the weakest links were Hanratty and Walker. He had to assume that because he had combat experience with the other two. So he was leaving Walker out in the car where he wouldn't cause trouble and he was sending Baraclough into the front of the bank with Hanratty so that at no point would Hanratty be alone. Hargit himself would be taking out the armored-car guards in the back room because that was the trickiest part of the operation, neutralizing those armed men, and he would have Burt with him because Burt was almost as accomplished a jungle fighter as the Major was himself. The two of them weren't likely to have much trouble with a crew of hick truck guards.

For himself, Walker had no objection to the arrangement. He had no desire to hog the limelight or the action. Sitting in the car was fine with him.

The Major put the guns away and zipped up the case. "You all know the operation depends on timing. They'll be setting off alarms, we can't stop that, and we'll have no more than four minutes to get in and get loaded and get out. But we'll do fine as long as everybody does his own job. I don't want to have to kick ass every half minute—if anybody hangs back too long he's going to get shot dead because we can't afford to leave any of you behind alive to talk. I guess you understand that."

It wasn't a threat. The Major wasn't the kind who made threats. He made logical statements and trusted that everybody could see the logic.

Walker felt chilled. He had begun to wonder why he had got along at all with Hargit during the Vietnam thing. At the time he had regarded the Major with respect and admiration —Hargit had been a bit of a legend out there. Now he saw that Hargit was as cold as any human being could be.

It wasn't that Hargit had changed; it was only, Walker

thought, that war gave men a common enemy, it threw them together so that men with nothing in common created between them a temporary brotherhood which was not false, but conditional. Now the conditions had changed and Walker was no longer a bystander to Hargit's feats but a part of them, and he understood why the men who had served under the Major had been terrified of him. With the Major around you didn't have to worry about the enemy, or in this case the police; you had to worry only about the Major, because if you made one slip you were finished.

"By this time tomorrow night," the Major said amiably, "we'll be crossing the Idaho mountains into British Columbia and we'll all be rich men. We have three automobiles staked out in the trees beside the runway up there. Baraclough and Sergeant Burt and I will take our share of the money and one of the cars. The other two cars are for Hanratty and Walker, and personally I don't care where the two of you go from there. By the time either of you gets a chance to blunder into trouble the rest of us will be halfway to Africa. But let me repeat one warning. Arizona still has the death penalty. I don't want anybody killed. I don't even want anybody bruised. They'll forget the money but there's no statute of limitations on murder."

At the time the warning had not meant very much to Walker. He didn't expect anybody would get killed.

10

There had been a hitch that had almost soured the whole thing but Walker hadn't found out about it until afterward, when Baraclough had told them about it.

Baraclough had cruised through San Miguel on Thursday

afternoon to have a last look around. Everything looked calm and he had driven across the plateau and up over the mountains to Fredonia to spend the night in a motel. There was no point hanging around San Miguel overnight because someone later might remember having seen him there; it made sense to drive a few extra miles and spend the night elsewhere. There would be plenty of time to drive back to San Miguel Friday morning and Baraclough had it planned nicely to arrive in San Miguel not more than twenty minutes ahead of time so as to spend as little visible time there as possible, waiting for the plane to land on the highway beyond town.

Only when he'd gone out after breakfast to drive away from the Fredonia motel, the Lincoln had refused to start.

By that time the rest of them were already airborne out of Reno and Baraclough didn't have a radio to make contact with them. He spent a few minutes angrily poking around under the hood of the Lincoln and finally determined the trouble was in the fuel pump. Nothing serious, but it would have taken time to get it towed to a gas station and even then there was not much chance this town would have the right parts in stock.

In a town that tiny it wasn't easy to boost a car. Baraclough had spent almost an hour in fruitless exploration and by the end of it he felt clammy and slightly panicky, sweating in the cool mountain air.

Finally the old Buick came down out of the pines and stopped at the curb and Baraclough watched the driver get out carelessly, leaving the keys in the car. The man walked half a block and turned into a café. Baraclough crossed the street and looked in through the window—if the man was just having coffee it wouldn't work.

The man was putting on an apron and going around behind the short-order counter.

Baraclough walked up the street, got into the Buick, drove back to his motel. He had a bad ten minutes there; he parked the Buick around the side of the motel where nobody was likely to see it, but he had to make several trips to transfer all the gear from the Lincoln into the Buick and that was hard to do without looking like a thief.

When he drove out of town he kept his head down and hoped no one would recognize the Buick or notice a stranger was driving it.

Nobody raised any alarums but by then he was running twenty minutes behind schedule and he had to push the old kluge up to its maximum—and a hick cop had pulled him over.

"I'd have shot the son of a bitch but he had a partner back in the car. Anyhow it takes a special kind of stupidity to leave dead cops around."

On his way into San Miguel he had watched the power lines and when they began to diverge from the highway he pulled off into a side street to follow them; tossed his rope over the high lines, tied both ends to the Buick and pulled the cables down.

Then he had driven straight through San Miguel, glancing at the bank as he passed it. It was just about lunchtime and there was quite a crowd of workers streaming into the place. That would subside by one-thirty or so and then the next mob would appear about three o'clock when the shifts began to change. They had settled on two o'clock as the best time to hit the bank.

He had sped through the fringe of hills, emerged on the flats and pulled over opposite the crescent grove of scrub the Major had singled out two weeks earlier. Baraclough had got out the wirecutters and portable chain saw and taken down forty feet of roadside barbed-wire fence. Then he'd pulled the power lines down and driven the Buick in through the hole in the fence, jounced across the flats and concealed the car behind the grove.

By then the drone of the Apache's twin engines was an insistent buzz in his ears and when he stepped out of the Buick he saw it making a sweep along the highway and pulling up and turning a slow gentle circle. Then he saw the stake-bed truck meandering along the highway.

The plane had to circle for ten minutes while three more cars and trucks went by. Then Walker had climbed for an altitude search, swept the highway in both directions with his inspection, and put the Apache into a fast nose-down descent. He made a quick low S-turn to come in final on the pavement and set the Apache down in a short landing which jarred the passengers but took the minimum time. He had judged the distance well; standing on the brakes he had the speed down sufficiently to make the nose-wheel turn into the gap in the fence and taxi straight across the flat, around the edge of the grove and into the little hidden pocket in back.

Baraclough had been standing beside the Buick with his palm out, knowing they'd be disturbed by sight of the unfamiliar car. When the rest of them climbed out of the airplane they had twenty minutes to spare before starting for town so Baraclough had told them his story.

11

On the leg into town Walker drove. He stopped a block short of the bank and Burt and Major Hargit got out, each carrying a B-4 satchel containing the stocking masks and weapons they would use inside the bank. Walker checked his watch and stayed put for seven minutes, giving the Major time to neutralize the armored-car guards. Waiting in the car,

Hanratty fidgeted nervously, hawking and snorting with catarrhal barks, and Baraclough chatted amiably about inconsequential things. Walker sat tight-lipped and sweating, one eye on his watch.

If everything was on schedule the Major and Eddie Burt were at the back of the bank by now, standing unobserved in the alley pulling the stocking masks over their heads and arming themselves with pistols and Mace. When they had cased the bank on two previous pay Fridays they had determined that the bank's rear door was not locked: the bank depended on the eight armored-car guards and the armed driver, and since the guards often went out one by one to cafés and shops, the door was left unlocked for their convenience. With the highway situation as it was, the bank felt secure. Hargit and Burt would have about five minutes to surprise the guards, disable them with the chemical spray, paste X's of adhesive tape over their mouths and lock them in.

When six minutes had elapsed Walker grunted and put the car in gear. Baraclough and Hanratty slipped stockings over their heads and bowed their faces until Walker rolled up in front of the bank and waited for two pedestrians to go by and gave an all-clear; then they exploded out of the car with shotguns, Baraclough dragging the empty duffel bags, and Walker watched them jump the steps three at a time and push inside.

He drove down the half block to the alley, backed the car into it and pulled out into the street again, heading the way he had just come. Pulled up by the corner in a twelve-minute metered space and got out of the car; went to the back of it and unlocked the trunk lid, but didn't raise it. He left it ajar barely an inch, went back and got in and revved the engine a bit to keep it warm. From the sound of it there was a bad sparkplug on one cylinder.

He couldn't see inside the bank. It was a sturdy brick structure with small windows set high up, covered with bar grillwork. The main entrance was set into a semicircular brick abutment like a medieval fortress tower jutting from the corner of the building: you couldn't see inside unless you were standing on the curb corner.

The shotgun blast was muffled but it made him freeze. His glance shifted up to the bank door and lay against it, riveted, alarmed. Time was stretching: he knew it would take about four minutes for the local cops to get down here—four minutes from the time the bank turned in the alarm. The alarms were wired direct to a panel in the local police station. Walker looked at his watch, sweating, and was amazed to see that only three minutes had gone by. Two people walked by, not hurrying; he had visions of the others charging out of the bank and crashing into the pedestrians. The gunshot echoed in his head: he had a sudden impulse to clear out—run for it, to hell with the rest.

Then they were coming out, tumbling across the curb Baraclough first. Yanking the trunk lid open, heaving the heavy duffel bag in; coming around the driver's side— "Shove over, that's a good boy." Walker slid across to the middle of the front seat and Baraclough got in, tossing a handful of rumpled trousers over the back of the seat, bashing Walker's ear with them.

Burt was coming around the side of the bank. Hargit backed out the door prodding Hanratty ahead of him. Hanratty was dragging two bulging duffel bags like cement sacks along the ground, bumpety-bump down the bank steps, walking backwards; the Major had a duffel bag over his shoulder and a shotgun braced in the crook of his elbow. In the stocking masks they looked like sinister creatures out of science-fiction films. The Major waited in the doorway, covering the room with his gun until Hanratty had dragged the two big sacks around behind the car, lifted them into the trunk and slammed the lid. Then the Major took the steps in one leap, tossed the last duffel bag into the back seat and crowded in beside Walker in front. Hanratty got in back, with the duffel bag between him and Burt. Doors slammed. Baraclough had already popped the transmission into Drive and run the engine up against the footbrake to prevent stalling; now the Buick squealed away from the curb and lurched wildly toward the head of the street. Under the mask Baraclough seemed white. He hurled a glance at Hanratty in the mirror. "You stupid fucking son of a bitch."

The Major said, "Everybody keep your gloves on." They didn't want to leave prints in the Buick.

The burn scar on Baraclough's wrist, on the wheel by Walker, seemed livid and pulsing. Baraclough uttered a snarl. "It was a piece of cake and you had to blow it."

Walker twisted his head toward the Major. "What the hell happened? Will somebody please tell me what happened?"

"You bought a ticket. You'll find out. Sergeant, where's the bag of nails?"

It was Baraclough who answered: "Somewhere on the floor back there."

"I've got it," Burt said. He twisted down the rear window on the left side of the car. They crested the last hill and swooped toward the flats. Hargit was twisted around in the seat, head low, looking for pursuit.

Hanratty's mouth flapped open and shut a few times, and finally he squeaked, "Shit and shinola, I didn't mean . . ."

"Shut up," Burt said; he was lifting the heavy canvas sack, pouring the twisted spikes out onto the road. He had his arms far out, spraying the tire-breakers from side to side to cover the width of the pavement.

Baraclough said with bitter contempt, "The smaller the man the bigger the gun, ever notice that? Hanratty, for two cents I'd . . ."

"At ease," the Major said mildly.

"Nuts. We could all take a fall for murder."

"Nobody is going to take any falls," the Major said. "Everything's right on schedule. Just keep calm."

"Schedule may get shot up a bit," Walker said. "Have a look at that weather up ahead."

"Nonsense," the Major said.

The bag of nails was empty. Burt discarded it. "So how'd we score?"

"Nobody's counted it," Baraclough said, "but it's big."

"As big as we figured?"

"I think so."

Walker felt a hard constriction in his gut. It was real: they had done it. He looked over his shoulder at the duffel bag on the seat between Burt and Hanratty. Hanratty had swept the crumpled men's trousers away and laid both hands on top of the duffel bag as if he wanted to make sure the money wouldn't get away from him. His eyes were fever bright and he was breathing through his mouth.

Walker said, "Look. Somebody got killed, is that it?"

Baraclough told him what had happened. It took a few sentences and then the Buick wheeled in through the gap in the fence. Spewed dust and bucketed toward the grove. Baraclough concluded, "There was no excuse. He got rattled and he blew the whole thing."

"That's a crock," Hanratty said. "He was trying to pull his gun—he wanted to be a hero."

"Stick it up your ass, Hanratty," Baraclough said.

The Buick half-skidded around the trees and stopped beside the plane with a jerk, its tail going up. The doors popped open and Hargit said, "Get the engines running. We'll carry the things." And Walker slammed into the Apache and reached for the controls. It was no time for a by-the-book preflight check; he started to flip levers, switched things on and fed fuel. The engines started with belches of smoke and he ran them up against the brakes while the fuselage bounced and sagged with the weight of equipment and money and men coming aboard. He heard the passenger door slam and felt the crack of a hand against his shoulder as the Major settled into the copilot's seat. "Go."

12

. . . Now they had turned to run before the storm, reaching for altitude to get above the mountains and never mind the Nellis radar. The weather front was uneven and when they crossed patches of it they were pitched violently around. Somebody— Hanratty?—was retching. The magnetic compass was not pointing at much of anything. A sudden downdraft, like the flat of a palm, pressed them sickeningly toward the ground and Walker's stomach surged up into his chest. He had maximum power now, rich mixtures, but in this air and with this dead-weight the Apache was heavy, sluggishly responding to his control. The downdraft had knocked them down more than fifty feet; the altimeter bobbed and flickered and began once again to climb through the "7" on the thousands dial but that was seven thousand feet above mean sea level, disregarding the variants in air pressure caused by the front, and up here the plateau was more than four thousand feet high and the mountains loomed eight thousand feet above that; Walker still had to pick up several thousand feet of altitude before it would be safe to turn across the razorback summit of the mountain range. With all this weight aboard he wasn't sure the Apache could attain or keep that kind of ceiling but it was that or turn south instead of north, and south was where the highways were, where the airports and Nellis AFB and the police were. . . .

He glanced at the gauges; the tanks were out of balance—there was more fuel in the starboard wing tank than in its mate—so he reversed the flow switches to close off the port tank and draw on the starboard one. Momentarily he recalled that the threads of the starboard filler cap hadn't looked good when he'd screwed it on after topping up the tanks this morning in Reno. But it would have to do. What the hell, another three or four hours and the whole plane could collapse for all he cared. But to make sure he leaned as far forward as he could without pushing the elevators down and peered around past the Major's shoulder, trying to get a glimpse of the tank cap on the starboard wing—and saw a plume of grey-white liquid pouring straight back from the wing.

Baraclough, at the window behind the Major, was rubbing at the pane and talking in a taut voice thinned by fear: "We're losing fuel."

The Major twisted around. "*What?*"

"That does it," Walker breathed. His hand shot forward. Switch back to the left-hand tank. Close off the leaking starboard tank. Bring up the trim.

He leaned forward to look out again. The Major was barking at him: "What is it, man?"

But the fuel was still streaming out. It would: the low pressure of fast-moving air over the wing would pull it out. And with high-octane flowing straight across the hot exhaust system . . .

It was no good. He flicked switches again—cut all starboard power flow, switch off magneto, feather starboard propeller:

the sudden drag pulled her severely around to the right and he had to stand on the rudder and crank the wheel left to keep her flying.

Hanratty was bawling and Eddie Burt exploded in oaths and Walker saw the Major's hands gripped white on the edge of his seat.

She was flying on one engine and the mountains were a looming threat off the port wingtip. The gasoline was coming out of the tank in a fine spray now and that was likely to keep up for a long time.

The Major grabbed him by the arm. "Captain . . ."

"Shut up." He shook off Hargit's hand. He was tipping her over on one wing to look at the ground below.

"What are you doing?"

"Looking for a place to land."

13

"You're out of your mind!"

"Major, it's not as if we had any choice."

"You're panicking. Any twin plane will fly on one engine—every schoolboy knows that."

"And every schoolboy knows what happens when you run high-octane vapor over a hot exhaust pipe in low-pressure air that's charged full of storm electricity. If we can get on the ground before that wing catches fire we'll be lucky."

And because it would have been anticlimactic he didn't add that the fuel remaining in the port wing tank would be hardly enough to carry them fifty miles single-engine.

The earth tilted away beneath the wing and then rose again, swooping, making Hanratty cry out. The ground was all buckled up—foothills. Walker made a tight economical turn to starboard without adding any unnecessary power and headed for the flats. Behind him Baraclough said, "What about that highway?"

"Too far. We must be forty miles north of it."

"No highway," the Major snapped. "Use your head."

He had about two thousand feet and the Apache was nose-up to the horizon, struggling, beating a jagged track through the turbulence; the stall-warning light was flickering a wicked red. He had to shove things forward to pick up a little airspeed. Flaps down full. "See those handles?"

The Major followed his pointing finger. Walker said through his teeth, "When I tell you, pull."

"What is it?"

"Landing gear. I'm going to have my hands full."

The hills were flattening out underneath. Nothing in sight but scrub. Cutbank gullies ran out onto the flats from groined foothill canyons and there were house-sized boulders scattered around like Easter Island statues.

Little shocks ran through the wings and the plane lurched: they were crossing the leading edge of the storm front again. Walker had one eye on the starboard wing: no sign of flames yet. "If anybody knows how to pray this might be a good time for it."

Baraclough said, "If you're half the pilot you think you are you'll get us down in one piece."

14

The sky was cut down the middle in two neat halves: black storm to the west, cobalt blue clarity to the east. In the cockpit it was cold and there was no more talk, only the gutteral growl of the port engine. The Apache had no more than five hundred feet and now there was a flicker of flame on the starboard nacelle. The wind whipped it away and for the moment it was gone.

He was looking for a flat stretch clear of boulders and uncut by gullies. The sun was behind the storm and there were no clear shadows; the bad light made it hard to judge the terrain. Walker's eyes whipped from point to point.

Flame burst from the nacelle again and Walker toggled the starboard extinguisher. He heard the hiss of foam; he didn't waste time looking. It wouldn't matter now anyway.

With all power concentrated on the port side the plane had a heavy tendency to yaw and tilt. The little airplane silhouette on the turn-and-bank indicator was all over the gauge. She still had a hundred and ten knots airspeed but even at that she wanted to corkscrew.

"Over there," the Major breathed. "Flat as an ironing board."

"Don't kid yourself. That's soft clay. But it'll have to do." He had to turn counter to the plane's tendency to spiral right; she fought him heavily and they were all pitched violently around in the cabin.

"You're going to overshoot," Baraclough hissed.

"Shut up. Gear down—*pull!*"

He could hardly budge the controls. His ears picked up the grind and thud of the landing gear going down. The straining port engine throbbed and chattered. "Brace," he said.

The ground came up slowly and she was beginning to tilt, banking into the beginnings of a spiral; at seventy-five feet he shot his hand forward to the board, snapped off fuel and ignition, punched the feathering button. Sudden silence: the rush of wind over the wings. *Hit this wrong and there'll be nothing left of us but a spot of grease.*

The greasewood clumps were bigger than they had looked

from the air. Silent flames began to flicker from the engine again. He shoved the nose down, dead stick, fishtailing with the rudder to reduce speed, and he thought *Christ I'm coming in too fast*. . . . He had overshot the first hundred feet and there was a gully running across their path up ahead there and he shoved the nose down savagely and only yanked it up at the last instant, hauling the wheel back into the pit of his belly. If the nosewheel hit first she'd flip right over on her back and crumple them all to jelly. No sound at all now, then the cracking of twigs, the earth rushing past and under them, waiting for the ultimate sickening grab and flip. . . . He had a vision of the gray Portland runway swooping up above his head as the old DC–6B had crashed—and he almost closed his eyes.

. . . She hit on her main gear: hit and bounced, nose-high, tailskid flicking off a bush. For an instant she was airborne again and then she settled in, main wheels snagging thickly into the soft clay of the earth, bringing the nosewheel down with a blow that slammed them all forward against their seatbelts. Greasewood rushed toward them and around them and against them. The starboard nacelle was fully on fire now and the wheels snagged against roots and rocks, rivets sprang loose in the airframe, a branch scratched the length of the fuselage with a wicked chatter. The gully was dead ahead and coming toward them too fast and so Walker did a groundloop by hitting the right footbrake and putting her into a spin. She whipped around in twice her own length and tried to stand up on her wingtip and there was a moment when he knew they were going over backwards. . . . And she settled back down, right side up on her gear, with a jarring crash that crumpled the port oleo and left her sitting in her own dust cloud on one main wheel and one wingtip.

He sat suspended, breathing in and breathing out. Finally

he reached for the extinguisher handle and started the pump. Foam smothered the flames on the starboard nacelle and covered the windows on that side like lather out of a pushbutton shaving-cream can.

Baraclough said hoarsely, "Holy Mother of God."

15

He unstrapped his seat belt and made an inventory of his bones.

The Major said mildly, "That was a shitty landing, Mister."

"Tough tit," he said absurdly, and found himself grinning like an idiot. "Major, any landing you walk away from is a good landing."

Baraclough stared at him out of blcak hooded eyes. "Walk away to where?"

CHAPTER

1

A town cop sat cross-legged in the corner analyzing the rope they'd picked up on the highway by the cut power lines. There was an array of objects on the floor around him. Clues.

Buck Stevens said, "Time's it?"

"Twenty to four," Sam Watchman told him. About an hour and a half since they'd discovered the abandoned Buick.

"Christ."

"Patience, white man."

Stevens' rookie eyes flashed at him. "You don't care much."

He thought of old Jasper Simalie. "I care. Just take it easy, Buck."

Radio microphone wires were tangled on the cluttered desk. Watchman stood near the front window, leaning a crook'd elbow across the top of the brown metal filing cabinet. Jace Cunningham was slumped at his desk and when Stevens paced angrily across the office Cunningham rolled his thin face around a few inches, without moving the palm on which his jaw and cheek rested. Cunningham's freckled face was morose.

The radio speaker crackled—the Highway Patrol dispatcher in Kingman. Because of the approaching storm the signal was weak and pulsing. Watchman walked over to the desk and picked up a microphone, pushed its Send button and talked and listened. There was no news. The Civil Air Patrol had planes in the air in three states and there had been a report from Nellis AFB radar that a blip had appeared briefly and then disappeared again somewhere near the mountains eighty miles west of San Miguel. Probably an ionized cloud; the storm was playing hell with radars.

"That FBI agent get there yet?" the radio asked.

"Negative," Watchman said.

"Keep a lookout for him. He should have landed in Kanab by now—he went up from Phoenix by Lear jet and he'll be coming down to San Miguel by helicopter."

"I don't know what he thinks he can do that we haven't already done."

"Just cooperate with him, Sam. We don't need to make enemies in that quarter."

"Well I wasn't planning to put his nose out of joint."

"Just do what he wants. Hold it—Ben just handed me this, we've got a make on that Buick. Belongs to a fellow named Sweeney runs a café up in Fredonia. He didn't even know it'd been swiped until Ben called him."

A fat lot of help. "What about Baraclough?"

"Nothing from Washington. We've sent a telex to the Military Records people in St. Louis, maybe get a set of prints on him if he was ever in the arm service."

It might come to that—the long slow hard way: trace Baraclough back, trace his known associates, gradually build a

picture through the FBI's resources. But that could take
months. Here it was hardly ninety minutes since the bandits
had fled the bank.

"Ten four."

Watchman put the mike down and went back to the
window.

Stevens leveled a pugnacious finger at him. "We ought to
be out there *doing* something."

At the desk Cunningham picked up a pencil and played
with it as obstinately as a bored child. Two of his deputies
were still down at the bank taking statements. A lot of detail
would pile up as a result but Watchman had a feeling it
wouldn't lead to much. This bunch had been smart—they'd
had it all worked out, every last detail except the bad luck of
one of them picking up a speeding ticket. Just the same, they
had to be *somewhere*—why hadn't anybody found that airplane yet and started tracking it? He scowled through the
window at the Feed & Seed store across the street. Maybe they
hadn't gone all that far, after all. Maybe they knew they'd be
tracked if they stayed very long in the air. The whole thing
might be a bluff: maybe they'd scratched out a landing strip on
some ranch close by, flown fifteen minutes and landed, and
hidden the plane in a barn. Maybe right now they were sitting
in a ranch house within fifty miles of this spot, counting the
loot and laughing up their sleeves.

Or it could be they'd decided to take a chance and flown
right into that advancing blizzard. Not much chance of coming through that in one piece—but it did offer perfect conceal-
ment for an airplane, if you could keep it flying. . . .

Too many ifs, too many maybes. There was nothing for it
but to wait, chained to the end of their prime umbilical, the
radio-microphone cord.

The phone rang and Buck Stevens jerked. Cunningham

picked up the receiver and grunted, listened, grunted again, and hung up. "They've got the phone lines fixed out east. Still working on the other one."

It was a small blessing. Watchman said, "Mind if I use it to call Flag?"

"Official call?"

"Personal. I'll pay the charges."

"Help 'self." Cunningham got up and made his way around the desk. He moved with a heavy deliberation in his tread. Watchman walked past Buck Stevens, who had the look of a potentially enraged Brahma bull, and took Cunningham's place in the swivel chair. He picked up the phone and listened for a dial tone and when he had one he put his brown finger in the dial holes and rang the number.

"Mogollon Gift Shop, may I help you?"

Watchman's face changed with disappointment. "Hello, Phyllis, it's Sam."

The woman's voice turned chilly. "Lisa's not here right now."

He'd known that already. If Lisa had been there she'd have answered the phone herself. Her sister-in-law only filled in now and then at the shop. "She be back soon?"

"Well she went up the street to buy a sweater. I'm minding the store for her. I don't know how long she'll be." The voice was cool with habitual disapproval.

Watchman said, "Tell her I probably won't make it back to Flag tonight. We've had a little ruction up here. . . ."

"I just heard about the robbery. On the radio."

He didn't want to talk about that. Not with her. "I'll probably get in tomorrow sometime."

"I'll tell Lisa you called." There was a beat of silence and then Phyllis said politely, "Be careful, Sam," and hung up. Phyllis was always polite and rarely said what she meant: *I hope you get your red hide in a wringer.* It was going to be an interesting clan to marry into.

It didn't matter. He could see Lisa clearly, her movements and poses and faces; he could hear the cadences of her voice and feel the warmth of their deep silences together, filled with confidences.

He put his hand in his pocket and closed the little velvet ring case in his fist.

Buck Stevens was writing the past hour up in his daybook. He was filling a lot of paper. In this business it was getting so you even had to make out reports on the reports you'd made out. Abruptly Stevens snapped the book shut and began to prowl again. "God damn it."

"Take it easy now," Jace Cunningham said. "Gentle down." It didn't matter to Cunningham; he had all the patience in the world and the first thing he'd done was see to it that everybody realized it wasn't his fault the bank had been robbed. Cunningham was going along with middle-aged caution, piling up the years toward his pension and a little ticktack house in a retirement community down in southern Arizona.

They heard the helicopter coming and Watchman said, "You suppose they know where to land that thing?"

"All them Kanab pilots know the drill," Cunningham said, reaching for his hat. "May as well get on up there."

2

The FBI man emerged from the bubble canopy and ducked to walk under the decelerating blades. A good deal of light had drained out of the sky and a chilly wind blew across the bald hilltop; only midafternoon, but electric lights were already coming on at the smelter on the hillside and in the town below them. Buck Stevens had his hands rammed in his pockets and was stamping from foot to foot. He said out of the side of his mouth, "Look out now for that masked man. He looks like he carries silver bullets."

"Dry up," Watchman said.

The FBI man had a sleek tawny handsomeness, somewhat dated, as if he required a slick part in the center of his hair and a cutaway coat to be in his element. In fact he was packaged in the Bureau's regulation gray suit, handkerchief in breast pocket, white shirt and subdued necktie. His shoes were absolutely brand new: stepping out of the helicopter he had revealed shiny tan leather soles, hardly scratched.

You could tell one by looking at him, always. The Bureau prescribed their standards of dress and stamped them like print-outs from a computer. Hair short, but not crew cut. Clean-shaven, short sideburns, exactly a quarter inch of white shirt cuff showing below the jacket sleeve. Side-vented jacket to allow quick access to the high-belted .38 in its stubby canted holster.

He had a rigid coin-slot mouth in repose but when he smiled he showed a double row of white teeth; the Bureau took them out of universities—all accountants and lawyers— and taught them to "look and act like gentlemen." This one looked young and vinegary, as if he was up to date in his field: confident, almost jaunty.

"I'm Paul Vickers, Special Agent." He had his I.D. wallet open in his left hand.

"Sam Watchman."

Vickers' handshake was perfunctory; perhaps he disliked being touched.

"This is Jace Cunningham, Chief Constable here."

..

Cunningham said, "Mighty nice to meet you."

Watchman turned. "And Trooper Stevens. My partner."

"Is he?" Vickers asked, and shook hands with Stevens. "That's fine—that's fine." He turned, brisk, putting the wallet in his pocket and rubbing his hands together rapidly. "That your car over there? Maybe we can get inside out of this wind and then you can bring me up to date."

Walking to the car Jace Cunningham said, "We wasn't sure if you'd want to check out the bank first or go on out to where they took off from in their airplane."

They climbed in and the four doors chunked shut. Stevens started the car and put it in low, crunching slowly down the steep gravel trail. The Special Agent asked a few questions to get things started. Watchman had not looked forward to a long-winded rehash of events but Vickers' questions were compelling and logical; he knew his job. He listened expressionlessly, skeptically, with stony unimpressed eyes. It seemed to disconcert Cunningham: the Chief Constable enjoyed exposition and kept beginning his pronouncements with the words, "Well, sir, I'll tell you," but Vickers kept cutting him off and hurrying him up and Cunningham muttered, "Yes, sir, uh-huh," to everything Vickers said. Finally Vickers turned to Watchman and got the story from him. By the time they reached the main street the high spots had been covered and Vickers said, "Let's skip the bank for the moment. The important thing is to try and nail the fugitives before they've had time to go to ground. Where's your communications center?"

"That's over to my office," Cunningham said.

Stevens turned the corner. Vickers said, "It's important that we get these fugitives and get them fast. In this kind of case you've got to do that—give the public an object lesson in quick justice, remind them that crime doesn't pay."

It had been an unnecessary speech and it made Watchman swallow a smile. How an FBI agent who presumably had spent a few years at his job could still believe crime didn't pay was almost beyond belief but actually Vickers was only conforming to type: these fellows had all been Melvin Purvis Junior G-men when they were kids.

The cruiser slid in at the curb behind Cunningham's parked traffic-cop car and they filed inside. On his way through the door Vickers said, "I want to try and get the search coordinated. I take it you've got contact with the Civil Air people and the enforcement agencies in Utah and Nevada."

"More or less." Cunningham showed his discomfort. "We ain't exactly got what you'd call a sophisticated communications network up here."

Vickers swept the room with his eyes. The old transceivers were stacked in the corner on an old table and microphone cords trailed over to the desk. The deputy constable at the radio table nodded to them and said, "Ain't nothing come in since you left, Chief."

But the phone was ringing and Buck Stevens, closest to it, picked up. "Police."

Then Stevens went stiff and his eyes whipped around toward Watchman. They all swung to face the rookie. Stevens listened hard and spoke two or three times and finally said into the mouthpiece, "Hold on a second." He lowered the receiver and cupped his palm over it. "Civil Air Patrol in Kanab. One of their scout planes reports a wrecked plane near the foothills about eighty miles west of here. Could be them."

Vickers strode past Cunningham and took the phone from him. "This is Special Agent Vickers, FBI. Is your scout plane still in the area? Are you in contact with him? . . . Ask him if there's any sign of survivors. I'll hang on. . . . Yes? . . . I see.

Well how bad a wreck is it? Did they crash or does it look more like a forced landing? . . . Fine. Now if you don't mind, ask him if he thinks they could have walked away from it. . . . Yes, I'm still holding. What's that? . . . Good, good. Ask him to fly a tight search pattern over the immediate area and try to spot any movement on the ground. Now can you give me an exact fix on the location?" Vickers lifted his head and turned, lifting his eyebrows at Cunningham, and said *sotto voce*, "Get me a map." Then he turned his shoulder to them and pulled out a pen to jot coordinates on the brass-frame calendar pad by the phone. Cunningham went around him and rummaged in desk drawers.

Watchman glanced at Buck Stevens and surprised a look of anxious impatience on his face: Stevens was closing and opening his fists.

Vickers said into the phone, "That's fine—that's fine. Now I want to get as many airplanes and choppers into that sector as we can get launched before dark. I want to blanket the area with searchers. Can you get on through to Las Vegas and Nellis and Kingman and pass on those instructions on my authority? . . . Now, look, the storm can't be all that bad over there if this scout plane of yours is still in the sector. . . . I see. All right, do your best. What's your phone number up there?"

When Vickers hung up Cunningham was spreading a Texaco road map out on the desk. Watchman had a look at the compass coordinates Vickers had scribbled on the pad. He put his finger on the map: "Right about there." He felt a surge of purpose. *All right—all right: now I've got a crack at them.* For old Jasper.

The map showed no useful detail and Vickers said almost immediately, "Is that the best you've got?"

Cunningham swallowed. "Well, sir, I ..."

Watchman said, "We've got a county topographical in the car. Buck..."

"Wait up," Vickers said. "We may as well all go—get started rolling. I'll use your car radio on the way. Let's not waste time."

Watchman flicked imaginary moisture from his mouth corners with thumb and forefinger and waited until Vickers had crossed half the length of the room. "You'll want a few things first."

Vickers stopped. His voice was metallic: "What?"

"You can't just head up in that back country with what's in your pockets."

"Trooper, you're wasting my time. Say what's on your mind."

"You'll want a jeep. And a pack of food and some heavy clothes. Rifles. Three or four walkie-talkies." He glanced at the Special Agent's feet. "A pair of mud boots wouldn't hurt." Turned to Jace Cunningham: "This is no time to play cute on this one so give me a straight answer. There must be plenty of night poachers in a town like this and you've probably seen them come and go. A few of them likely have snooperscopes —infrared. I want one."

Cunningham scraped a hand across the abrasive stubble on his jaw. It sounded like sandpaper. "I reckon I could scare one up."

The look in the FBI agent's eyes was unreadable.

3

Cunningham and his deputies had gone out to assemble equipment. Watchman started taking rifles down from the locked gun rack and inspecting them and finding ammunition. Vickers had gone to the telephone and was talking, arranging relay contacts through the Highway Patrol dispatcher and the FBI District Director in Phoenix so he could keep in touch with CAP coordinators in three towns and sheriffs' offices in two Nevada counties and one in Utah. Vickers had a brisk command voice and there was no faulting the efficient precision of his maneuvers to coordinate the search and start drawing up a tight net. "I want State Highway 793 sealed off at interval points and I want the roadblocks maintained until further notice. . . . Keep every plane you can up there. I want every inch of ground air-searched before it gets too dark out there. They're on foot if they got out of the wreck at all—I'm going out there myself but it'll take at least an hour to get there. This damned copter pilot of mine won't take me out there, he says the storm's too close to that area. I can't force the son of a bitch to do it."

Buck Stevens came in with an armload of coats and gloves and boots. "Bummed these from the deputies. See if you can find stuff that fits."

Vickers was still talking—evidently to his superior in Phoenix. "Yes, sir. I think we ought to take all these bits and pieces of information we've got up to this point and run them through the I. D. classifications on the computer in Washington. It may help to get a make on these people. We can try all the usual openings—modus operandi, identity of possible twin-engine airplane pilots, access to military stores of chemical Mace, tracer on that abandoned Lincoln up in Fredonia where they stole the Buick—that was a last-minute switch, the Lincoln broke down on them. It's probably stolen too, but it's worth a try. And I'd like some assistance up here as soon as you can provide it. We'll need to go over the witnesses' stories and run checks on recently discharged employees—whoever planned this operation had to know a great deal about the situation here and you often find an ex-insider in on these jobs. I'd appreciate getting a good lab crew up here as fast as possible; they seem to have dusted everything for prints but the local equipment is pretty shoddy and they haven't got any real technicians up here. . . . Yes, sir, I realize it's expensive and possibly redundant but there's a good deal of cash involved. . . . Traceable? I don't think so. Not easily. According to the Chief Constable here they only had a list of serial numbers on the big bills, the hundred-dollar bills, and we all know how easily those can be passed in foreign countries. . . ."

Watchman stopped listening. Vickers was touching all the correct bases. He knew the regulation methods, had a command of the situation and a willingness to make decisions and set things in motion. But there was a weakness in it: the weakness a regular army met when it tried to close with guerrilla terrorists. Computerized organization and modern technology were fine for sealing off elaborate superhighway networks or city streets, or closing in on clues and identities, but Watchman was dubious about how well the technocrats' methods were going to work in the desert with a high-country blizzard ramming down toward them.

4

The storm was ugly and black and they were driving straight toward it. The cruiser was convoyed by the mining company jeep, Cunningham driving; their speed was limited by the jeep's but even so the tires snickered on the sharp bends. Watchman's arms felt constricted by the bulk of the borrowed sheepskin-lined mackinaw. When he judged the spot right he pulled over on the shoulder of the highway. "End of the line. We swap here."

A truck snored by, heavy laden. The jeep waited behind the cruiser, its engine idling roughly. Cunningham stepped out, letting the canvas door flap behind him, and stood with a bland incurious expression on his freckled cheeks.

Vickers took charge. "Constable, you'll stay here in the Highway Patrol car with one hand on the car radio and the other hand on your walkie-talkie. You're going to be my only contact with the rest of this search so I'll want you on your toes. You can handle it."

Watchman looked on with the amusement compressed inside him. Vickers must have read somewhere in a Bureau manual that it was a good idea to compliment local officers and persuade them to give utmost cooperation: but it didn't come naturally to him, he had a heavy hand with the butter-knife and old Jace wasn't fooled; he just stood there with his glance fixed on Vickers as if he was waiting for Vickers to serve a subpoena on him.

It unsettled Vickers; finally he said in a different voice, "You know how to work these radios, don't you?"

"I reckon."

"Fine—fine. Well, then, let's get on."

They got into the jeep, Stevens in back with the knapsack and the walkie-talkies. Watchman handed the folded map to Vickers. "You'll have to navigate. Watch the compass."

It hung in a black plastic shell from the windshield divider, below the mirror. Watchman put the floor stick in low gear and went grinding up over the hump of ground beside the highway shoulder; turned north, away from the highway, and went up through the gears fast, bumping across the brush-studded hardpan at a speed that made everything rattle.

"You don't need to shake us to pieces, Trooper."

"Maybe you'd rather get there after we run out of daylight." Vickers cleared his throat.

The dust lifted high and the jeep's passage exploded gray wrens out of the bushes. After a little while Vickers said, "I think you want to head a few more points to the left—more over that way." He pointed and Watchman adjusted the course, weaving among brush clumps and a spindle tracery of cactus and catclaw. In the half light the mountains were vague and hazy out ahead. Vickers kept his finger on the map in his lap and watched the compass; his finger moved a fraction forward every now and then, marking what he thought was their present position. "It shows a ranch back here in the foothills. What's that supposed to be?"

"Monument Rock Ranch. It's a tourist outfit—they run horseback pack trips and hunting safaris back into the mountains."

"Safaris?"

"Mountain elk, antelope, mountain lions."

"I gather you don't approve."

"Hunting a near-extinct animal with a telescope-sighted high-power rifle isn't what I call a sport."

"I see. What *do* you call it?"

Watchman flicked him a glance. "I guess you like to hunt, don't you."

"I've hunted deer a few times. In New Jersey."

"That where you come from?"

"Leonia, New Jersey. You'd be surprised the deer population back there. If it wasn't for the hunting season the damn deer would eat up every farm crop in the state."

There was no point in starting an argument and Watchman thought he had let the subject die, but Vickers revived it: "I like venison, you see."

"That's more than you can say for most of the customers they get up here."

"I get you. The type that wants a head of antlers to hang over the fireplace."

"I don't even think most of them care about that. They just like to shoot at something that moves."

"Well that's a primitive instinct in all of us, isn't it," Vickers said. "Most people work behind a desk all year and don't get much chance to act like natural men. I guess that's a pet theory of mine—man is a hunter-killer by nature, the paleontologists have proved that."

Watchman tried to make his voice sound friendly. "Out here we get plenty of anthropologists full of theories about the nature of primitive man."

"I didn't mean to step on any sore corns."

"Forget it."

"A little bit to the right now. Try guiding on that sawtooth peak." Vickers buried himself in the map. The jeep rattled and bounced; Watchman squinted, peering through the bad light for gopher holes and sudden cutbanks.

There was an X penciled on the map and Vickers' fingertip was inching closer to it. Westward, over Watchman's left shoulder, the storm obscured almost half the sky and great arms of cloud shot forward from its crest. The wind bucketed the canvas sides and top of the jeep. Vickers reached back for one of the walkie-talkies and got it going by his ear. "Cunningham? Can you read me?"

Watchman heard it squawk faintly and Vickers said, "Fine, I'm just testing it. Any word?"

There was more squawking and Vickers made a face. When he handed the instrument back to Stevens he said, "They've recalled the search planes on account of the storm. No sign of the fugitives."

"Not likely there would be. If they're on foot they'd hear an airplane coming—plenty of time to hide."

"I thought they might be able to see tracks from the air. Footprints."

"In this hardpan?"

"Well you know the country better than I do." Vickers said it in a conciliatory voice but it was evident he felt stung by the mild reproof.

5

Far off in the eastward distance an Air Force jet made a sound like slowly ripping cloth. The silent engine of the jeep made a pinging sound, heat contraction in the cold air. Watchman stood rocking heel-to-toe, considering the crippled remains of the airplane. The landing gear had collapsed on one side and it left one wing sticking up in the air at a high angle. The wind whipped at dried remains of foam where they had used the pressurized extinguisher to put out a fire—the starboard engine nacelle was blackened along half its length. Vickers had already got on the walkie-talkie and directed Cunningham to pass the word to get a team of technicians out here. That was all right; necessary procedure; but it wasn't likely to find the fugitives for them. Watchman doubted the bank robbers had left any clues to their intended destination aboard; they'd done a thorough job of stripping the plane of everything usable—emergency water bottle, fire ax, maps. They had left several air charts behind, showing this morning's weather and the radio navigation ranges of all stations in the tristate area, but the pilot had made no position-fix marks on his charts and there was no way to judge where they would plan to go, or where they had been planning to go before the plane had crashed.

Vickers came up from the jeep, new shoes creaking and squealing, and stood restlessly beside Watchman, bouncing on his arches like an athlete waiting to compete. After a while he cupped both hands around a match and hunched his shoulders to light a cigarette, blew smoke unnecessarily at the match and conscientiously put it in his pocket. "You know we may be jumping to conclusions. Maybe this wasn't an accident. Maybe they planned it this way."

"You think they *planned* to crash?"

Buck Stevens, ten feet away, got up from his haunches and came over. "What do you mean?"

"Look at it this way," the FBI man said. "You get five or six professionals together and you lay out a plan to rob a bank. The bank itself is a pushover but there's a hitch, there always is—this time it's the getaway route. Only one highway through town. So you lick that problem by using an airplane to make your getaway. But you also know the police are going to figure out that you used an airplane. You're not going to have much more than half an hour before everybody in three states starts hunting for you in the sky. Radar, search planes, ground spotters—an airplane's a very easy thing to spot and a very hard thing to hide, as long as it's in the air."

Buck Stevens said, "You're saying they landed here on purpose. They planned it this way from the start."

"It's possible. Or take another possibility. Say this wasn't the getaway plane at all."

Stevens said, "No other planes have been reported missing. It'd be too coincidental."

"Not if our bank robbers planted it here deliberately. Look, they knew we'd be looking for an airplane. So they've given us

one. It's possible they hired some out-of-work stunt pilot in
California to crash-land here and make it look as if he had an
engine fire. That fire could have been set after the plane
landed, you know. Then the pilot walked away, knowing we'd
find him sometime soon but knowing he wasn't going to be in
too much trouble—he was hired to do this, he doesn't know
any more than that. In the meantime while we're chasing the
son of a bitch the real fugitives are halfway to Mexico."

Watchman said, "It's a mite fanciful."

"Sure it is. The whole caper showed imagination—making
them all take off their pants."

"I suppose you've just told Jace Cunningham to get the
planes back in the air and keep searching for the real getaway
plane."

"That's right. I admit it's a long shot but it's worth trying."
The polite smile rode smugly on Vickers' satisfied face.

"It's a cute theory," Watchman said. "There's only one hole
in it."

Vickers' smile coagulated. "Such as?"

"The way I read the signs, four or five men walked away
from this plane. Probably five."

6

The smile disappeared completely and instantly. Cigarette
smoke trailed slowly from Vickers' mouth and nostrils and
whipped away in the cool wind. He said slowly, "You let me
go all the way through with it before you stepped on it."

"I always like to let a man say what's on his mind."

"I don't like being made fun of, Trooper."

"It's an old habit. Hang around and you'll get used to it."

Buck Stevens said, "Wait, Sam."

Vickers threw his cigarette down and ground it out under his toe, making the movement fierce and violent. "Trooper, let's grant you're clever, in your toe-in-the-dust way. Let's grant you've got a sense of humor. I've seen all the movies where the Westerners let the dudes make jackasses out of themselves—maybe you think I'm that kind of dude. I've only been out here a few weeks, I've got things to learn. All right; but I'm a quick study and if I wasn't capable of handling my job the Bureau would have replaced me with somebody who was."

Buck Stevens reached for Watchman's sleeve. "Sam, it's no time to be a porcupine."

Watchman shook his head. The wind across his face was sharp with chill: he turned his collar up against it and said in a hard clipped way, speaking each word as if he had coined it on the spot, "You've sent a lot of airplanes up into bad weather to hunt for something that isn't there. You could have asked me before you went sprinting for that radio—you could have asked me first but you jumped right in the pool without looking to see if there was water in it. The super G-man—it doesn't fit into your neat strategy to look for advice from a seminomadic food-gathering folk primitive. But this is still my home ground and nobody's taken my jurisdiction away yet. Look—it was my friend who got butchered in that bank. And I can't risk any more stupid . . ."

Vickers cut him off harshly:

"Let's get this straight right now. I appreciate advice but the decisions are up to me—you know the statutes on Federal crimes as well as I do. We're dealing with bank robbery, it's an FDIC bank, and we've got attempted interstate flight. The ultimate responsibility is the Bureau's. It's not your case—it's not a private war. I know the old man was an Indian and I could see the way that made a difference to your constable

back there, but I'm not Cunningham and I haven't got time
to play that game with you. Don't get thin-skinned with me. I
don't care if you're red, black, or green. Your partner's right—
it's no time to get contentious, we're both on the same side. I
understand your feelings. I understand about the old man.
Hell, I had an Indian great-grandmother myself, I think."

*Oh God. You understand Innuns, yes indeed. That great-
grandmother of yours was probably a Cherokee princess,
wasn't she. They always are. If you had time you'd tell me how
you sympathize with the plight of the poor Innun and you'd
pull out a Bible and flagellate yourself to atone for the sins of
your ancestors against the red man—but right down at the
bottom underneath all that crap you know for sure you're just
a little bit better than I am, don't you, and you think . . .*

Damn, he thought, *quiet it down to a war whoop, Tsosie.*

Vickers had stopped to glare at him but now added, "We
need to get this straight right now—later on we may not have
time to stop and get our chain-of-command sorted out. Ordi-
narily the Bureau doesn't muscle in, we just ask politely for
cooperation and we usually get it; but if you want to drag your
heels you'd better let me know right now."

"So you can pull rank?"

"Trooper, I represent the United States Government."

Watchman laughed at him—brittle. "I'm not your ward,
Great White Father."

"I didn't mean that and you know it."

Watchman turned around, breathing hard, putting his
shoulder to Vickers and contriving to deal with the sudden
anger that had burst in him unexpected. He had never in his
life been that kind of resentful Indian before: why now?

Jasper, he thought. Jasper and that crazy bit of a conversation on the phone with Lisa's cool blonde sister-in-law.

It was enough to turn an Uncle Tomahawk into a raging Red Power militant.

And this was just a fine time for that.

He said, "If it turns out I'm wrong I'll apologize."

But he didn't turn back to face Vickers and in the end Vickers was forced to walk around in front of him, shoes squeaking; Vickers touched Watchman in the chest with his fingertip—"This is my party, Trooper. Not yours." And he wheeled away. Went thirty yards past the jeep and crouched down to search the ground. The light was so dim now he could hardly be seen. He began to move slowly around, crab-wise. The wind was down now and the air was thick with a heavy layer of silence that muffled the crunch and squeak of Vickers' movements. The jagged black shoulders of the mountains stood vague in the near distance like wreckage on an abandoned battlefield. The smell of dust and distant snow hung in Watchman's nostrils.

Buck Stevens came over close and stood facing away from Vickers, talking over Watchman's shoulder in a voice calculated to reach no farther than his ears. "That look on your face would've made quite a blaze if you'd touched a match to it. Listen, what'd he *do?*"

"Maybe I got rattled." But that wasn't all of it: suddenly he saw what he'd been missing. "I had to kick him in the teeth with it, Buck."

"What the hell for?"

"We can't let him go on thinking he's going to wrap this up with radios and helicopters and their computerized crime lab."

"I don't get it. He looks pretty good to me."

"Most everybody looks pretty good until you put them to the test. Then some stay good and some don't. This one won't. He's going to run out of sand, Buck."

How did you explain things to the rookie? This Vickers worked for an agency where you could get in trouble for turning in reports with bad spelling. They all went by the book. It was rigid, it came down from Washington, none of them was allowed to think for himself. They cared more about sticking to orderly procedures than about getting the job done —because the important thing was to be able to show in your report that you hadn't made mistakes.

And out here in the mountain states you got the worst of them. Because when an agent got in dutch they assigned him to a district office in the sticks. They called it "going to Oklahoma City" but Oklahoma City was paradise against Phoenix, which was Coventry.

So this Vickers had got his fingers burnt for some transgression. That was what Watchman had known all along in the back of his mind: it had only just come to the surface and it explained Vickers' eagerness to fall all over his own feet in an anxious rush to muster the minions of the law and summon all the manpower and machinery in three states when the coming blizzard was going to ground all that precious machinery and drive all that manpower into shelters. It was going to leave a lot of big holes for the fugitives to escape through, but Vickers wasn't thinking that way because he hadn't been programed to think that way: he was nervous, caught up by the fever of self-importance and the need for redemption. He wasn't about to innovate, he wasn't about to take chances. If he had to swat flies with a sledgehammer that was what he would do to get back in Washington's good graces. Even if the sledgehammer missed the flies Vickers would be able to prove he'd done everything correctly.

But there wasn't time to articulate all that. What Watchman said was, "Us Innuns have a name for people like him. The name is Custer."

Vickers had gone back to the jeep and picked up one of the walkie-talkies. Watchman walked around the far side of the jeep, pulled the door back and began reaching inside and taking things out and distributing them on his person. He could hear Vickers talking into the hand radio:

"On the map I see a park headquarters and three ranches within fifteen or twenty miles of here in various directions. Get men into all those places and tell them to keep their radios open. And keep those planes in the air as long as you can—there's still some daylight east of here. . . . They did? That's fine. All right, we're going to wait here until we get word. It's a central spot and the fugitives can't be too far from here."

You could hear it now—the storm was beginning to move, the air right here was very still and heavy and there was a faint growl coming from the west.

Buck Stevens came around the jeep. His boots crunched pebbles and seemed very loud. "What's up?"

"Time to move." Watchman handed him the knapsack and a five-cell flashlight. He shouldered into the heavy night-fighter's battery pack and slung the 'scoped Weatherby rifle, with its red-lamped projector, in the crook of his elbow.

Vickers came in sight with his small mouth tight. His eyes whipped from Stevens to Watchman and he made an obvious effort to be civil:

"I gather you've got something in mind."

"Sit here and wait if you want to. We're heading out."

"No. I need you right here." Vickers' jaw crept forward. "What do you think this is—every man for himself? If a call comes in we've got to move fast and move together. It's stupid to divide our forces when they've already got us outnumbered."

"You've got reinforcements headed out this way. You won't

be alone long. A couple of hours at the most, but that's a couple of hours' head start they add onto what they've already got if we wait that long."

Vickers was very cool. "I've got two dozen planes up. Eleven roadblocks. Men heading into every ranch and building within walking distance of here. When the storm hits they're going to have to take shelter and they'll walk right into our people's arms. But when that happens we've got to be ready to move in—I can't have you way the hell out in the boondocks."

Watchman smiled at him with the lower half of his face. "I guarantee you when that happens I'll be closer to them than you will."

"Tracking on foot? Two against five, with this weather coming?" The FBI agent shook his head. "We've already got seventy-five people hunting. By morning it'll be two hundred. We'll find them. You'd be wasting energy and taking a chance of getting caught in the open when the snow starts. I say it's better to stay by the jeep and wait. Either they'll head for shelter and we'll catch them or they'll try to wait it out in the open, in which case they'll probably end up frozen to death— but even if they don't they won't have got far and we can find them after it blows over. No—you're just taking an unnecessary chance. I won't authorize it."

Watchman looked at the sky. It wasn't moving fast; he might have half the night before it hit. The fugitives were hauling maybe two hundred and fifty pounds of loot, plus whatever they'd decided to salvage from the plane. They were traveling heavy and there was a chance to catch up before the weather socked down.

Buck Stevens said, "Maybe the man makes sense, Sam."

"I don't say your idea won't work," Watchman said. "I'm just saying there's a chance it won't work. I want to plug that hole. If they know how to handle themselves in this kind of weather they might just find ways to get clean out of the country while your whole army's bogged down and blinded by weather."

"That's far-fetched."

"I haven't got time to stand here arguing all night. Look: are you giving me advice or are you telling me flat out not to try this?"

That put it out in the open. Raw meat on the floor. Vickers had to make the choice now. If he made it a direct order and Watchman went ahead and disobeyed it, and if Watchman then caught up to the fugitives and nailed them, it would make Vickers look a prime fool. On the other hand if he left it at "disregarding my advice" and Watchman didn't produce any results, Vickers could always write up an "uncooperative officer" memo that could get Watchman in plenty of trouble. Technically Vickers didn't have authority to give orders to a state police officer but they both knew that was beside the point.

It really wasn't a choice at all. In the end Vickers had to leave himself the opening. "All right. I'm advising you not to do it but I'm not telling you what to do. It's your own funeral. If I need you later on and you're not here, it's going to sit heavy on you."

"Understood."

"What about you, rookie?"

Watchman snapped, "We don't play that game here. He's under my orders."

"I'd like to hear what Officer Stevens thinks," Vickers said. Stubborn about it because if Stevens went on the record as disapproving Watchman's action it would add ammunition to Vickers' arsenal later.

Buck Stevens' eyes went from Vickers to Watchman and

back to Vickers. Suddenly he was at the point of an unpleasant triangle. Then his head lifted: "I don't mean anything personal. I know Sam Watchman and I don't know you, Mr. Vickers. If Sam says it's the right thing to do then I believe him."

"Your faith and loyalty are very touching. I hope they're not misplaced." Vickers' mouth was like a surgeon's wound. "I wish you both luck." He said that expressionlessly and Watchman was reminded of old British war movies in which the Air Vice Marshal said something like that to his pilots just before he sent them up to be shot down by the Luftwaffe. The thought made him grin; he hunted for the snooperlight switch and turned to walk away.

The infrared projector wouldn't throw any light that the fugitives would be able to see but it would light up the ground like a floodlamp when you looked through the lens of the snooperscope: plenty of light to pick up indentations in the hardpan clay—light to follow tracks by.

Stevens was adjusting the walkie-talkie around his shoulders by its strap. When that was done he came away from the jeep. Ten feet from it Watchman turned to look back and said to Vickers, "We'll keep in touch. Listen, I'm not saying we'll get to them first, I'm just saying we've got to cover this bet."

"I gather you know how to build a shelter if you have to. It's my opinion you'll end up sitting out the storm in one." Then Vickers turned his back deliberately and reached for his walkie-talkie and Watchman smiled slightly, touched Buck Stevens' arm and walked out into the dark desert.

And Stevens said, "Git 'im up, Scout."

CHAPTER

1

Walker's legs felt rickety. He slipped the deadweight of the duffel bag off his shoulder and let it drop to the ground. It made a muffled sound and Baraclough snapped at him. "Take it easy with that. We break a hole in one of those bags and you know how long it'll take to chase down every last ten dollar bill in this wind."

The Major said, "Five minutes, no more."

Hanratty was sitting on his fat butt. "You think they're following us already?"

"Not following. Chasing." The Major was on his feet, turning a slow circle on his heels, trying to burn away the darkness with the heat of his stare. He kept moving his head quickly, like an alert animal. *He's made out of poured concrete,* Walker thought, partly in awe and partly in resentment. Major Hargit had the endurance of a truck horse: he didn't look tired at all.

Hanratty said, "Christ, my feet's killing me." Hanratty need-ed a thorough laundering: the creases of his neck looked begrimed, his clothes were rumpled like a beggar's, the lobes of his ears gleamed dully with a grease of old sweat.

By a trick of meteorological caprice the storm hadn't hit them yet. Either it had stopped in its tracks or it had changed direction radically. A few clouds had drifted over east but there were enough stars shining through from that half of the sky to throw a faint illumination across the pale ground. Walker could make out the heavier silhouettes of the moun-tain sawteeth, the silver crest of a hill directly ahead of them, the faint glitter of the Major's eyes when they came around and touched him and went on, sweeping vigilantly.

It was cold; it was still. Gusts came up now and then but the silence in the intervals was leaden. The chill seemed to irritate Walker's sore tooth and he kept sucking on it with his tongue to warm it.

"We should only have about two miles to go," the Major said. "Let's get going."

"Jesus Fucking H. Christ," Hanratty complained.

"You're wasting wind," the Major said mildly.

Eddie Burt got up and shouldered his sack and prodded Hanratty with his toe. "Get your ass moving before I put a boot up it."

"Shit, I just sat down. Give me a chance to get my breath."

Baraclough walked over to him and peeled his lips back from his teeth. "Hanratty, you drag ass just one more time and I'll feed you to the birds. Now get on your feet." Baraclough said it in a sibilant whisper; turned on his heel and went back to pick up his duffel burden. When Baraclough straightened and looked at Hanratty the man was on his feet. Hanratty turned to the Major and grabbed the Major's sleeve and began to say something in his whining voice; the Major said, very soft, "You want that arm broken?" And Hanratty dropped his hand. The Major had spoken without heat but he had a driving, elemental thrust of hard personality and competent brutality and you knew he could have broken that arm without half trying.

Walker was sweating lightly in the cool air. He stayed out of it, to one side, not wanting anyone's attention: he didn't trust any of them. Least of all the Major. Because the Major no longer had any real need for him except as a beast of burden to help carry the money. There was no plane for him to fly and that was all he'd been recruited to do. Fortunately the rest of them were still too angry with Hanratty to think about Keith Walker but when they got around to it he wouldn't be surprised if they started thinking about his expendability.

It wasn't greed Walker sensed in the leader. Hargit wouldn't murder him for his share of the loot. Hargit wasn't that kind of doublecrosser. It was just that three could move faster than five, especially when the three were all ex-Green Berets accustomed to long fast treks through wilderness country in all kinds of lights and weathers. Walker didn't fit into the group.

The only thing he saw in his own favor was that he was a lot less expendable than Hanratty: Hanratty was past fifty, he was out of condition, he was a whiner, and he had made irrevocable trouble for all of them by shooting that God-damned guard.

Hanratty didn't care. He was an ex-con with nothing to lose —a three-time loser. The Baumes Act: one more conviction and Hanratty would get put away in hock for good, regardless of whether the charge was armed robbery or felony murder. They'd throw away the key: no chance for parole. So it hadn't made much difference to Hanratty, killing the guard. But it made a lot of difference to the rest of them and even though Hanratty sometimes acted as though he'd been taking stupid pills he wasn't dense enough to be ignorant of the way the rest of them felt. Baraclough had made it clear in a dozen ways. And the fact that Hanratty was Eddie Burt's ex-brother-in-law didn't cut any ice, not even with Burt.

Hanratty was on his feet now with the bag across his shoulder and his free hand locked around the grip of the big revolver in his waistband. He hadn't taken his hand more than six inches from the gun since they'd left the plane. Maybe it made him feel a little safer. Walker knew it didn't matter much to the rest of them: the Major could take the thing away from Hanratty without blinking an eye whenever he got ready to. But it made Walker nervous, Hanratty clutching the gun all the time. Hanratty had already proved he was a triggerhappy fool.

"Let's move out," Baraclough murmured, and they started walking.

2

They lay in a line at what the Major called the military crest of the hill—just below the top so they wouldn't be skylined. They moved forward on their bellies. Like some kind of exercise in Basic Training. The Major had studied the maps and had said the place was just over this hill and he was right: they'd seen the glow of its lights in the air above. Now Walker reached a point from which he could see it.

The dirt road came up from the south and dead-ended in the yard. There were lights on in one building and half a dozen buildings dark. He could make out the lines of corral fences. There was a grove of trees behind the main house. Wires came in along the road on poles—electric power, telephone, or both. There was the faint sound of a motor pulsing:

probably a water pump for the well. Windows in the main house splashed enough light around the yard to show the arrangement of buildings: a row of dark cabins, probably tourist accommodations, and a scatter of outbuildings—barn, tack shed, smithy lean-to, a three-car garage with half a dozen roofed carports extending out from one side of it. No cars in sight. One of the downstairs windows in the house showed a bluish reflected glow—possibly a television set. There was a tall spidery aerial on the roof.

Someone touched his ankle. He jerked.

It was Baraclough. The rest of them had already slid back off the hilltop. He crawled backwards down the slope and sat up.

They were gathered in a little knot. The Major spoke in an undertone.

"They know we're in the area so we have to assume they've posted cops in the place to ambush us. So we go in light and take care of them. No noise. Sergeant Burt stays here with the money. Hanratty, you're on me—if you drift more than six feet from me I'll garrote you and I don't want a single word out of that mouth of yours. Walker, stick to Baraclough."

It was clear the Major had thought it out and taken the least undesirable option. The Major didn't trust Hanratty and didn't wholly trust Walker; that was why he refused to leave them near the money. He wanted both of them along where he could keep watch on them. Burt could be trusted with the money; no one else could, except possibly Baraclough, but Baraclough was needed if there was trouble below.

The Major said to Baraclough, "You go down first and check out the garage. I'll come through the barn and meet you at the back porch—the dark corner on the northeast side Then we'll take the windows."

They had probably had plenty of practice in Vietnamese

hamlets. Walker hadn't; he'd been an airman to whom the face of the ground war had been remote.

Baraclough touched his arm. "Move."

3

It seemed to have been a long night but when he looked at the luminous dial of his watch he saw it was only a little past ten o'clock. They'd been walking since, what, half-past three? Quarter to four? He had been by no means a physical wreck but there was a blister now on the back of his left heel and he felt flatfooted and weak, his back was like a boil from carrying sixty-odd pounds of canvas and paper money, there was a twitch in his right shoulderblade and he had developed kinks in his fingers from holding the duffel bag across his shoulders and back. The Major had set a hard pace. Remotely he knew how Hanratty must feel by now—very old, very weak, sick.

Baraclough seemed alert and energetic. To him, as to the Major, it must have been a stroll. Walker followed Baraclough's narrow back, sticking close; they went around the long way, around the end of the hill, down the little valley toward the ranch, keeping that grove of planted trees between them and the buildings. At the edge of the trees Baraclough stopped and drew the automatic pistol out of his belt. Walker felt it pressed into his hand.

"How good are you with one of these?"

"Just fair." It was an Army issue, 9-mm. Smith & Wesson. The Green Berets preferred them to the big forty-fives. He had used one only two or three times on the qualification range every six months or so, but he'd carried one just like it every time he'd flown a plane in Indochina.

"Don't use it unless you have to."

"What about you?"

"I won't need one," Baraclough said. "Keep it quiet now."

Well that was something. At least Baraclough, unarmed, trusted him with the gun.

A stupid thought. If there were cops around here and he used a gun on Baraclough he wouldn't get far. Baraclough must know that—must be counting on that.

Following Baraclough into the woods, silent as he could, he wondered if he was being paranoid about it. Maybe it was all in his mind. Maybe they owned a lot more loyalty than he thought: they weren't commonplace thieves. He'd held up his end of it. The Major had been angry for a little bit back there but it wasn't Walker's fault the storm turbulence had busted that filler cap loose. The Major had to see that. In fact they owed him their lives: it had been a good landing. A very good landing. Nine out of ten pilots would have killed everybody on board trying to set down with a shoehorn in soft clay like that.

He hoped the Major appreciated that. It might be worth mentioning later on.

They went forward very slowly; it was pitch dark in here. Baraclough was guiding on the light from the house windows. Walker kept close, ducking now and then to pick up Baraclough's silhouette. Baraclough moved like a cat. Quickly from tree to tree; then stand and listen; then move again.

They went past the back of the house, fifty feet from it, screened in the trees, and angled toward the garage. The overhead doors were shut; there was a small window at the narrow end and Baraclough was headed for that. Walker shifted the automatic to his left hand and wiped his sweaty right palm on the thigh of his trousers, and shifted the gun to his right hand again. His thumb rested on the safety.

Baraclough motioned him to halt with a swift descent of his outstretched, downturned palm.

Walker waited there, ten feet from the end of the building, while Baraclough went right up against the side of it and put his ear against the wall.

It seemed a very long stretch of time, nothing moving. Then Baraclough straightened slowly and edged his face to the window to peer in with one eye, cupping a hand around his temple to block night reflections on the glass.

When Baraclough turned to wave him forward his teeth were showing. Walker eased up beside him and Baraclough whispered, "Have a look." He seemed in an odd good humor. Walker made a mask of his two hands to look in through the window. It took a moment to sort out the darkness inside. Very faint streaks of light came into the garage, lamplight from the house coming through cracks under the doors. He saw an old DeSoto station wagon, wheelless, up on masonry blocks; a horse trailer in the far stall; and in the center space between them, a white police car with a big translucent red globe on its roof.

"We'd better get out of here."

Baraclough was amused. "What for? Come on. No noise, now."

Right by the corner of the garage, leaning against the building under the shelter of the roof overhang, stood a hand-painted sign which evidently had been stored here under cover for the winter: MONUMENT ROCK RANCH— HORSES FOR HIRE—PACK TRIPS & HUNTING SA-FARIS—BEN & MARIANNE LANSFORD, PROP'S.

Baraclough led the way back into the trees and around through a slow arc toward the rear corner of the house where the trees came up close to the porch. It was a plain stucco house like a cube, Spanish tile roof and screened porch tacked onto the back. Baraclough halted just within the trees and when Walker looked to his left he saw something moving beyond the house, toward the barn. His thumb tightened against the pistol's safety catch but Baraclough pushed his hand down and shook his head with a grimace of exasperation. Well all right, it was probably the Major, but how could Baraclough be so sure?

It was the Major. He came up through the fringe of trees with Hanratty and Baraclough breathed, "They're being cute They hid the cop car in the garage."

"Waiting for us to walk into an ambush," the Major said "Check it out—Walker, wait here with me."

Baraclough moved off, disappeared around the corner and was gone, silent as an eel, and Walker stood listening to the pound of his own pulse and the uneasy rasp of Hanratty's breathing.

He felt weight behind him and wheeled in panic but Hargit's fist had closed down over his gun: it was Baraclough, coming around the far end of the porch after making a complete circuit of the house.

Baraclough reported in a taut whisper, lisping because it was the sibilants that carried. "Jutht one cop. Making himthelf comfortable in the living room with the woman."

Walker said, "How do we know there aren't more of them hiding around here?"

"Coffee cupth in the kitchen. Two of them and one hath lipthtick on it."

The Major made a few hand signals and Baraclough took Walker in tow and led him to the far end of the porch. Walker plucked his sleeve. "Maybe you ought to tell me what we're putting over."

"Well we want to take that cop out, don't we. Let me have that thing back a minute, will you?" Baraclough took the gun and smiled vaguely, and led him around the corner along the side of the house. Walker banged his shin on a water faucet that protruded from the foundation; he almost cried out, bit his tongue, limped after Baraclough.

Lamplight spilled out of two windows on this side of the house. Baraclough ducked under the first one and went right by, toward the front of the house. When Walker came by the first window he had an oblique look inside, saw a refrigerator and overhead cabinets, and ducked his head to hunch below the windowsill going past. The well pump started up with a muffled clatter somewhere off to his left. Up ahead Baraclough had frozen by the front window and as Walker approached a buzzer rang, very loud in his ear—it made him jump and tremble and then he recognized it for a telephone.

Between rings a woman's voice said, "It may be for you," and the second ring was cut off in its middle and the woman's voice, closer to the window now, said, "Monument Rock."

The window was open an inch. Baraclough was down on his haunches below it, listening patiently. Walker stopped and breathed shallowly through his open mouth.

The woman had one of those husky smoky voices and made him think of those sunwhacked sun-streaked blondes you saw around expensive California swimming pools.

"Hi, Ben, how's it going? . . . Oh crap, that means you'll have to stay over and wait for the garage to open in the morning, is that it? . . . No, darling, nothing's happened but I doubt I'll get much sleep tonight all the same. Isn't this ridiculous? It must have been like this for the old timers when they knew there was a pack of renegade Indians loose in the countryside." A throaty laugh, and then the voice dropped, became low and intense; Walker could barely hear her now: "Of course he's still here. What do you want me to do, throw the poor man out in the cold? . . . Darling, he's a perfect gentleman and he's an officer of the law. . . . What? No, he's one of Constable Cunningham's deputies from San Miguel."

Now Walker could hear the crackle of a voice on the

telephone earpiece: he couldn't get words but the effect was angry; the woman's answer was a hiss. "Ben, don't be childish. He's right here in the living room and I really can't discuss it with you. Now just calm down and be a good fellow and I'll see you in the morning, chastity intact. . . . My *word?* You want my *word?* For God's sake this is the last straw, Ben Lansford!"

The telephone jangled when she slammed the receiver down and Walker saw the crooked grin on Baraclough's face; Baraclough shook his head with amusement and slowly uncoiled his legs to stand up beside the window. Baraclough's left hand took a grip on the lower sash, ready to heave it open.

The woman's footsteps clicked across the floor and her voice, receding from the window, climbed on a false-gay note that masked the anger underneath: "It looks like our old pickup is really on its last legs. The generator's all burned out. Are you sure you wouldn't like another cup of coffee, Frank?"

And a man's voice, uncomfortable, edgy: "Why thank you, Miz Lansford, I don't mind if I do." Then: "Maybe I really ought to spend the nat out to the barn, ma'am."

"Don't be silly. It's cold and damp and you'd have bats all over you."

"Yes, ma'am. Maybe better bats than Ben Lansford."

The woman's dry nervous laugh was cut off by the crash of the front door slamming open and Major Hargit's voice, hard and crisp:

"Freeze."

4

Then Baraclough was sliding the window open and poking the 9-mm. pistol inside, elbow resting on the sill, and Walker stepped out behind him to see into the room over his shoulder. Baraclough said, to draw attention, "Don't move, you're whipsawed."

It was a big comfortable room with exposed rafters and heavy Spanish furniture of dark wood and leather. The deputy was a big man gone soft, belly sagging over his belt, wearing a blue uniform and a black Sam Browne belt. His hands were flat against the leather couch cushions as if to propel him to his feet but he was arrested in that strained attitude, fearful glance rolling from the Major to Baraclough.

The woman stood in the middle of the room, one foot on the bearskin rug in front of the fireplace. Her head was turned, she was staring at Hargit. Her nostrils flared but she didn't speak. She had walnut-brown hair and she wore it proudly, like a lion's mane; she was encased in a vertically striped shirt with pearl buttons and a pair of bleach-blue Levi's, long of leg, tight and round at the hips. She had a starkly sensual face—prominent bones, heavy mouth, big eyes surrounded by sun tracks.

You could see what it was that made her husband the jealous type.

The Major's voice clacked abruptly, breaking the ugly silence: "All right, Steve." And Baraclough put one foot over the sill and climbed in.

Walker went in after him. Baraclough had walked across the room, going around behind the woman, staying out of the Major's line of fire; now he went behind the couch and bent over to unsnap the flap of the deputy's holster and pluck the service revolver out of it. Then he stepped back and tossed the revolver underhand toward Walker. Walker caught it awkwardly in the air and turned it around in both hands, got his grip adjusted and pointed it vaguely in the woman's direction.

A corded muscle rippled in her cheek. Baraclough was staring at her, frankly and obviously undressing her in his mind. His expressive lips pulled back slowly in a smile.

The woman slid her glance off Baraclough as if he were some kind of zoo animal. "All right. What do you want?"

"Keep your lip buttoned," the Major said mildly. Hanratty came inside and closed the door behind him. The Major said, "Hanratty, find a bathroom and see if there's any surgical tape. A few wire coat hangers. Go on, now."

The woman said, "You're going to tie us up?" She was controlled and angry but underneath that she was a little relieved: if they were going to tie you up they weren't going to kill you.

Baraclough put one of his menthol cigarettes in his mouth and got a lighter from his pocket.

The deputy's hands came together in a prayer clasp. Hanratty left the room and the deputy said, "Look, y'all ain't got no way to get clean out of this. We got this whole area surrounded and they gon close in on you. Y'all give yosevves up to me and it mat go a whole lot easier."

The woman said, "You're wasting your breath, Frank."

"Very astute." Baraclough was standing against the wall, shoulder tilted, smiling slightly, the smoke of his cigarette making a vague suspended cloud before his long face.

The woman turned without hurry and settled on the edge of a chair. She seemed incredibly calm; she acted with complete aplomb, perfect attention, absolute control—control so rigid, in fact, it seemed quite possible to Walker that she might begin to scream at any moment.

The Major said conversationally to Baraclough, "I counted eleven horses in the barn," and then Hanratty came into the room with a handful of coat hangers and a white roll of first-aid bandage tape.

Baraclough handed the second pistol to Walker. "Keep both eyes open." And went over to bind the deputy's wrists and ankles with coat-hanger wire.

5

They tied the deputy to the steam radiator in the corner of the living room. Baraclough said, "Come on," and took Walker outside with him: they left the Major and Hanratty standing guard over the woman and the deputy. Baraclough led the way up the hill.

Before they reached the crest Baraclough sent his call out ahead: "Gentle down, Eddie, it's Baraclough."

Burt was waiting with an expression of mild impatience on his brutal broad face. "What took so long?"

"We had to get the jump on a hick cop." Baraclough made gestures. "All right, everybody load up. Let's see if we can cart all this stuff down there in one trip."

The money sacks seemed to have gained weight in the interval. Walker staggered under two of them and they paused every few yards on the way down.

"Dump it here, it'll be all right."

They left it piled in a heap in the middle of the yard and went into the house.

The Major had found the rancher's arsenal. There was an array of hunting rifles laid out on the coffee table. Two of them were 'scope-sighted .30–06's. "Pick yourselves a weapon." There was a pile of ammunition boxes.

Walker said, "What are we planning to do, stand off a siege?"

"Hardly."

The woman sat in the chair with her legs crossed and her eyes heavy-lidded. "I don't suppose it matters but those rifles cost us a lot of money."

Baraclough said, "In this land of Western hospitality, what's yours is mine."

The Major said, "Now who's had experience with horses?"

Walker turned, looked up from the rifle collection. "I've had a little. Grew up on a farm."

"Fine. Pick us out six mounts and saddle them up. If you can find a couple of pack saddles put them on two more."

"Six?"

"Just do it," the Major said. "Steve, you might go on out to the garage and see what you can pick up on the police radio. Sergeant, go upstairs and see what you can find for us in the closets by way of coats and hats and overshoes."

Walker started for the door but then he hesitated. "Look, why can't we use the police car?"

"Because every road within fifty miles of here is blocked off."

"They'd let a police car through."

"With five of us in it? Forget it. You'd better get moving, Captain. Take Hanratty with you and show him what to do with the saddles—we've got to keep moving. They'll be closing in on this place by morning."

"But what happens to these two?" The cop and the woman.

"Just saddle the horses, Captain."

"In a minute, maybe. First I want to know your plan. Maybe the rest of us won't like it. We've got a say in this."

"Captain, I'm trying to get all of you out of this fix with whole skins and you stand there arguing with me."

"All I want is a simple answer."

"You'll get it in due course." Hargit's hard eyes penetrated him. "We agreed from the beginning this was a strictly military operation. Now I'm in command of this party and I don't put decisions to a vote. If you keep arguing with me I'll assume it's because you want to find out how much of a beating you can take—I'm sure Sergeant Burt will be happy to accommodate you."

Walker's toes curled inside his boots. He went outside.

6

It had been a long time since he'd fooled with any kind of livestock. Fortunately the horses were kept in separate box stalls and he didn't have to chase them all over a corral to catch them up. He had several bad moments getting bridle-bits into mouths without having his fingers chewed. The saddle blankets were soft worn Indian fabrics and the hulls were solid Western saddles, heavy wooden trees with a lot of leather on them, double-cinch rigged, leather *tapadero* boot-guards around the wooden stirrups, a lot of concho strings and saddle pockets. Each one of those saddles had probably cost five times the price of a good horse. He found a stack of X-frame pack saddles built on old Army McClellan trees, with open slots down the middle over the horse's spine; he cinched up two of those on big horses and tied lead-ropes to their bridles.

He showed Hanratty how to smooth down the blankets and settle the rigs in place before cinching them up. Under the yellow forty-watt barn bulbs Hanratty looked pale and unhappy, afraid the animals were going to stomp him or bite him or kick him in the belly. He wasn't much help but in the end Walker had the eight horses strung out on a picket line of nylon rope and he led them out into the front yard and tied the picket rope to the front porch of the house. Horse smell was oddly, pungently nostalgic in Walker's nostrils.

Inside he found Burt and the Major trying on coats and galoshes. They had strewn the couch with clothing. The woman sat watching them without blinking and the cop had his head back against the wall; he sat awkwardly on the floor with his knees drawn up and his hands out to one side, wired to the radiator. His eyes were closed but he was breathing in and out very fast.

Baraclough came in. "You were right about the roads. They've got us sealed off but good."

The Major nodded, not surprised. "Anything else?"

"I gathered there are a couple of state troopers trying to follow our tracks on foot and the FBI seems to have summoned a vast army of people to pounce on us once we've been fixed for them."

"Any weather report?"

"The storm could hit any time. Hell you can see that for yourself by stepping outside."

Hanratty was rooting through the pile of clothes, tossing discards on the floor.

The Major said, "We'd better start tying down the loads. Sergeant, scrape together whatever you can find in the kitchen by way of provisions and utensils. Sack them in something we can tie on a horse. Captain, did you find any rifle boots in the barn?"

"Any what?"

"Saddle scabbards for rifles. It's a hunting resort, they must have them somewhere."

The woman said tonelessly, "You'll find them in the tack room."

"Thank you kindly," Baraclough said.

Walker went out and found the scabbards. Took five and strapped them to the saddles. Baraclough and Hanratty were tying down the duffel bags on the pack saddles and Walker said, "You'll want diamond hitches over those to keep them on—I'll show you."

When they had finished loading the animals he looked at his watch. Just past midnight. He went inside and shoved his feet into a pair of Wellington boots, found a plaid hunter's coat and a pair of mittens, and helped himself to one of the blankets piled on the couch. There was also a stack of oilskin rain slickers Burt had brought downstairs and he collected one of those. He put an earflapped hunting cap on his head and picked up a Remington .302 rifle, shoved a box of cartridges in his pocket and said, "I guess I look the part." He was feeling hazy, disoriented, vaguely euphoric as if drugged.

The Major was sitting at an old rolltop writing desk with a pencil in his left hand, printing a note on a piece of ranch stationery. Hargit was right-handed, writing with his left hand to disguise it. When he was done he handed the note to Baraclough. "Pin it on him. Don't make noise—we don't know who's in earshot by now." Then he turned with a sweeping motion of his arm. "Everybody outside now. You too, Mrs. Lansford. Please equip yourself from your wardrobe here."

Numb, dulled, Walker drifted outside with Burt and Hanratty. They stood near the horses. The light in back of the house went out; the living-room windows stayed bright. The faint cool miasmic breeze that came down the hill seemed to get inside Walker's skin and scratch his bones. He knew what was about to happen inside the house and he knew he wasn't going to do anything about it, and in his fatigued state of listlessness he no longer had the power to rationalize away the knowledge that he was, in this instant of time, sinking to a level of inhumanity from which there was no return. Everything else up to now had been defensible: you could bluff yourself into justifications—the money was insured, nobody got hurt; Hanratty killing the bank guard, that was nobody's fault but Hanratty's and Walker wasn't going to wear emotional sackcloth and ashes the rest of his life for that mistake that hadn't been his own; surprising the woman in her own home, stealing her husband's horses and saddles and clothes and food, trussing the cop—all these were necessary to self-preservation and since nobody was irrevocably injured by these acts they could be dismissed.

But now the Major came out onto the porch, holding Marianne Lansford by the arm, walking her down the steps into the yard. The woman's lower lip was clenched between her teeth; she looked steadfastly at the ground ahead of her. It left Baraclough in the house with the cop, and finally Baraclough came outside tugging his gloves on. "All set."

Walker's vision lost focus and he swayed against the porch. Gripped the rail for support, closed his eyes and fought the nausea.

An iron fist gripped his upper arm. He opened his eyes, looked at it: Baraclough's fist.

Walker's eyes rode up to the face. Baraclough looked heavy-lidded, detached—as if sexually released.

Baraclough said, "We could argue about it if we had time."

"Could we."

"They'll know we were here, of course, but that won't tell them who we are—what we looked like. The cop was the only one who could have told them that."

So the cop was dead, strangled by the wiry fingers that gripped Walker's arm, and the note pinned on the dead cop's shirt would tell the other cops what the Major wanted them to know. Walker had seen the note when the Major had handed it to Baraclough: *Keep your distance. We have Mrs. Lansford. She stays alive as long as we are not harassed.*

Walker said, "You were the one who said it was stupid to leave dead cops lying around."

"That was before Hanratty killed the old man, wasn't it." The sensuality of Baraclough's little smile made him turn away.

The Major had the woman over by the horses. She hadn't

heard Baraclough and there was no reason to think she knew the deputy had been killed. She wasn't supposed to know: ignorance would keep her more tractable.

The Major was talking to her:

"Hanratty here isn't much of a cowboy. Can you pick out a horse for him? Which one of these animals is nice and slow and gentle?"

Mrs. Lansford made a point of avoiding the Major's eyes. "I suppose that one." She nodded toward a sleepy-looking sorrel; then she threw her head back: "The penalty for kidnaping is damned severe, you know."

"Possibly. When you're already wanted for murder it doesn't matter all that much any more." The Major tugged his cap down tight. "We've got very little to lose, you see. We're desperate men." He said it deadpan. And before the woman could speak again he added, "And please don't tell us we won't get away with it. Now please pick out a horse for yourself and get mounted."

The woman thought about arguing with him, thought better of it, turned and looked over the animals. Without much hesitation she walked toward the big blue gelding at the head of the string. The blue's ears were upright, alert; it watched her approach and the hide along its flank quivered.

"Fine," the Major breathed; and lifted his voice like a whip: "Stop right there, Mrs. Lansford."

She turned around. "What now?" Lovely eyes full of anger.

The Major flicked his glance toward Walker. "Can you ride pretty well?"

"I used to. Long time ago."

"It comes back to you, doesn't it? Like riding a bike."

"I guess so."

"You ride the white horse, then."

The woman opened her mouth; the Major cut her off: "And

you ride the old sorrel, Mrs. Lansford. The one you picked out for Hanratty. Obliging of you to point out the slowest horse."

The woman's face changed. Now for the first time it was genuine hate. The Major had tricked her and she was too proud to accept that.

Walker went over to the blue—what the Major had called the white horse—and picked up the reins. The woman turned slowly and went stiffbacked toward the old sorrel and began to adjust the stirrup length for herself. The Major spoke to her back: "Understand this, Mrs. Lansford. We're miles from the nearest help, there's no one within screaming distance. You've got a slow horse and if you try to run for it Captain Walker will have no trouble running you down. Then we'd have to tie you and put a gag in your mouth. It wouldn't be very comfortable. You understand?"

She spoke without turning her head. "I understand." She buckled the stirrup leather and let it drop. "I'd like to know where you're taking me."

"You're entitled to know that."

Instantly the Major had everyone's attention. He lifted his arm toward the heavy darkness of the mountain peaks to the north. "We're going up there."

Silence: Swish of horsetails, thump of hoof. Hanratty squeaked. "Shit. You must be out of your gourd."

Walker took a step forward. "Major, we'll get buried under a ton of snow up there. You don't know these mountains."

"I've spent a good part of my life in montagnard country, Captain. I'll keep you alive."

"It's insane. It's a dead end."

The woman wheeled. "Your friend is right. No one goes up in those mountains after the first snow. It's suicide."

The Major said, "I certainly hope the police are as convinced of that as you are, Mrs. Lansford."

Baraclough came past Walker and climbed into a saddle. When he had his feet settled in the stirrups he said, "Major Hargit knows wild country survival better than any man alive. He's right. Now let's quit arguing and start moving."

When Walker turned to put his foot in the stirrup he somehow caught the eye of the woman and for that brief instant their glances locked with tremendous impact: an exchange of sudden shared understanding, of bleak and hopeless regret.

Hanratty said, "Somebody help me get on top of this animal."

CHAPTER

_____

1

Through the infrared scope they showed up plainly: boot-heel indentations, scuffed ground, a patch where the pebbles had been disturbed when they'd set down their burdens to rest or reconnoitre.

"Watch yourself now. Monument Rock just over the hill."

"Okay, *kemo sabe.*" The knapsack made Stevens look hunchbacked.

Sam Watchman covered the last twenty yards on his belly and took his time looking it over. There were lights burning in the front room of the house. He didn't see anything move.

After he had completed his naked-eye inspection he lifted the Weatherby to his shoulder, switched on the infrared beam and put his eye to the scope.

The snooperscope was designed to make heat visible. The image on the lens revealed contours of temperature rather than light. The warmth of the earth made it red; the relative coldness of the air made it green. The buildings, which stored less heat than the ground but more than the air, were an indeterminate mauve. The heat of lamplight against the front window made it show up very hot. The trees behind the house were a madras patchwork of shades.

If there had been human flesh in the beam's line it would have shown up heavily red on the lens.

Watchman made a hand signal and the rookie handed him the walkie-talkie. He spoke into it with low-voiced clarity: "Watchman to Vickers. You still reading me?"

"I hear you."

"How long since you've heard from the deputy at Monument Rock?"

"I haven't heard from him at all. Hold on, I'll check with Cunningham."

Watchman put the scope on the tracks going down the hill. It took a few minutes to sort out the spoor. Four of them had walked down the hill. Two had walked up again. Three, carrying heavy loads—the indentations were deeper—had walked down again.

The FBI agent's voice sputtered in his ear. "No word from Deputy Foultz since eleven o'clock."

Watchman twisted his wrist to check the time. Almost two in the morning. "Then you'd better get over here and bring some people with you."

2

"Let's go down and scout around."

"Wouldn't it be better to wait for Vickers to show up?"

"If they're still inside the house they'd hear the cars coming." Watchman backed off the hilltop. "We'll go around and come in through the trees."

When they got near the house he played the scope around and made out patterns of footprints inside the grove; it was no good sorting out tracks on the open earth of the yard because the ground had been scuffed up by years of use. Watchman crept to the back of the house and used his ears. Heard nothing but the thrumming of the well pump; signaled Stevens forward and went around the side of the house, moving without sound, forward along the wall to the lighted front window.

When he looked inside he turned stiff in his tracks.

3

One of the FBI technicians offered a pack with a half-extended cigarette and Vickers, nodding thanks, took it and put it in his mouth and poked his face forward to take a light from the technician's cupped match.

The technician waved his hand to extinguish the match. "Been dead two and a half, three hours. Not more." He turned to Watchman: "The front door was open when you got here?"

"Yes. It looks like the kind of door that's never shut." Watchman's eyes went beyond the technician to Vickers. "While you were on your way here I called Olsen's horse ranch. Asked them to send a couple of four-wheel-drive trucks and horse trailers over here. All right?"

Vickers looked up at him; he had been bending down to look at the one-millionth-scale contour map on the table. "You think you can catch them in this country with trucks?"

"We can get fifteen miles back in there and use horses from

there. We'll gain at least an hour."

"They've probably got three hours' jump on us."

"And they've got the woman," the technician said. He was down on one knee, spreading a blanket over the dead deputy.

Watchman turned to Buck Stevens. "They left three horses in the barn. Let's get saddles on them."

4

The yard filled with cars and trucks—police, FBI, horse trailers, Dodge power wagons, Vickers' jeep.

A big red-faced man drove a poorly stuck-together convertible into the yard. There was no wind. The dust settled just where it had been kicked up. The big man exploded out of the car. "What the hell is all this?"

Vickers stepped forward. "You're Lansford?"

"You're God damn right I am. What's everybody standing around for?"

Vickers was flashing his identification. "We're busier than we look, Mr. Lansford."

The rancher whipped his hat off. It had indented a red weal across his forehead; he rubbed it with the side of his index finger. "They took my wife, is that right?"

"I'm afraid it is."

"And you're standing around." Lansford's eyes narrowed into a fighter's squint. "Okay. Help yourselves. Stand around all night if you want." He turned with a quick snap of beefy shoulders and began to tramp toward the three horses tied up by the barn.

Watchman blocked his path. "Take it easy, Mr. Lansford."

"Take it easy!" The man had a good loud bellow. It rang around the yard.

Vickers said, "Try to calm down. Let us handle this, Mr. Lansford—we don't need amateur help."

"You've got it whether you want it or not."

"Do you want me to place you under arrest?"

"On what God damn charge?"

"Protective custody if you like."

"Piss on that. Those are my horses. You don't go an inch on those horses without my permission."

"All right," Vickers said. "I hadn't planned to use them anyway."

Watchman turned; stared at him.

Vickers took two paces forward so that his face picked up the lamplight that splashed off the porch. "These five men have attempted a wave of terror. They've killed two men, one of them an officer of the law. They've abducted a woman. They've stolen almost a million dollars. Washington and Phoenix have agreed we can't tolerate terrorism on this scale. We've traced the background of one of these men and it looks like we're dealing with a well-organized group of former United States Army officers who were recently cashiered for acts of extreme brutality and savagery in Vietnam. The government regards this as a critical situation because we don't know how much organized paramilitary support these men have and we don't know how many more acts of violence they're planning to execute. For that reason the federal government and the Governor of Arizona have agreed to mobilize the National Guard."

5

"By morning," Vickers continued, "a cordon of police officers and National Guard troops will have this mountain range completely surrounded. We're establishing roadblocks on every road and trail that comes out of the range. If the storm holds off until daylight, the troops will begin to move into the mountains from all sides, and we'll have helicopters up there to locate the fugitives. We've got them bottled up in there—they've got no way out. It's only a question of time now."

Ben Lansford's outdoor eyes squinted at Vickers. He made a half turn and rubbed the back of his neck nervously, bobbing and ducking his head. A lot of excited talk ran around the yard. Lansford met Sam Watchman's glance, ran a hand through his hair showing his desperation, and said in a lower voice than he'd used before, "You mean you've got these horses saddled right here and you're not going in after them."

Vickers stepped in. "Mr. Lansford, they're only three horses. There are at least five heavily armed men out there. I don't see taking the kind of risks we'd run with a three-man scavenger hunt." Vickers made an elaborate sweeping arc with his arm and looked at his watch. "Once the fugitives have satisfied themselves there's no way out of those mountains past the cordon of troops they'll have to see the logic of releasing your wife and giving themselves up."

"Will they?" Lansford said. "Would you?"

"Naturally."

Lansford's mouth clamped shut: rage swelled behind his eyes. You could see the obsession that had him in its grip. Five toughs had his wife. One look at Ben Lansford—bluff, loud, impatient, arrogant—and you knew the kind of conclusions he must have jumped to.

And it was little comfort knowing they might be the right conclusions.

Vickers said, "Try to relax, Mr. Lansford. We'll keep you advised of every development. But right now there's nothing for any of us to do but wait."

Watchman's hair rose. He had tried to convince himself it wasn't going to come to this but that had been stupid. Obviously it was going to happen the same way every time Vickers found a theory that pleased him. Vickers and his kind had this marvelous ability to find ways to make all the facts fit the theory.

Vickers was continuing in his clumsy reassuring voice: "If the storm passes by we'll move in right away at dawn. If it doesn't, the fugitives won't be going anywhere either. In either case, Mr. Lansford, thousands of men will ridgewalk every inch of those mountains if it becomes necessary. We're good at what we're paid to do. Trust us."

Watchman turned. "I'd like a word with you."

"Go ahead."

"In private." He turned past Vickers, went by the horse trailers and chose a spot behind the jeep.

6

Vickers came around the jeep, paused to step on the stub of his cigarette, looked up quickly as if to catch an unguarded expression on Watchman's cheeks. "All right. What is it?"

"I've said this to you before. You're not going to get this job done with armies and helicopters. Use your head—you got a make on them, you know they can take care of themselves in the woods. They're not going to blunder into any traps. They've got a blizzard coming and they'll use it."

"If it pins us down it pins them down."

"No. It gives them time to get ten thousand miles from here."

Vickers just watched him with the patient attitude of a man giving him enough rope to hang himself.

Watchman showed his anger. "Do you have any idea of the size of the circumference of this range?"

"I've seen the map."

"And you think you can seal it off with a cordon of troops?"

"Don't be an idiot. We know the general area. We're stringing lines of troops across the mountains ten miles east and ten miles west. We've got them boxed into a square, ten miles on a side."

Watchman was unimpressed. "Forty-mile perimeter—how many troops, two thousand? Fifty men to the mile? A hundred feet between each man? And you don't think five Green Berets can crawl through a hundred-foot gap in a blizzard without getting spotted?"

Vickers kept his face rigid with suppressed feelings. "Trooper, you're in trouble with me."

"Oh wow."

"One. They've called out more like four thousand troops— so that narrows your gap a little, doesn't it? Two. Our cordon won't be standing still, it'll be moving—and that means converging, the gap between men growing narrower all the time. Three. Even assuming somehow the fugitives did slip through the lines, they couldn't get far on foot and if they tried stealing a car they'd be stopped by a police roadblock. Every road within forty miles of here is blocked at ten-mile intervals. No: let me finish. This is the last time you're going to try and make a fool out of me. I don't know what I've done to rub you the wrong way but you've thrown your last banana peel at me. Understand this: if I thought I was the wrong man for this job I'd step out. If the time does come, I'll know before anybody else does. In the meantime I want no further interference from you. As far as I'm concerned you can go home right now and amuse yourself practicing your fast draw."

"Not good enough," Watchman said. "You've made a long

speech. Fine. Now I'll take equal time. One. They've got that man's wife with them. What happens if they walk right up to your National Guard lines with a pistol at the woman's head and use her as a hostage for safe conduct to the nearest Army helicopter? How many weekend soldiers do you know with balls enough to put up a fight when they're using a woman for a shield? Two. Any Indian with a brain knows enough to get down on his belly and let a cordon walk right past him and then get up and fade into the landscape behind them. At least give your Green Berets credit for that much sense. Three. When the five of them get away scot-free and leave you with Mrs. Lansford's dead body on your hands you won't need any help from me to make a fool out of yourself. End of speech."

7

When Watchman came around past the back of the trailer he saw Lansford sitting on the porch steps, dry-washing his clasped hands. Watchman signaled Buck Stevens and went to the horses. Untied two of them and began to lead them toward the horse trailer. Stevens trotted over to it and let down the tailgate ramp and Watchman went inside to lead the horses into the box. Stevens lifted the gate behind them and latched it shut, and Watchman climbed out over the slats.

Vickers was standing there. "What do you think you're doing?"

Watchman glanced toward the house. Lansford sat holding his head as though it weighed half a ton. He was out of earshot. Watchman said, "I'm going to try and get his wife back for him."

"Very noble."

"No. It's my job."

"You're living in the past, Trooper. This isn't a one-man job. It isn't one of those movies where the stalwart Indian scout goes out to rescue the captured white woman from the savages. You're two men who put your pants on the same way I do and you think you're going to win out against five well-armed soldiers who've got all the guts and all the technical know-how there is. They're organized—you're not. It takes a bigger organization to stop them. You'll just get yourself killed—and probably get the woman killed too."

Watchman checked the tailgate latches and turned. "You could try to stop me if you want."

"Suppose we put a call in to your superiors and see what they say."

"Go ahead."

Vickers showed his surprise. "I will. You'll wait right here until I have an answer." And began to turn away.

"I guess not," Watchman said, and went toward the cab of the truck.

Vickers gripped him by the arm and turned him back. "God damn you for a stubborn man. Do I have to put handcuffs on you?"

Watchman just looked at him. "You could try."

"Trooper, one shout from me and we'll drive you down into the ground like a tent peg."

"Do that. And then explain it to the Bureau after you come up with nothing in your hands but Mrs. Lansford's corpse."

"You are wrong."

"Maybe I am. If I'm wrong I'm wrong. If you're wrong you're dead wrong. You've got a stupid way of figuring up odds, Vickers. If I was taking bets on you I wouldn't even bother laying them off." Watchman opened the door and climbed up into the cab.

Vickers stepped back. He didn't say anything more. His hooded eyes pushed at Watchman.

Watchman triggered the starter and the engine caught and began to rumble. He reached for the headlight switch and then the passenger door opened and Buck Stevens climbed in. "Weren't you going to wait for your faithful white companion?"

"You don't have to make this run, Buck."

"Who says?"

"If I make a mistake up there he'll have my head in a basket. If you're with me he'll have yours too. I'm not going to ask you to stick your neck out."

Stevens pulled the door shut. "Okay, you didn't ask me."

8

When he jammed the levers into four-wheel drive the transmission made a harsh whining growl. Watchman flicked on the high beams and they stabbed the hills, swinging wildly like searchlight beacons. Jouncing along high up in the cab of the old power wagon he had no trouble following the tracks of the eight horses: nobody could conceal evidence of that much traffic on this soft clay.

"*Kemo sabe,* maybe I'm a wet blanket but what if they look back and see our lights?"

"I hope they do."

"You do."

"Can't hurt to keep them nervous."

The borrowed jacket was tight across his shoulders. He cracked a window against the heater's stuffy warmth. The hoofprints angled up into higher foothills and the truck engine strained on the grade against the weight of the horse trailer. Half-past three in the morning: it would be dawn soon, if the blizzard held. Along the hilltops here the wind was bending the scrub and an occasional snowflake drifted against the windshield but the edge of the storm was holding still, circling, a visible black-on-black wall eight or ten miles to the west. He had known storms to sit still like that until they blew themselves out. He had also known them to sit still like that until they had gathered maximum centrifugal strength and then burst forward like nuclear explosions, ripping out trees, peeling roofs off houses, overturning trucks, shoveling livestock into steep canyons by the ton. Two years ago they'd had an early fall blizzard in the high country that had stranded ten thousand Navajos and wiped out half their sheep; and the other half had been saved only by massive air drops of feed.

It was the kind of night on which you wanted to be home snug in bed. In bed with a healthy firm-haunched young Lisa lying warmly against you, idle talk or long easy silences until she felt stirred to make love again. The nerve-ends of his hands and lips remembered the textures of her. Right now she would be asleep but in a few hours, getting up and going downtown to open the shop, she would be ripping off a few choice words about his absence. Lisa was not your average housewife worrying about stubborn kitchen sink stains. Nor likely ever to become one.

Thinking about her unsettled him. In fact he was unsettled merely by the fact that he was thinking about her at all. Not the time and place for it.

He bestirred himself. "You put the stuff in the truck?"

"You betchum. But you sure as hell don't plan to travel light. Snowshoes, Sterno, blankets, axes, ropes—I didn't know we were outfitting a Polar expedition."

"Just minding the Boy Scout motto."

9

It began to get rocky and the power wagon pitched and skidded on the stones. They had covered eight or nine miles in an hour and that had cut the fugitives' lead but they were going to have to abandon the truck soon. The hills were beginning to buckle and heave.

He swung the grinding power wagon up a steep grade, all four wheels scrabbling at the pebbled surface. At the top the hoof tracks turned across the sand shelf into a wide thicket of scrub oak and piñon that twisted up the spine of a razorback fin toward the pine-wooded heights. Watchman set the hand brake and switched everything off. "Unload the horses and get everything packed on them."

When he pushed the door open against the wind a blade of cold stabbed into the truck. He turned his collar up and climbed down; got the ax from the truck bed and went out into the scrub with it. Without much discrimination he hacked down a succession of three-foot bushes and dragged them into a pile on the hardpan fifty feet from the truck and downwind. He wasn't satisfied until he had a good big stack. He whacked half a dozen thick hard scrub trees apart and scattered the logs judiciously on and inside the brushpile and when it looked satisfactory he brought both five-gallon gasoline cans from their fender-runningboard brackets and drenched the woodpile with fuel.

Gasoline stink was raw in the wind. He was sweating from his exertions; he lifted his hat and dragged a coatsleeve across his forehead. The wind roughed up his hair. Stevens was standing by the horses, packed and ready, watching him with a long face. After a moment Watchman put his hat on and walked over to him, slipped the leather scabbard over the head of the ax, and strapped it to the saddle. "I hate a noisy silence,

Buck. Say what's on your mind."

Deep breath in and out: Stevens put his head down, thinking. In the end he said, "The truth is I don't like the odds all that much."

"You can stay here. You can go back."

"No. But it would help to know what we're trying to do, kemo sabe."

"Trying to keep Mrs. Lansford alive, mostly."

"How?"

"Keep pressure on them."

"You said something like that before. I don't follow."

"If they thought they had a long lead and a good chance to get out clean then they'd have no reason to keep her alive. They took her for a hostage but you only need a hostage when somebody's pushing you."

"I see. You want them to know we're pushing them. But I still don't see where that gets us."

"Maybe with a little luck it gets us in close enough to get her away from them."

"That'll take a lot more than luck, kemo sabe."

"Now that depends on the weather, doesn't it."

"I see that. But it's still two against five. I don't see why you figure it's up to you and me to tackle it by ourselves. Like the FBI man said it's not our responsibility, it's his."

"Well you need to have some reason to get up in the morning, Buck."

"I'll put that in your obituary."

"I'll tell you the way I was thinking. I was thinking suppose I was that poor son of a bitch Ben Lansford and the woman they took was Lisa."

Stevens' head lifted and Watchman caught the swift cut of his eyes. "You don't really think you're going to get her back from them alive."

"I think I'd like to try."

Stevens' head nodded up and down slowly. "I may not be much good except to hold your coat but I'd like to watch you try. If I don't get killed I might learn a thing or two."

10

"One more thing I don't understand," Stevens said when he reached for the reins. "Why'd Vickers get so upset about it?"

"Because he was wrong." Watchman took off a glove to dig for his matches. "Those guys aren't used to having anybody tell them they're wrong. Most folks seem to think of them the same way they think of Motherhood and the Flag and God. Of course nowadays none of those items drag down the kind of veneration they used to, but the Bureau just chalks that up to an epidemic of Commies and radic-libs."

Stevens smiled with slow wickedness. "Maybe when he turns in his report you'll turn out to be the first un-American Indian in history, *kemo sabe*."

But Watchman wasn't listening. The corner of his vision had picked up the bouncing glow beyond the ridgeline behind them and he turned quickly and squinted down toward it.

In time the headlights burst over the crest and swung wildly across him and dipped below as the truck growled over the lower hilltop and came gnashing forward with its horse trailer clanking and wobbling.

"Looks like we've got help."

"Aeah—but whose?"

It downshifted again and came wheeze-whining up alongside the parked power wagon. The door opened and Agent Vickers climbed out of the cab, straightened, jabbed his fists into the small of his back and arched his body backwards.

"Jesus. My kidneys."

"It must be the cavalry," Stevens said. "Coming to the rescue."

Watchman said, "Since you're waiting for us to ask, to what do we owe the honor?"

The FBI man's face was not readable in the sudden darkness after the switching-off of headlights. His voice issued from the shadows as he moved forward. "Maybe I decided to play it your way. On the theory that it's not wise to change even horses' asses in midstream." He came into slightly better view behind the horse trailer and lowered the tailgate ramp. "Somebody want to help me back this beast out of here?"

Watchman said, "I seem to remember a speech you dropped on Lansford back there. We don't need any amateur help."

"And I seem to recall he answered you've got it whether you want it or not." Vickers turned: his face picked up a bit of illumination from the sky and seemed remotely angry, bitter. "I may as well tell you. If we live through it you'll find out anyway. They've called off the National Guard."

11

"Why in hell would they do a thing like that?" Stevens asked.

"Politics and money. The State Attorney General got to thinking it over. Decided in the first place it's a criminal case —not a military matter—and in the second place it would cost five times as much to mobilize the Guard as the bank lost in the holdup."

"And in the third place," Watchman said, "they probably wouldn't have done us much good in the first place."

"You're wrong about that, you know."

"All right. We had that argument before."

"Let's get this horse out of here and get moving, all right?"

There were a lot of things Watchman felt like saying but he only waited while the rookie backed the saddlehorse out of Vickers' trailer and tightened up the cinches. Vickers seemed to have bundled himself up in half a dozen mismatched layers of borrowed clothing. He danced around quite a bit with one foot on the ground and one foot in the stirrup before he got purchase on the saddlehorn and heaved himself aboard.

There was no point belaboring it with questions. Vickers was here because if he hadn't come along he'd never be able to claim credit for the outcome, whatever it might prove to be. Obviously he had considered it from all angles and ended up with the judgment that Watchman's chances for success, however dim they might be, were still the best chances anyone was offering.

Among police officers the FBI was notorious for its hunger to hog glory but Vickers' decision had grown from something more basic than that: survival. He had already been on a kind of probation before this case had erupted; he'd been shipped to the boondocks and no doubt he was being watched by his superiors—one more foul-up and he'd likely be discharged; the Bureau wasn't noted for forgiveness toward its agents. So to keep his job Vickers had to bring in a winning score on this one. That was why he'd overreacted, mobilized enough machinery to fight a medium-size war. Then they'd kicked his National Guard props out from under him and when that happened he must have realized that if Watchman didn't nail the fugitives there was an excellent chance they wouldn't get nailed at all. Watchman's warning—*You'll come up with nothing in your hands but Mrs. Lansford's corpse*—must have gone around in his mind like a palmist's ghastly prediction of doom and in the end Vickers had forsaken by-the-book caution and chosen to throw in with the only players left in the game. It was a long shot but when it was the only shot you had, you had to shoot it.

Watchman wasn't going to argue: he needed another pair of eyes, another gun.

Watchman put the kitchen match between his teeth and went around to the front of Vickers' truck. Lifted the hood, felt around for the distributor, unsnapped it and lifted out the rotor. He removed the power wagon's rotor as well, closed both hoods and went to his horse, shoving the rotors in his pocket. They bunched up against the little velvet case that contained Lisa's ring.

He gathered the reins in quick synchronization with his rise to the saddle and took the wooden match in his hand.

Vickers said, "Why the woodpile?"

"I didn't have any neon signs handy."

"For what?"

"To keep our friends up there from feeling too lonesome." Watchman turned his horse along the slope just below the woodpile. "I don't want you pitched off when the fire starts. You two ride up there a little. I'll catch up."

"Old Inyun trick," Stevens said solemnly. "You betchum."

"First you disable the trucks," Vickers said, "and then you build a bonfire big enough to be seen from the moon. I don't see your point."

Watchman explained it for him because Vickers would be more help with his mind cleared of distracting mysteries. "I'm gambling the blizzard will hit them before they get to the top. When they're hurting enough they'll remember they saw these trucks down here and they'll remember they saw us ride away from them. They'll start to think about doubling back—circling down past us and getting to the trucks ahead of us."

"So you're sending out an invitation."

"That's about it." Watchman waited for the two of them to gig their horses into the scrub oak. When they had ridden two hundred yards and almost been absorbed into the night he snugged a tight saddle grip with knees and left hand and said a few quiet words to the horse and scratched the wooden match across the steel saddlehorn.

It cracked alight and was still fizzing when he tossed it down into the little runnel of gasoline that had trickled downslope from the woodpile.

The spark caught with a sedate *whump* of sound and burst into a pale yellow-blue flame that ran uphill instantly into the pile of brush and logs. There was a louder thud of noise and Watchman kept one eye closed, the other slitted, guarding against night-blindness in the face of the sudden high daylight blaze, while the horse bunched itself and whickered in fear and went three feet straight up into the air and came down running.

He kept his seat. Clamped his free hand down on the pommel and fought the horse down to a semblance of control: reined down from dead run to gallop to canter and went crashing into the scrub, branches whipping at his legs.

Down to a trot by the time he caught up with the others. Behind them the fire was a magnificent beacon, showing up the two silent trucks in hard silhouette. Even at this distance the heat touched the back of his neck and his own shadow on horseback splashed out across the trees and earth ahead.

There was a little streak of grey-pink on the eastern horizon; opposite, toward the storm, the sky was dark and wild. Watchman tugged his hat down and pointed the horse toward the high country.

CHAPTER

1

They rode across a tilted clearing dusted with threadbare snow. At the upper end Walker hipped around in his saddle to look back. He could still see the glow of the bonfire but it was slowly being overwhelmed by the spreading sunrise.

At the head of the column the Major looked back. "Come on—come on. Keep it closed up."

"Just looking to see if they're still following us."

"Of course they are. What difference does it make? Three yokel cops with their noses to the ground. Come on, Captain."

They moved on. The woman on the sorrel gave Walker a brief glance and then turned her face away; her heavy rope of hair swung forward and masked her.

The storm was starting to move. He could feel it, it made him hunch his neck into the collar of his coat; he could see it, higher mountain peaks being absorbed into its scudding blackness as he watched. The wind began to whip little flurries of powder snow off the surface of the ground. Walker's blue could feel it too: he had to hold in the nervous prancing horse.

All the vibrations were bad, he thought. When you found yourself absurdly and unexpectedly on horseback in a stormy wilderness you began to think in simplistic truisms and it occurred to him for the first time that he was one of the Bad Guys. He hadn't thought badly of himself until that moment back at the farm when Baraclough had stayed behind, inside the house with the doomed deputy, and Walker knowing what was going on had not lifted a finger to stop it. That was the point at which it had all crumpled. Up till then, even though they were things he was doing himself, they seemed more like things that had been happening to him—the preparations, the caper, the escape—as if he had been in an audience watching himself, an actor in a movie, acting out events that had no reality. But now it was real enough and the reality was pain. They were the real Bad Guys and in the end the Bad Guys always got killed by the Good Guys. In these chilly mountains he convinced himself that he was about to die.

Once you started thinking about your own death it was hard to stop thinking about it. He kept seeing himself on a mountain rock somewhere with the blood draining out of him, going cold and without life.

The wind dropped. They crossed a bare slope and penetrated the pine forest. The big trees shut out a great deal of light. The wind died altogether; the horse laid its ears back along its head and hoofs crunched softly in the silent pine needles. Goosebumps ran along Walker's arms; the flesh of his chest quivered. Jingle of bit chains, squeak of saddle leather—the gray air hung cold and motionless.

Back in these mountains it felt as if civilization was a thousand miles and a thousand years away. The heaped-up summits loomed vast above them, timber and boulders and loose shale slides. They climbed the side of a long S-curving ridge and stopped briefly while the Major got out the topographical map and held it up with both arms wide, glancing up from it at intervals to check his bearings. The temperature was dropping sharply all the time now: the horses' breath had begun to steam. The air was getting thicker, more gray, and it was getting noticeably more difficult to make out the outlines of the peaks against the sky. But the still silence persisted.

The Major checked his pocket compass and snapped it shut and turned around to look them over. Eight horses, six riders. The Major's heavy beard stubble had grown perceptibly overnight.

Baraclough finished field-stripping the stub of his menthol cigarette and put the butt filter in his pocket, not for neatness but for security.

Eddie Burt's thick waxy face was upturned as if to pray: Burt was watching the sky.

Jack Hanratty's pitted face was averted, pointed meaninglessly toward the trees to the left: Hanratty wanted to avoid meeting anyone's eyes for fear of what he would find there.

The Major said, "Captain, let's have the clothesline."

Walker dismounted, holding the blue by the reins, walked back to the pack animals and hunted for the coil of nylon line. He had forgotten where he'd put it and it took a while to find it.

The Major said, "Run the line through the bridle bits."

"All of them?"

"All eight horses."

"What for?"

"In a little while you won't be able to see the horse in front of you, Captain."

Walker's eyes jerked toward the sky. Most of it was a seething obscurity.

The Major said, "Now we'll have a little lecture in survival. Pay attention. You've all been up for twenty-four hours and you're tired. That's too bad. Fall asleep in this weather and you're dead. Think about that and remember it. When you feel yourself starting to fall asleep, or when you begin to feel a funnybone tingle in your feet, get off your horse and walk. Stamp your feet when you walk, keep the circulation going. I recommend you tie your horse's reins to your wrist with a slipknot so that if you happen to trip and fall you won't get lost. If you haven't seen mountain weather you may find it hard to credit this, but take my word for it you won't be able to see your hand in front of your face at noon today. Just hang onto your horse and let the horse lead you. I'll be at the point, breaking trail, and I'll have a rappel rope running from my belt to the saddle horn on my horse, so if I happen to walk over any cliffs you won't lose me."

Walker said, "If we're traveling that blind how will you know where you're going?" He was threading the line through Mrs. Lansford's bridle and he caught the edge of the woman's bleak glance before it whipped away.

"Dead reckoning," the Major said. "I've got a compass."

Eddie Burt said, "Don't fret it none. The Major's never got lost in his life."

Walker ran the nylon through Baraclough's bridle and handed the free end up to the Major, who threaded it through his bridle bit and ran a double hitch around his saddle horn; he had about a dozen feet of slack left over and he let most of it go, coiling it and hanging the coil over his saddle horn, tying the butt end through the belt-loops of his trousers and knotting it around his hips. It was a three-eighths-inch nylon clothesline from the Lansford barn and it probably would test out at five hundred pounds or more.

Walker didn't go back to his horse just yet. He stood beside the Major's horse and tried to sound calm. "I wouldn't mind knowing what our plans are, Major."

Eddie Burt snapped at him from the rear of the line: "The Major's kept you alive this far."

"Nobody said he hasn't." But Walker kept his eyes on the Major, as stubbornly as he could.

"You have a right to know." Major Hargit's hatbrim lifted: he had everyone's attention. "We'll keep moving as long as we can, and then we'll keep moving a while longer. The map shows a ranger station on that peak up there—a fire-lookout tower. I'd like to get at least that far but if it becomes impossible we'll just have to rig shelter and wait it out. At least the pursuit won't be gaining on us—they'll be stalled in their tracks. If those are ordinary hick cops back there they won't have enough woodcraft among the three of them to build a Boy Scout fire—maybe they'll die out there. Maybe they won't. Whatever they do they'll be too busy staying alive to worry about catching us for a while."

Walker's mouth twisted.

"As soon as this lifts," the Major went on, "we'll cross the range. The storm will have covered our tracks and if the weather clears enough to permit aerial search sweeps they won't see us as long as we've got the sense to stay under the trees. By the way forget those trucks we saw back there. That's a trap.

"Once we've crossed into Utah we've got four or five roads to choose from. There'll be roadblocks. We'll raid one of them, confiscate their patrol cars, make our way into one of the villages over there. We'll have plenty of opportunities to mail the bank money to ourselves in a series of small first-class packages, after which we'll separate and find our way individually to Reno. The police are looking for five men and several hundred pounds of loot—if we travel separately without large quantities of cash we ought to be able to survive a few stop-and-search checkpoints. Bear in mind that the secret of a successful escape operation is not to hide but to blend into your surroundings. We'll become ranch workers, itinerant mechanics, café dishwashers for a few days if we have to—by the time we get down there we'll look disheveled enough.

"But first we've got to get there. Steve, you might tie the lady's hands together and leash her to her horse. Then let's get moving."

2

Walker felt the numbness of his ears and nose and hands and feet. The wind almost tore the hat from his head and he tied it down around his chin with a ripped-off concho thong. The wind was a swirl of snowflakes and foaming mist; he batted his gloved hands together.

The wind was a sound now, he could hear it frothing through the pines, beating the branches together. It wasn't yet carrying very much snow; most of it had vaporized into a whirling chalk-dust fog. Walker's flesh trembled inside the coat: he tried to hunch himself down inside it for warmth.

Burt and the packhorses trailed him on the nylon rope; the woman was in front of him—then Baraclough, then Hanratty, finally the Major in the lead. He could barely make out the Major's grayish shape swaying in the mist.

The Major had assigned the order of placement and it was easy to see why. It put Hanratty between the Major and Baraclough; it put the woman between Baraclough and Walker; it put Walker between Burt and, at one remove, Baraclough. All the unreliable ones accounted for—and Walker right behind the woman, responsible for her: the Major had told him in a mild voice, *Anything that happens to her happens to you. Bear that in mind. If she tries to break for it you had better bring her back. If she gets away from you don't bother to return—you can forget your share of the money.*

Baraclough had wound coat-hanger wire around Mrs. Lansford's wrists and twisted the ends together with a pair of pliers. Not tight enough to cut the skin but too tight to be slipped. The nylon rope ran from Walker's bridle through Mrs. Lansford's wrist bindings to the bridle of her horse. She could get down and walk but she couldn't get free of the rope.

The wind was against his left shoulder and the horse wanted to turn; Walker had to fight it with the reins. The white horse's coat had a curious pigmentation that he had seen on a few horses before: when it was wet the white hair turned pale blue—some kind of secretion in the hide underneath. It came up dappled, like drops of blue ink on a white background; that was why this sort of white horse was called a blue roan.

He scrubbed his ears and tied the scarf up around his nose and mouth. An arm of cold wind got into him and shot dry agony through the tooth cavity in his upper jaw.

There was no reckoning the passage of time. The sun was gone, light was draining out of the day. The only way to tell direction was by compass and the Major had the only one of those. Walker closed his eyes up to slits and blinked back the tears of icy wind. They were climbing steadily along the side of a steep slope that seemed endless, doing switchbacks now and then when the Major decided it was time. Walker could feel the shifts by the changes in wind direction. Probably the Major was tacking—so many steps right, so many steps left, trying to keep a balanced compass course somewhere between. But the wind hit the exposed face of this south slope with wicked fury and Walker wondered when they would get behind something that would help break its force.

A swift blast of gale swayed him to one side and he grabbed the saddle horn wildly and when he righted himself he could only just see the whipping tail of Mrs. Lansford's sorrel four or five feet ahead. The mottled pointillism of whipping snow enfolded him that quickly: now he could only see the blue's ears, he couldn't even see the ground, and he bent forward low over the withers in a useless try at evading the hard clout of the blow. Disoriented, he couldn't tell if they were still climbing or if they were descending. He clung to the saddle and closed his eyes and tried to hide his head between his shoulders.

3

He blinked sluggishly and jerked himself upright. No good going to sleep. No good. His legs felt rubbery and he was having trouble keeping his knee-grip on the saddle. He tested the knot with which he had tied the reins to his right wrist. He couldn't see it until he brought it up within a few inches of his face.

He lifted his right leg over and slid to the ground. Almost fell; kept his grip on the saddle, straightened, felt his way along the reins to the bit and found the nylon rope. Took a grip on that and staggered ahead.

He kept his eyes closed because there was no point in trying to see anything. His nose and lungs burned with the in-and-out rasp of frigid air. All the layers of clothing didn't seem to help: the wind came up inside his cuffs, inside the sleeves of his coat, under the coat skirt, down the back of the neck.

His feet burned and tingled when he stamped them on the ground. He would put a foot out and test his footing and then stomp down hard and bring up the other foot. It got to be like that: you thought about each step and you took time executing it. It meant the others were going just as slowly. But that made sense: the Major had to find the way, had to keep from blundering into trees, keep from falling over precipices.

The earth seemed to change its tilt underfoot but it was impossible to tell which way it had shifted until he detected an almost imperceptible drop in the force of the wind. They must be on the backside of a slope now. Going down, or at least going around something. He kept walking into the rump of Mrs. Lansford's horse and in a dulled way he began to worry that he might do it once too often and get kicked in the belly by the horse.

He kept the reins wrapped around his glove and whacked his hands together with energetic sweeps of his arms.

He stumbled over something and went down. The horse made a vague sound that was whipped past and away on the wind; he felt a jerk of reins against his hand and scrambled for footing, got one leg under him and tumbled forward, dragged by the reins. Terror hit him: the rest of them were going on regardless, they couldn't see him or hear him, he'd get dragged to death. His feet spun and scrabbled and finally he got upright after a fashion and lurched forward: found the saddle, hooked his arm around the horn and let the horse carry him along a little way while he sawed icy air in and out of his laboring lungs and fought down panic.

The wind tumbled and howled, beating at him like fists. He walked alongside the horse's head with his grip on the reins choked up tight: if he fell again he would be able to pull himself up.

His boots were sliding a little; feathery soft snow on slippery pine needles made a treacherous footing. The wind was a vast pounding thunder in his ears; it flayed at him willfully. He knew what it was like to be a blind man now. Tingling pinpricks of sensation burned in his feet and hands. His ears hurt him with a sharp agony; he took a long clumsy time untying the scarf and snugging it down over the top of his hat, tying it under his chin, tucking the ends into his coat and wrapping the collar around.

4

It was madness. Every animal had the sense to get shelter and hide out a blizzard.

No way to judge the passage of time but his extremities were almost without sensation and fatigue had set in; he could hardly lift his knees. And then the tilt of the ground changed again, for the fiftieth time, and the wind almost knocked him off his feet. The noise was earsplitting. He had a handkerchief wadded in his mouth and he was breathing through it but it was beginning to clog with ice. He kept one hand clutched over his nose. He couldn't feel his fingers.

He walked into the sorrel's rump again and stopped, waiting for it to go on, but it didn't move away. The line had stopped. Something wrong. The Major—had he fallen down? Not Hargit; nothing knocked Hargit down.

Something tugging the nylon rope. He turned, afraid, puzzled. Something banged into him and he recoiled; a hand gripped him and Baraclough's voice rasped an inch from his ear.

"We're here. Follow the rope inside. There's room for the horses."

And Baraclough was gone, finding his way back along the rope toward Burt.

The rope stirred again; the sorrel was moving. He took the

blue by its headstall and felt his way forward. Bruised his fingers against a wall, felt around and found the doorway. And led the blue inside out of the wind.

5

He didn't hear the door slam but the thunder of the wind dropped away abruptly and the cold air became still. A voice —the Major's, but hoarse: "Everybody hold still."

After a moment Walker heard the distinctive click of Baraclough's Zippo lighter and saw it explode into flame like a little bonfire.

They were crowded into a dirt-floored shed. Burt, near the shelves tacked to the far wall, reached up and got down a long cardboard box. "Candles."

The flame was transferred from the Zippo to half a dozen candles which Baraclough and Burt placed on the two-by-four crossspieces between the exposed joists.

"See if you can get that stove going, Steve."

It was an old potbelly stove on claw legs with a black pipe chimney that went up the wall. Behind the stove the corner of the room was stacked with short-cut chunks of firewood.

Walker hooked his arm over the saddle and sagged against the horse. *Oh Jesus God.*

6

"Watch those candles. We don't want to burn the place down."

Burt started moving around, obeying. The woman was just

standing there with her head down, raking fingers through her hair to get the ice out of it. Hanratty and Baraclough had got the stove going and sat down beside it. The wind banged and screamed around the place. Icicles hung from the horses' flanks and fetlocks and their coats were frosted white; snowballs had formed on their tails where they had dragged through soft whirling drifts.

Things were starting to get thawed out and the room was beginning to smell rancid. The breath no longer poured from the horses' nostrils like steam. Walker stripped off his gloves and held his palms toward the stove. He watched the Major make his way between horses to the foot of the ladder that went up the side wall to a trap door in the ceiling. This had to be the ranger station and the ladder had to go on up to the fire-lookout tower.

The Major said, "Steve."

"All right. I'll check it out." Baraclough hadn't removed any clothes yet. He got up and climbed the ladder and pushed at the trap door. The wind got a finger inside and blew out all the candles and Baraclough said mildly, "All right, all right. I'll close it in a minute."

The wind got louder and began to blow around inside the room: that meant the trap door was wide open. Then it slammed shut again. Walker thought Baraclough had climbed up through it and so it surprised him to hear Baraclough's voice: "Forget it. If there's a ranger up there he's not coming down that ladder before this lets up."

"Good enough," the Major said.

Burt went around lighting the candles. The Major went to the stove and began to shoulder out of his coat. "Get out of your boots and put them by the stove. Hanratty, put together something for us to eat. We may as well eat our fill and get some sleep. Sergeant, you'll take the first watch. Be ready to pack up quickly and move out of here the instant the wind drops."

7

Walker came awake and the first thing that drew his attention was the aching stiffness in all his joints. He was saddlesore, his feet hurt, he felt as if he had arthritis in his knees and charleyhorses in the tendons of his ankles and calves. And he was still cold. Not frozen numb as he had been before, but chattering painful cold.

He was lying on his back wrapped in two blankets with his sock feet toward the stove. The shack was thick with a steamy moisture that came off the drying hides of the horses and smelled foul.

Probably there were a lot of things to think about but his mind wasn't tracking well. He lay on his back and rolled his head slowly from side to side to look around and see how things looked. The inside walls looked flimsy and there was no insulation but the wind wasn't getting inside; it was probably a split-log cabin, well chinked on the outside. He could hear occasional brittle cracks outside against the steady drumming of the wind—icicles breaking off. Well there probably wasn't any ranger up in the tower. From what he had seen of forest watchtowers they weren't anything but six-foot-square platforms surrounded by plate glass. They had probably recalled the ranger when they knew there was a big blow coming.

The potbelly stove had a flat top with a handle sticking out of it. That was where the ranger did his cooking. One narrow bunk built against a wall—the Major was asleep on it now, his face poking out of the blankets. A sheet-metal enclosure in one corner beyond the stove flue—that would be the plumbing, one of those portable shower-toilet-sink arrangements, probably brought in by helicopter. There would be a water tank outside. They didn't equip these places for winter use; firewatching was a summer–fall job.

There was one comfortable reading chair, lightweight but well cushioned. Eddie Burt was in it, fast asleep, his chin down on his chest.

Half a dozen shelves above the stove with tins of food. A little office-size refrigerator behind Burt's chair. Probably a diesel generator outside somewhere: there were electric light fixtures hanging from the rafters but the current wasn't on now. The windows were boarded up from the outside: possibly the ranger had closed up for the winter.

On the floor just inside the front door lay a broken padlock and that explained how the Major had got in.

Someone—Baraclough—had run the nylon rope around two of the upright roof-supports and anchored them to windowsill coat hooks to make an enclosure that kept the horses in their area. Their area took up three quarters of the floor space. There was left only the L-shaped sector from the stove to the lavatory to the bunk. Hanratty lay on the floor at the foot of the bunk, snoring with his mouth open. Baraclough sat on the floor with a rifle across his knees, smoking. Mrs. Lansford was sitting with her back against the lavatory wall, arms wrapped around her knees, brooding toward the stove.

Walker rolled his head, still not getting up, and looked at the horses. The cinches had been loosened but they had been left saddled. There was nothing to feed them. They were docile, asleep on their feet; probably thankful to be in out of the wind, too exhausted to feel their hunger.

He looked over at Mrs. Lansford and then at Baraclough. Baraclough had turned his head: he was staring at the woman, eyes hooded and erotic and amorally detached—amused, yet reflecting vicious thoughts. That cold stare of Baraclough's could mesmerize you.

If Mrs. Lansford was aware of Baraclough's stare she gave no sign of it. She sat with her forehead against her drawn-up knees. Her hair hung damp and heavy against her cheeks, hiding her face.

Baraclough flicked a cigarette against the back of his hand; yawned and patted his lips.

The blizzard made a great battering racket against the cabin. It muffled the occasional stirrings of the horses. Walker kept his eyes slitted and pretended to be asleep; he had Baraclough and the woman in the narrowed range of his vision and now his brain began to work.

There were hunters and there were killers. Sometimes one man could be both but the qualities were separate and Baraclough was a killer: he took pleasure in it, it gave him something like a sexual relief. Walker had seen it when Baraclough had come out of the ranch house and left the cop dead inside.

This whole thing had gone sour. Walker's tongue sucked his sore tooth and he saw the way Baraclough's hands rested on the rifle in his lap, and it was obvious that when the time came to murder Mrs. Lansford it would be Baraclough who would do it.

There hadn't ever been any doubt in his mind that she was going to be killed. It was possible that by now the cops had put some kind of tracer on them and begun to get clues to their identities, but they'd all been pretty careful about that and most likely the cops still didn't know who they were chasing. That was what would make it possible for them to separate in Utah and melt into the itinerant traffic that flowed endlessly toward California. They had to safeguard their anonymity and now Mrs. Lansford was the only outsider who could identify them. Obviously the Major wasn't going to turn her loose to talk.

He probably wasn't going to turn Hanratty loose either. The spine had melted out of Hanratty a long time ago and if you found the right button and pushed it Hanratty would spill out everything he knew like a computer spilling out reels of programed tape.

And Walker. Walker wasn't one of the inner circle either. The three of them, the Major and Baraclough and "Sergeant" Burt, had their plans all neatly worked out to go someplace in South Africa or Latin America and use their share of the loot to finance the mobilization of a private army so that they could go out into chickenshit little countries and play little war games. That was fine, but it wouldn't work out that way if anybody remained behind who could finger them for the American law, because there weren't many countries in the world that wouldn't cooperate in their extradition when it turned out they were wanted for multiple murders and assorted federal crimes. Hargit and Baraclough were deliberate, methodical, careful; they didn't take unnecessary risks, they didn't leave loose ends lying around to be picked up, and at bottom they didn't trust anybody except themselves.

They were going to kill him. He had tried to talk himself out of the notion, tried to chalk it up to fear and paranoia and the general sinister portentousness and unreality of the past twenty-four hours; but when he looked at it with cold logic it always came back to the same thing: they weren't going to leave him behind because he might slip up, he might get caught, he might for any number of reasons decide to spill his guts to the cops, and if there was even a remote chance of that happening they would plug the hole.

They weren't going to do it now. Not now and not here in

this place. It was still possible the cops would catch up, in which case they would need their hostage alive and they would need all the guns they could muster. All right then, they weren't going to kill him in the next ten minutes or probably the next ten hours. But sooner or later, before they got out of these mountains, they were going to do it.

And he didn't see any point in hanging around obediently waiting for it.

8

The woman sat with her knees against her breasts and her head tipped to one side on her folded arms. He realized she was watching him. Looking right at him.

He let his eyes open a little wider.

When she knew she had his attention she sat up and began to do something with her hair: pulled it back from her face on both sides and tied it in a horsetail knot at the back of her head. He could see tautness and pain ground into the lines across her eyes and mouth. She kept darting glances at Baraclough and the others: she had the look of a boxed-in animal trying to watch five converging wolves at once. It was clear she was near the perilous edge of breaking, keeping herself rigidly under control.

Baraclough stood up, leaned his rifle against the wall, stretched, and bent forward a little to massage his thighs. His thin face glowed in the chilly air and his cynical eyebrows arched when he looked at the woman.

Walker watched him as he might have watched a barracuda.

His gut ached. He looked at the woman again and saw in her bloodless face the knowledge of what was going to happen to her. He suspected she'd known all along—she wasn't stupid

—but she'd probably found some way, just as he had, to keep herself from believing it. Until now. Now the defenses were down and she knew. Looking at Baraclough she knew.

It was like a hunk of concrete in Walker's stomach: fear.

His slitted eyes moved and locked on the woman's. Her face turned until it was no longer in Baraclough's view but she held Walker's eyes with her own and now her expression changed and they had between them that same unspoken shared understanding he had felt in the ranch yard, a sudden impact of communication and contact: and her eyes went wide, full of silent pleading, desperate need, a voiceless cry for help.

Almost imperceptibly Walker nodded. It was more in the drooping of eyelids than in any movement of his head but he was sure she caught it and understood it; she almost smiled.

It wasn't important that she trusted him. What was important—in a way he sensed but did not really comprehend—was that she thought she knew him well enough to trust him. Something he had said, something he had done, something in the way he had looked at her: he had revealed enough of himself to give her that idea. And if he let her down now it wouldn't just spoil her picture of him, it would spoil his own picture of himself. He didn't have much self-respect left to his name but what was left he cherished.

So he knew he was going to try.

9

He sat up without hurry. Yawned, scratched his face. Tugged his boots on, got to his feet as if still groggy and extended his arms; stretching, he heard the crackling of his own musculature.

He felt his face color under Baraclough's stare but he

managed a short meaningless smile, shrugged for no particular reason except that it seemed a disarming sort of thing to do, and turned to the shelves on the wall to run his eyes over the canned-food labels. He still had the heavy coat on; he thrust his hand under it, down the sleeve of his leather flight jacket, and extracted a cigarette from the bicep pocket. He lit the cigarette, inhaled, choked, recovered, took down a can of stew and set it on the stove. During all this he never once looked at the woman.

Burt and Hanratty snored away. The Major was deeply asleep as well: the trek had been hardest, most exhausting, for him.

Baraclough must have had a few hours' sleep and then relieved Burt on watch. He looked a little droopy but not likely to fall asleep.

Power of suggestion, Walker thought: he went into the sheet-metal lavatory and urinated into the john. The cubicle was no bigger than an airliner's rest room.

He flushed the toilet but the noise was almost obscured by the steady roar of the blizzard against the log walls.

He stepped out of the cubicle zipping up his trousers and went back to the stove to test the temperature of the can of stew; left the can on the stove and sat down against the wall, midway between the stove and the woman. Baraclough sat beyond the woman, smoking; he had left the rifle leaning against the wall.

For a moment Walker thought it wasn't going to work. But then Baraclough stood up, caught Walker's eye, nodded toward the girl as if to say "Watch her," and went into the lavatory. Baraclough was the kind of man to whom superficial manners were important: he probably killed politely. Walker had counted on that: Baraclough closed the door.

The moment the lavatory door was shut Walker scooped up

his hat and mittens and crossed the room. Past the woman, moving swiftly and without sound. He picked up the rifle Baraclough had left tilted against the wall, and turned to sweep the rest of the room with a wary inspection.

Nobody woke up.

The woman was on her feet without a word, coming after him.

He had one mitten on. He put the other one in his coat pocket to keep his hand free on the rifle. Ducked under the nylon rope and walked between the horses to the front of the shed.

The woman's face was upturned, alive, expectant. He pointed to the horse nearest the door and when the woman reached for its reins Walker made a signal with a jerk of his head to indicate that she should go first. With his mittened left hand he reached out and gathered up the trailing reins of the blue roan. Then he backed up against the front door and collected the lead-rope of one of the packhorses and wrapped that in his left hand along with the blue's reins. Finally he nodded to the woman, braced the rifle across the crook of his elbow and slid the wooden crossbar back out of its slot. And shoved the door open with his boot.

The wind slammed in, banged the door back against the outside wall; the candles guttered out and he felt the woman go by, urging her horse through the doorway. The horse didn't want to go out into that. Walker whacked it with the rifle—whacked where he thought the horse was, and seemed to hit it because it jumped and went rushing past him, almost knocking him over.

"What the fuck?"

"Jesus . . ."

"What's going on?"

The lavatory door slammed open with a tinny clank. If

there were other sounds they were swallowed in the rock-crushing growl of wind.

Walker was through the door, outside, head bowed against the blast. Pulling the blue's reins and the packhorse.

But something got stuck. He couldn't see but it had to be that the two horses had wedged together in the narrow door. One of them screamed, a high whickering neigh; he felt the leather reins slide out through his mitten. Trying to grab for them with his right hand he dropped the rifle. And missed the reins.

Now all he had was the packhorse's lead-rope and somebody inside the cabin started shooting.

Shooting at the door because they thought they were being invaded.

Walker dropped flat on his belly and rolled out of the line of fire.

He'd lost the rifle and he'd lost both horses. What he rolled into was a deep bank of loose snow that the wind had piled against the side of the shed. The gale had packed it semi-firm but the flakes were quite dry and didn't adhere to one another, so that his body penetrated the drift and a small avalanche tumbled down over him. A sense of burial, of drowning, of being sucked under: impossible to get his breath.

He swam out of it and crawled on his hands and knees, shaking himself like a wet dog. His knuckles banged into something solid and when he felt for it he found the corner of the cabin: he crawled around into the lee of it and got to his feet.

Somebody fired two or three more gunshots and he heard a fellow bellow—the Major?—and the shooting stopped.

It occurred to him he could go back inside. They hadn't seen anything; they'd never know he had tried to get away. But he had let the woman go and they would kill him for that.

Then he felt a thud and heard the slam as if from a far distance, and knew he no longer had the choice of going back inside: they had shut the door and now they would be lighting candles, counting heads.

He was behind the cabin; the woman had gone in the opposite direction. He had to find her. He had no horse, no blanket, no gun, no food. She had all those things except a gun.

He reached the corner and stepped into the shrieking wind. There was a little light, it was gray rather than black, but the grayness was opaque. He had to feel his way forward along the side of the cabin and when he reached the front corner he hesitated, half expecting the front door to slam open and the others to come charging out with guns. He stood paralyzed by that fear until the realization crept into him that they weren't going to come out after him: they couldn't see any better than he could out here.

The woman had gone straight out from the front door. He stepped away from the cabin, only two paces but it seemed to put him in the middle of nothingness. The wind came at him against the front of his left shoulder and if he kept the wind on that quarter he ought to be able to keep moving in a straight line toward the woman.

If she had stopped: if she was waiting for him. But why should she?

He had to find her. Find her or freeze to death out here all by himself.

10

The next hours never came back to him clearly afterward. He moved in a disoriented daze with the icy wind driving right through him. It kept blowing him off his course, or so he kept thinking. He rubbed the palm of a glove over his face, scraping off frost. Needles tingled up his legs as his feet hit the ground and his bowels were knotted with unreasoning hollow terror: a child's awful fear that not only is the house empty but nobody will ever come back to it. Hunger, and the thought that the beans he'd eaten in the cabin had been his last meal. Shoulders and head butted into the blast, he had the feeling he was only treadmilling in his own former tracks.

The wind was a grating roar, a deep rumble like a heavy artillery barrage, and the snow driven upon it never reached the earth: it flew horizontally, beating his cheek, rolling against him with a steady weight that made him lean into it to keep balance. The world spun drunkenly. He lost sensation in the flesh of his face and tiny icicle fringes hung like sweat beads from his nose and ear lobes and eyebrows. In one lucid moment he estimated that fifteen minutes more would mark the farthest limit of his strength: find shelter or die.

Like debris torn loose from anchor he flapped through the snow and somewhere in that run of seconds or minutes he remembered the woman's name and began to shout with the full power of his lungs: "Marianne! Marianne!"

And could hardly hear his own voice as it whipped away. He beat his hands together, staggered with numb legs. . . . He jerked himself erect and discovered that he had fallen; yanked his body forward with the desperate knowledge that he had to keep moving as long as the muscles would pull.

A spasm of agony wrung him out. It was unendurable. So stiff with cold he could hardly move, he kept sawing painful breath into his chest to call her name and the pitch of his voice climbed in panic.

Most of the time he moved with his eyes shut, keeping the

wind against his left cheek, trusting the pain in his feet to keep him moving. When the pain made way for no feeling at all that would mark the end of hope.

Now when he passed them he could vaguely see trees bending in the wind. Must have descended in the lee of a mountainside, out of the full blast of it.

His foot caught, he went down again. His belly churned; his thinking wheeled as if in a dream. He lay where he was, unable to rise and wanting sleep, and he fought a battle there and won it and forced his frozen body up. Now a strange question came to him: were his legs really moving or were they not; was he lying in the snow imagining he was walking? Something whipped his face, tingling sharply yet distantly, and he reared his head back, supposing he had run into a branch. He felt the lash of it again and blinked.

It was the woman, standing vaguely before him, slapping his face. Putting her lips by his ear: "Stop shouting. I'm here. Stop shouting."

He realized he had still been shouting her name.

Laughter bubbled out between his stiff lips.

"Come on—come on." She had him by the arm and he felt himself being dragged along. When she let go his arm he fell to his knees. His hand had fallen on the horse's fetlock and the horse stirred, frightening him, but when he looked up he could make out the horse's ghostly gray outline against the paler background, the tops of windbent pines. He could see his hands and the ground under them.

When he looked up again the woman was standing there against a tree, slumped, her stomach thrusting forward, and another bundled figure stood on two widespread legs looking down at him. Hargit, he thought. Major Hargit. You could never get away from that man. Sudden tears came in a scalding, bursting convulsion and vomit pain twisted his stomach and he fell flat on the frozen earth. . . .

The man was bending over him, stripping off a glove, laying his fingers behind Walker's jaw hinge. Walker felt his own pulse beat against the man's hard fingers, and he heard the man's voice—not the Major's voice, not any voice he'd ever heard before: "You'll be all right. Come on." And the man was picking him up under the arms, lifting him onto his feet.

11

At first he thought it was a cave they dragged him into but when he looked around he saw it wasn't quite that. A rock cliff, a slight overhang, an improvised lean-to of dead logs and saddles piled cleverly to form a kind of triangular shelter. The wind was not canceled, but at least it was reduced. Two men squatted inside; the woman went in and crowded between them for warmth and the man who was dragging Walker pushed him inside and he collapsed on the ground, drawing his knees up foetally.

The woman was crying. "Look at me. I can't stop."

"Take it easy, Mrs. Lansford."

Walker felt dizzy; he couldn't breathe. The man who had dragged him inside turned and Walker glimpsed his face. He looked like an Indian.

The others were huddled together watching him. The Indian said, "Vickers, your horse is just about done anyway. Bring him here."

"What for?"

"Do it."

And one of the men got up with a grunt and went out,

stepping across Walker. The Indian was kneeling beside him again and began to slap his cheeks. Walker tried to jerk his head away but the Indian kept slapping him. "Got to get your circulation going, man. Don't fight me."

His cheeks began to sting dully. The woman said, "There's no way to build a fire?"

"Not till the wind lets up."

The other man came into sight leading a horse that was limping badly where balls of ice had formed in its hoofs.

The Indian went back into the shelter and reappeared with a rifle and Walker's face crumpled. The Indian stood up and shot the animal in the head.

The horse fell right beside Walker and the Indian put the rifle away and came out again with a hunting knife. Faint streaks of light flashed fragmentarily from the blade when it moved toward the horse and plunged in, opened a great slit in the dead horse's belly. The Indian methodically gutted the horse, throwing the insides away in the wind, and the smell of escaping gases made Walker turn his face away. He began to lose consciousness, not unpleasantly; sleep drifted vaguely into his mind and somehow his concentration focused on the numbness of his bad tooth.

They were shaking him violently. He tried to push them away but they kept shaking him and finally he cursed thickly and opened his eyes.

The Indian said, "Come on—get inside."

"Inside what?"

The Indian began to tug him toward the dead horse. He saw a gaping maw: flap of hide folded back, several ribs torn away. "Inside," the Indian said. "Pull it shut over you. It's going to stink like hell but it'll get you warm, keep you thawed out."

The smell nauseated him. The woman was kneeling beside him. Her slender fingers reached out. "Thank you." Eyes full of concern.

The Indian shoved him into the carcass. The hide flapped down, closing him in stinking warm darkness. The heat enveloped him and there was no wind. He sagged against the sticky wetness of his black cavern and gagged on the stench. He felt an insistent hammering behind his eyes; the beat of his heart was loud; needle pricks quivered the flesh of his hands and feet and face, and sleep rolled his head against the warm rib cage of the dead horse.

CHAPTER

7

1

Watchman batted his hands together and thrust them under his armpits and squeezed into the lean-to. The woman was lifting the mess-kit cup of instant coffee off the Sterno. She sucked at it and passed it on to Buck Stevens and said to Watchman, "Do you charge extra for the coffee or does it come with the rescue service?'

"The coffee's free. So's the weather."

"Do you think he'll be all right?"

"He'll be fine." Maybe a touch of frostbite, but not serious. The temperature wasn't all that low; it was the wind effect that seemed to drive it down. Without shelter you could die out there but the pilot would pull through now.

Paul Vickers was blowing his nose, giving Mrs. Lansford a bloodshot look. He was taking the weather badly. He had lost his hat in the blow and his hair stood out in wild disorder. "I'd like to know what really happened up there—why this man helped you get away. What he expected to get out of it."

"Maybe he found a streak of humanity in him." Mrs. Lansford said it a bit sharply, as if in rebuke.

"I don't see that. I don't want to put down your gratitude to the man, Mrs. Lansford, but if he thinks that will get him off he's mistaken. Two men have been murdered—by this man and his friends."

"I don't think they're his friends."

"Then why was he with them?"

Buck Stevens stirred in the back of the shelter. "Can't you leave her alone? Why don't you just shut up for a while?"

Vickers' head whipped around. It was the first time the rookie had talked back to him and it seemed to catch him off guard: he didn't know whether to bluster or sneer or ignore it. He twisted his gloved knuckles, looking cranky.

Watchman's voice was rusty, tired; it had been a bad day for them all. "Let's all settle down and try to get some rest."

Vickers turned to him. "They're right up the mountain there."

"Then go get 'em, tiger."

"I know my limits, Trooper. I couldn't find that cabin in this storm to save my life. But you could."

"Look at your watch, Vickers."

"What's that got to do with it?"

"The sun's going down. Another half hour and what little light we've got will be gone. We're not going anywhere for a while—neither are they."

2

It had to be the fire-lookout station they were heading for; Watchman had known that by midmorning, before the blow had hit, following the tracks and seeing which way they were heading. They were boxing themselves into a series of step-up mountain passes that could only lead them toward the ranger cabin and once he had determined that much it had become unnecessary to track them; he had been able to keep moving after the blizzard had wiped out the tracks. Vickers, who was an indifferent horseman and a stranger to mountain weather, had slowed them down but they had kept pushing it until the middle of the afternoon when Vickers' horse had gone lame with ice-split hoofs and they had come under the lee of the cliff. By that time Watchman had no clear idea of their position but he had a feeling they were not too far below the summit; the trees, briefly glimpsed in slack flurries of snow, were stunted up here and that meant they were close to timberline. It might have been possible to continue but with odds of three against five, with the woman being held hostage, and with the blizzard likely to confuse things beyond control there was no point in trying to close in on the cabin.

The fugitives most likely believed they had left pursuit far behind. If they had reached the shack ~~at all~~ it could be assumed they wouldn't leave it again before the storm blew over: its comfort would be too compelling and there was nothing outside except the risk of dying in the snow.

Of course there was a good chance they had never reached the cabin. Maybe they had got separated in all this madness and were perishing one by one on the exposed flanks of the mountains. Maybe they had given up their try at the summit and doubled back, passing their pursuers unseen in the wheeling murk, heading back down toward the plain. But if they had done that they would run into police lines sooner or later and Watchman doubted they had tried that; when they hadn't fallen for the bonfire invitation he'd set by the abandoned trucks he'd accepted the idea that the fugitives were well led by a man confident of his wilderness skills.

Probably they had reached the cabin. If they had they weren't going anywhere for a while. Here under the cliff he had called a halt and built the shelter.

The woman had stumbled right into their camp for several reasons, but mainly because this was the only way down from the south face of the summit—the rest of it was too jagged, too crowded with boulders—and because it was a reasonably narrow trail, the same trail the fugitives had gone up. Mrs. Lansford had meant to come this way, it had been no accident of fate; it was the way she had arrived, it was the way home. She had known that if she managed to get down the trail a little way she would find at least a bit of protection from the wind because there were trees and boulders and mountain shoulders to hold back the storm.

Once out of the full brutality of the wind she had stopped and waited for quite some time on the trail, waiting for the pilot Walker, but he had not appeared and she had known she couldn't wait forever.

In the end she had had to assume Walker wasn't coming: either he wasn't coming this way—he had gone down the other side of the mountain or taken shelter somewhere near the cabin—or he wasn't able to come at all because the others had retrieved him or killed him.

She had been very bitter when she had wandered into the steep cut leading her horse and had almost trampled Buck Stevens. There had been a few moments of confusion there, Vickers ready to start shooting at the intruder, but it had got sorted out and they had brought the woman inside their shelter and fed her hot liquids and she had told them pieces of her story.

She was a remarkable woman, full of endurance and spirit, but women who chose to live isolated lives on the fringes of the wild country tended to be strong characters. At one point

Vickers had told her how anxious her husband was about her and Mrs. Lansford had given him a twisted look and said, "How intrepid of him," and looked around as if to emphasize the fact that Ben Lansford wasn't here, hadn't come after her. It was evident, and therefore sad, that Mrs. Lansford despised her husband; Watchman found himself regretting that because it violated his sense of orderly romantic neatness: a woman is in peril, you rescue her from it, you prepare to return her to her man, and you want her to look forward to that reunion with ecstatic joy. For a moment he resented Mrs. Lansford, he made her out to be an ingrate for obscure reasons, he even felt that her attitude somehow threatened everything good between himself and Lisa.

It was a brief passing irrationality and he had no time to dwell on it. Mrs. Lansford was just getting herself thawed out and beginning to answer questions coherently when they had heard the faint sounds of a man shouting. She had got up quickly and left the shelter before any of them had time to move. Watchman had gone after her; she had for some reason picked up the reins of her horse and was leading it along with her, and Watchman only just caught up to her when she found Walker and began to slap his face to stop his hysterical shouting.

Now they had Walker bundled into the stinking carcass and Vickers was talking to the woman in his methodically polite FBI voice: "Now Mrs. Lansford if you don't mind I'd like you to tell us everything you can about those four men up there."

The woman began to talk and Watchman listened with close attention. A corner of his mind marveled at her resilience; mostly he just absorbed her words, forming a picture of the four men. The images of two of them were only vague outlines—the older man, Hanratty, and the one called Burt; but she had reacted sharply to the one they called only

"Steve" and the other one, "Major." From the information Washington had sent, Vickers supplied their names: Baraclough, Hargit. When Mrs. Lansford talked about those two men there was a change in her voice; the mannerisms of country drawl fell away, the syllables tightened up. These men had frightened her: frightened her in a different way from the kidnaping itself. When you were abducted your fear was likely to be self-focused—*What's to become of me?*—and Mrs. Lansford had reacted that way but in time she had worked up another kind of fear, induced by Hargit's awful predatory indifference and Baraclough's sadistic malice, and she was not surprised when she learned that the police deputy had been left dead in her house: she recalled that Baraclough had been the last one to leave the house and remembered the look of satisfaction on Baraclough's strange face.

After a while Vickers' voice ran down with fatigue. They fed themselves and Watchman checked the pilot's condition —the man was dead asleep, almost comatose in his rancid cocoon—and they wrapped up in a huddled knot and slept.

3

Watchman came awake fully and instantly. It was still night-dark and the wind still howled; for a moment he had trouble deciding what had disturbed him but then he listened to the wind again and discovered that its tone had changed.

Its direction had shifted around and the pitch of it had dropped; the air in the lean-to had a keen cold edge but it didn't whip at him as it had before. As near as he could judge, it was coming up from the southwest now and that meant they were on the trailing edge of the storm's circular flow: the blizzard was moving on east.

He had to adjust his blankets and peel back several layers of sleeve cuffs to see the luminous face of his watch. Just past five o'clock in the morning.

He turned, disturbing Vickers; heard Vickers grunt in his sleep and saw a shadowy figure sitting up in the mouth of the lean-to, wreathed in blankets and looking like one of those old photographs of Plains Indians sitting outside their tepees. That was Buck Stevens, keeping watch on the pilot.

Watchman touched him on the shoulder and went past to have a look at Walker. Then he began to dig around in the snow for firewood.

It took a long time to gather enough wood. It was quite wet but he built the fire on top of a burning Sterno can and that dried it out sufficiently for it to catch. He built it close against the rock face of the cliff, under the corner of the lean-to, and the wind whipped up the flames and carried the smoke away up the cliff.

Vickers and Mrs. Lansford moved close to the fire and Watchman lifted back the flap of horsehide over Keith Walker. The hide had frozen and it cracked when he bent it back. The embryonic figure moved: blinked and muttered. Stevens brought an aluminum cup of coffee and they got it inside the pilot. Walker's face, when they brought him to the fire, was bloodless and slack, and his jerky rictus smile flashed on and off—the nervous reaction of spasmed relief, the smile of a survivor who had met death.

Mrs. Lansford gave him a grave look. "How do you feel?"

"All," Walker said, and had to clear his throat. "All right. Like a cheap watch somebody forgot to wind up." He shrank back against the heated rock as if to remove his offensiveness from the rest of them: the smell of dead flesh clung to his hair and clothes. "I guess I was pretty far gone."

Vickers said, "You're in bad trouble, Walker."

Mrs. Lansford's face came around fast. "For God's sake." She went back to Walker and her voice changed: "Do you think you can eat?"

"I'd like to try. I don't know if I can hold it down." His eyes were full of fear, darting from face to face, ready to flinch.

Vickers said, "Are you ready to talk?" in a no-nonsense voice.

Mrs. Lansford was building a plate for him and Watchman said, "Let the man eat something."

"We haven't got a whole lot of time, Trooper." Vickers swallowed coffee and addressed himself to the pilot. "It may make a difference to the prosecution if I can tell them you came forward voluntarily and told the whole story to the FBI. But you're not required to make any statement in the absence of your attorney and you—"

"Never mind the recitation. I know my rights."

"Then you've been through this before?"

Walker had turned sullen. "Nuts. I look at television." Mrs. Lansford got up to take him his food and stayed there beside him, making a point of it, showing Vickers her defiance.

Walker ate slowly with the concentration of a monk attending his breviary. Watchman thought it was because Walker was in no frame of mind to take anything for granted just now: the feel and sight and taste of each morsel was reassurance that he was alive.

Vickers said, "You have information we need, Walker. There are four men up there—how are they armed? What are their plans?"

"I don't know—I'm not sure. Things are screwed up, you know?"

"I won't accept that for an answer."

"You know what it's like when you wake up and you know you've had a bad dream but you can't remember the details?"

It had a counterfeit sound but Watchman thought it was probably true; you didn't always remember clearly things that happened in panic. Walker said, "I'm just not thinking straight. It's not that I'm trying to hide anything." He was no longer sullen; he wasn't angry at all. His expression had the false serenity of withdrawal.

Vickers said, "Lansford said they'd taken some rifles. Are they all armed with rifles?"

"Maybe. Probably. I don't know."

Mrs. Lansford's eyes flashed. "Can't you leave him alone?"

"Don't waste your pity on this man, Mrs. Lansford."

"He saved my life."

"If it hadn't been for him and his friends your life wouldn't have needed saving." Vickers had a nice neat way of drawing lines and putting people on one side or the other. Watchman saw the effect it had on Walker: it closed him up and he quit talking.

Vickers had a veneer of competent sophistication but underneath he was clumsy, insensitive. He let arrogance take the place of understanding. It wasn't hard to guess the kind of mistake he must have made that had got him exiled to the boondocks; it was a wonder the Bureau had kept him on at all.

Vickers said, "I had a look in your pockets. You were their pilot."

"Aeah."

"The name on the license isn't Walker."

"Is that a fact."

"Clamming up now won't do your case any good, friend."

"What will?"

"I will," Mrs. Lansford said. "I'll testify for him."

Vickers said, "You're not thinking straight. Think about the police officer they murdered in your house. Think about the bank guard they shotgunned to death."

"Walker didn't kill them."

"He did in the eyes of the law." Vickers got to his feet. "I can see he's not in a mood to cooperate. That'll go in my report. Now I suggest we saddle up and move in."

Watchman was picking up the blankets he had slept in. He walked around the fire and draped the blankets around Walker's shoulders. The pilot looked up at him, showing thanks, and murmured, "The Major and Baraclough. You want to look out. You're Indian, aren't you?"

What did that have to do with anything? "Yes."

"Then maybe you know a little something about snares and traps and ambushes. But I'll tell you this—Hargit maybe knows more than you do. And Baraclough. Maybe they're better Indians than you are. You want to look out."

Vickers, listening close, made a scoffing sound. "Don't let them assume monolithic proportions, Trooper. They're just soldiers gone bad."

Walker looked up at him. "You go on thinking that way and I won't have to worry about what you put in your report because you won't live to write it."

"All right, they've thrown a scare into you. But you're imagining things. They're on the run—they're just as scared as you are."

"Don't bet on it," Walker said.

Mrs. Lansford said, "He's right." She said it to Watchman as if she knew there was no point talking to the FBI agent. Vickers had a genius for tuning out what he didn't want to hear.

Vickers was lifting his saddle off the lean-to. "Come on, Trooper. Your partner can stay here and watch the prisoner and look after Mrs. Lansford."

"They can look after themselves," Watchman said. "We'll need Buck with us."

"And let this man make a run for it as soon as we're out of earshot? You know damn well Mrs. Lansford wouldn't lift a finger to stop him. Hell she'd probably go with him."

Mrs. Lansford's face reddened; she didn't speak. Walker said drily, "You could always handcuff me to a tree."

"I thought of it," Vickers said. "But there's a chance we might not come back."

"You mean a chance of getting killed."

"Yes." Vickers was stubborn about rules, about going by the book. It wasn't his sense of humanity, it was his sense of reputation. It wouldn't look good in his obituary to have it pointed out that he had left an unattended prisoner chained to a tree to die in a blizzard.

Watchman shook his head. "Trooper Stevens is under my orders, not yours. He comes with me. You can come or stay, that's up to you."

"I don't like your implication, Trooper."

"I'll spell it out in short words then. I trust Buck not to make mistakes up here. He grew up in the Arizona hill country—he's been hunting out here since he was ten years old. Wl.en his daddy gave him two cartridges he was supposed to bring back two cottontails and he did it."

He caught the grin behind Stevens' hand. Stevens didn't make any comment but when Vickers replied, Stevens' eyes sought inspiration from the sky: *Good God*.

"I've done my share of game hunting," Vickers said. "I've told you that."

"In New Jersey?" Watchman tried hard to keep the acid out of his voice. "You fellows have a very big crime-busting reputation and it's probably deserved, mostly, but can you navigate these mountains in this weather? Can you make sense out of sign? Spot an ambush in the woods? You heard Walker, he knows these men. Hargit may be a better Indian than I am; he's bound to be a lot better Indian than you are."

Stevens drawled, "Better red than dead, Mr. Vickers." His grin was amiable.

Vickers flashed an irritable glance toward the rookie. "Next you're going to tell me he can smell a white man in a blizzard."

Watchman said, "I also grunt and wear feathers and consider myself a member of the Ten Lost Tribes of Israel. Now if we're through with the ethnic discussions let's get these horses saddled."

4

Helping him rig the horses, Buck Stevens said mildly in a voice too low to reach Vickers, "And I don't even have Medicare. *Amigo*, one of these days they're going to come and get you with a butterfly net. I hope they don't write this up as *kemo sabe's* folly."

"What's the matter, white man, you fresh out of silver bullets?"

"Sam, the first time I ever laid eyes on you I knew you'd be one of those guys who had to do everything the hard way. You know damn well that story about me and the two cartridges and the two rabbits was as phony as a plastic flower. I wouldn't be surprised if old Vickers is a hell of a lot better at it than I am."

"The difference being, I can depend on you at my back."

"You really think he'd cut out on you?"

Watchman shrugged. He doubted Vickers was a coward but he had no confidence in Vickers' private idea of priorities. When you were in the middle of a play you didn't want your pass receiver to change his mind and head for the wrong end of the field. Vickers might get that sort of wild-hair notion; Buck Stevens wouldn't. He could be depended on to be where he said he'd be, when he said he'd be there, and to stay there until told to move.

Stevens smoothed the saddle blanket and heaved the saddle up. "You know Walker won't be the only one gets reamed out in that report of his. The way you keep needling him you could end up unemployed."

"I don't want to lose these jokers on his account."

"You're making it into a crusade."

"Jasper isn't any less dead today than he was yesterday," Watchman said, but then he had to think about that. He hadn't been raised to believe in eye-for-an-eye retribution; that was a white man's concept. Indian law didn't lean hard on revenge and punishment; it emphasized compensation of the victim instead. But you couldn't compensate Jasper Simalie. The question had run through his mind at odd intervals in the past two days and although he had never developed much of an introspective habit he was beginning to realize what was behind this dedication of his that had come out of nowhere and taken him by surprise and stripped away a good many superficial layers of easygoing indifference. When you came right down to it, it didn't seem to make a whole lot of sense: they had killed a Navajo, therefore they needed to be caught by a Navajo. It was a streak of—what? nationalism? tribalism? —he had never thought he had in him. And there was another idea, too, hard to articulate: somehow he needed to demonstrate that they couldn't be allowed to kill a Navajo brother and get away with it.

He looked across the horse's withers while he was snugging the cinch and saw Vickers by the fire, shouldering into his heavy coat. It didn't strike Watchman until a moment later that ten minutes ago he hadn't been able to see that far through the driving snow. Now the camp was quite clearly visible. Snow was falling at a slant, not too heavily, and the wind was breaking up into gusts, with intervals of near-silence. He turned, hung onto his hatbrim and threw his head back to look up. The cliff receded into a mottled gray haze of drifting snow but he could make out the rim a hundred feet above him and the bellies of fast-moving clouds.

Vickers tramped over to him, boots kicking up little powder flurries. The snow was settling quickly onto the exposed flats, which it had not done before; until now it had blown across the open ground and collected in high drifts against wind-breaks.

"We'll all go," Vickers said.

"Them too?" Watchman was astonished.

Vickers shook his head. "I didn't mean that. We've only got three horses. They'll be on foot—they wouldn't get far in all this snow. I told them we'd come back for them within twenty-four hours. I think I impressed it on Walker that his best chance is to stay here and wait. If he doesn't he'll be run down and caught eventually. He's not as important as the other four right now."

"All right," Watchman said, not displeased that Vickers was using his head for a change. "We'll leave some of the provisions here."

"I've taken care of that. Are we ready to go?"

"As soon as you saddle your horse."

Vickers' expression changed a little—a pinching of mouth corners. Evidently he had expected somebody to saddle up for him. Watchman didn't take the hint. He was nobody's hired wrangler.

Getting to be a pretty proud Innun, aren't we. He chastised himself silently for his childishness and went over to the fire to gather his things. Mrs. Lansford was trying to comb wet tangles out of her walnut-brown hair with her fingers; she looked up at him and her smile showed him the same resilient strength he'd admired last night. "Thanks for what you've done, Officer."

He said impulsively, "My name's Sam Watchman. Sam."

"All right. Thanks, Sam."

Keith Walker said, "Remember what I said about the Major and Baraclough."

"I will. Listen, if we're not back here by daybreak tomorrow you'd better start down the mountain. And watch your footing in the drifts."

Mrs. Lansford said, "You'll be back."

"They may have headed down the back of the mountain by now. Don't wait past morning. All right?"

"All right, Sam."

Walker only nodded bleakly and Watchman walked to his horse.

5

It wouldn't have taken half an hour to reach the ranger cabin if it hadn't been for the drifts. A good part of the way the horses were up to their bellies in snow. Twice Watchman had to double back and find another way around.

At the summit the wind was still brisk but nothing like the previous day's gale. Ramps of snow lay against two sides of the cabin all the way to the peaked roof line. The spindle tracery of the wooden watchtower loomed above the cabin in silhouette against the clouds. Watchman signaled a halt at the side of a twenty-foot boulder and took a good long time to look the place over. He didn't see any smoke at the chimney but that didn't need to mean anything. The blowing snow had almost erased a line of indentations in the crust that emerged from the cabin door and made an abrupt right turn and disappeared down over the far crest. It could mean they had moved on; it could mean they had laid tracks to invite their pursuers into an ambush. Watchman dismounted and dragged his rifle out of the saddle boot. Without the need of instructions Buck Stevens got down with his rifle and braced his aiming arm against the abrasive side of the boulder, training the rifle on the cabin door. Watchman nodded to him and struck off on foot to make a wide circle and come in at the cabin from its blind side. When he looked back he saw Vickers coming after him.

The scatter of boulders made it possible to keep cover until he had come up within twenty feet of the cabin. When he stopped Vickers bumped into his back and muttered, "Sorry."

"Keep a little distance," Watchman said, and swept the summit with a careful inspection. Nothing stirred except the wind and snow. He looked across the little flat and made a hand signal to Buck Stevens, and Stevens' hat lifted and fell in acknowledgment. Watchman stripped off his right glove and put it in his pocket; fitted his hand into the rifle's trigger guard and sprinted for the side wall of the cabin.

He was ready to drop and slide but his run drew no fire. Against the cabin he spent a good while listening. Heard nothing and glanced back. Vickers was still in the rocks, training his rifle on the cabin. Watchman nodded to him and Vickers made his run, skidding to a stop beside him.

Watchman went along to the front corner of the log shack and poked his head out. Stevens had the door covered but that didn't keep anyone in the farther rocks from having it covered too.

The snow right in front of the door had been churned up

and was brown with mud, thinly covered with a fresh white fall that had coated it since the tracks had been made. Watchman tried to judge how long that might be but it was hard to estimate—ten minutes, maybe two hours; the cabin roof overhung it and a lot would depend on the changes in the wind during the past hour or two.

A few blunt icicles hung from the edges of the roof. Watchman eased around the butts of the corner logs and moved along to the door, and stood there studying it and studying the rocks beyond. Vickers' head appeared at the corner, an inquiring lift of eyebrows, and Watchman held up a palm to keep him where he was.

There was a padlock hasp, badly bent; no lock. What held the door shut was a wooden throw bar, a dowel handle of which protruded through a slot in the face of the heavy plank door. You had to slide the dowel about eight inches to the right. Watchman thought about that for a while, not touching the door, and after he had considered the temptations he went back to the corner and said, "Wait here. Don't touch the door." And looked both ways and jogged over to Buck Stevens' post in the rocks.

"What's up?"

"Nothing, I hope. Hand me that coil of rope, will you? Thanks."

"Want me to stay put?"

"Yes. Make noise if anything moves."

Watchman carried the lariat back to the cabin door and dropped it on the ground. Vickers was scowling at him. Watchman said, "Be a good idea if you went over to those rocks for a minute."

"Why?"

"Just prudent," Watchman said. He picked up the noose

end of the rope and pulled it down tight into a small loop. Then he made sure the coil of rope lay properly on the ground, and gently hung the little loop on the dowel handle of the door bar. He did this very gingerly. Finally he reached down for the free end of the rope and began to pull it slowly. The rope began to uncoil, not disturbing the latch.

Vickers had gone over to the rocks and Watchman backed toward him slowly, paying the rope out. It was a fifty-foot lasso and he went back into the rocks with the end of it. "Duck down behind that rock now," he said, and Vickers finally got the idea and took cover.

Watchman pulled the rope around back of a boulder and kept pulling until he heard the door latch begin to scrape in its slotted guides. It looked as if they hadn't booby-trapped it after all, but he didn't regret taking the time to be sure. . . . And then the rope met resistance, he gave it a brief final tug, and a blast of explosives blew the cabin door out.

6

Just inside the doorway the explosion had dug a little crater in the dirt floor. Vickers picked up a small piece of metal and dropped it quickly because it was still hot. "Shrapnel. It was a fragmentation grenade."

Watchman nodded. He fingered the charred end of the dangling piece of wire by the door frame. They had wired the grenade to the post and hooked the tripwire around the latch, to pull the pin when the door was opened.

"Now that raises an interesting question," Watchman said.

"Such as?"

"Just how many more of these handy little goodies do you suppose they're carrying?"

7

He felt the potbelly stove—still warm. They hadn't been gone very long.

He made a quick search. The explosion had littered the front of the room with wooden debris and it had knocked a few shrapnel holes in the walls. But the fugitives didn't seem to have left anything behind except for a few discarded empty tin cans. Well, they'd had an extra horse—the one Walker had left behind; they had plenty of space to pack everything they wanted.

He went back to the jagged-edged doorway and stepped across the remains of the door. Vickers was coming out behind him and Buck Stevens brought up the horses. Watchman could see vaguely the shapes of lower summits down the north slope.

Vickers said, "They can't have got far. Look at those tracks. What would you say, half an hour ahead of us?"

"Something like that."

"Let's go, then."

"Take it easy a minute," Watchman said.

"What for? Four men, seven horses—they can't travel in this snow without leaving tracks. We've got them now."

"Or maybe they've got us."

"What are you talking about?"

"They may have heard the racket up here. They know we're close behind them. They can't count on wiping all of us out with one grenade so they've got to figure they've still got some of us on their trail. And like you said, they know they can't hide their tracks."

"So?"

"So put yourself in their shoes. They're going to do two things. First they're going to set themselves up in a place where they get a good long view down their own backtrail so they can count us on their fingers when we come in sight. Then when they know how many we are they'll go on down the mountain a little way, lay some nice tracks for us to follow, and they'll double back around their own tracks and set up a fine little crossfire for us to walk into."

A crimson flush suffused Vickers' cheeks. He got busy lighting a cigarette.

Buck Stevens said in his matter-of-fact voice, "How do you want to work it, Sam?"

"No point in playing the game by their rules. I think we'll cut over east a little way. Go down behind that ridge line and ride north."

"You mean try to get around in front of them."

"It's worth a try," Watchman said, squinting across the mountains.

Vickers said, "You're talking as if you can anticipate which way they're going. It's all very well for us to go on ahead of them and try to ambush them, but what if they don't walk into it? What if they go another way entirely?"

"Then we'll just have to send them an invitation, won't we?" Watchman walked past him and mounted his horse. "Of course you can go right on after them if you want. I don't much recommend it but you can please yourself." He nodded to Buck Stevens and led the way down off the summit, splitting wide away from the dimpled tracks the fugitives had left in the snow.

Behind them Vickers climbed onto his horse and gigged it nervously. When Watchman looked back Vickers was coming right along after him. Watchman smiled a little and turned to face front.

CHAPTER

1

The napalm burn on Baraclough's wrist was supposed to be dead scar flesh but it had a way of itching sometimes. He scratched it viciously, enjoying the pain.

Eddie Burt said, "I don't think they're coming."

"They're not stupid," Major Hargit conceded. They'd seen three men start down off the skyline by the cabin. Three men had left the bonfire by those two trucks down on the flats night before last, and if it could be assumed these were the same three men then none of them had been hurt by the booby-trap grenade in the cabin. If they were smart enough to avoid that one they were pretty good.

But it had been a good twenty minutes since the three horsemen had disappeared over the summit half a mile above, and they should have showed up long before now if they were following the tracks.

Hanratty took it badly. He dragged his gloved palm down across his face with an abrasive rasp of stubble and began to shake. He had shaken like that an hour ago, coming down into this timbered cut, when the Major had halted the group and said, "The pack only chases a prey that runs. We'll turn and face them."

Now Baraclough said, "I guess they want to flank us."

Eddie Burt grinned. "They ain't bad for country cops."

Major Hargit nodded. "They're not bad, Sergeant, but they're no A-team. Their friends will be taking the three of them down off this mountain in canvas bags. All right, gentlemen, let's go find them."

2

The wind had just about died but it was still quite cold and Baraclough had stripped down to his windbreaker because he took a kind of pleasure from the discomfort. They followed the Major along a steep hillside, keeping under the pines where the snow hadn't drifted very deep. The Major checked his compass at intervals and finally turned his horse straight up the northeast face of the mountain and they clung to their saddles, leaning far forward to balance the horses. Hoofs scrabbled in the loose footing and the horses lunged and heaved their way toward the top.

At the military crest they tied the horses to trees and crawled to the top. Baraclough waited for the Major to hand him the field glasses. The Major completed a sweep and handed them over. Baraclough lifted them to his eyes and said, "See anything?"

"No. Your try."

But Baraclough saw nothing either.

Hanratty said, "Jesus, let's don't just lie here. I'm fixing to freeze my ass off."

"We'll wait," the Major said.

3

Half an hour drifted by. Baraclough was mildly offended by the rank smell of his ~~own~~ wet clothes. The temperature had risen considerably since dawn; the wind seemed cold but everything was melting around him. Snowflakes drifted lazily through the air but they were thin enough to cause no problem of visibility; he could see one peak, east along the range, that must have been eight or ten miles away. The sky beyond it was dark and wild where the storm had gone, but overhead now little salmon streaks of color showed through where the clouds were thinning and beginning to break up. Baraclough suspected they'd have sunshine before the end of the day.

A brittle thin sheet of ice clung to the shadowed side of a rock near Baraclough's shoulder. It cracked like a rifle shot and Hanratty almost jumped out of his skin.

"Oh Jesus. I can't stand any more of this cocksucking waiting. My balls are froze." Hanratty's voice sounded unhinged. When Baraclough looked over his shoulder he saw Hanratty starting to get up.

He rolled over, crashed into Hanratty's knees, knocked Hanratty down.

Hanratty uttered a little cry. Eddie Burt said, "You God damned fool, Jack. Stay off the skyline."

Baraclough flicked a glance toward the Major and the Major nodded slowly; the Major looked at Hanratty and said with icy contempt, "It was my mistake to trust a civilian. I won't make it again."

Hanratty's eyes were pouched. He looked at the Major and he looked at Baraclough and his head skewed back; he understood the unspoken order that the Major had issued to Baraclough.

Pulsebeat drummed in Baraclough's temples. His scalp contracted; he felt the familiar anticipatory knot in his groin.

Hanratty turned to stare at the Major. "Look, I didn't mean—"

Baraclough caught him from behind, clamped a hand around his face. Jerked Hanratty's head back and chopped his free hand across Hanratty's throat. The bladed chop to the larynx snapped Hanratty's hyoid and when Baraclough let him drop to the ground Hanratty was dead.

Baraclough's breathing was just a little unsteady; his eyes grew heavy and he rolled over in the snow and reached for the field glasses.

4

After half an hour more the Major stirred. "They're doing a good job of keeping out of sight."

"They've got to be somewhere in this district."

"Granted. But we're not locating them this way. I think we'll move to that peak." The Major pointed with his finger. The peak was about a mile due east of them, a little lower than the one on which they lay.

Eddie Burt said, "What about Jack? Leave him here?"

"No. We'll throw him across his horse and bring him along. I think he'll be useful."

5

Shards of sunlight began to stream through apertures in the clouds. On the uphill slope little trickles ran down past them, cutting through the snow. There was a smell of pine resin and the woods echoed with the tiny cracklings of breaking ice.

When they stopped and dismounted Baraclough made a methodical inspection of the money sacks to make sure they had not worked loose of their packsaddle lashings. "Walker did a good job tying these down."

Eddie Burt said, "I wonder if he's still alive."

"Not a chance," Baraclough said.

They wormed to the top and made a slow circuit of the perimeter on their bellies, scouting the surrounding slopes a sector at a time with the Zeiss glasses the Major had liberated from the ranch house forty hours ago.

Baraclough took his turn and let the lenses ride slowly up and down, covering the district in a checkerboard sweep. Abruptly the binoculars steadied in his grip and he fixed the point in his vision and handed the glasses to the Major. "That little patch of open snow between the pine groves. Eleven o'clock—down a little lower now. Got it?"

"Yes. It could be their tracks. You've got good eyes, Steve —I missed that."

Baraclough took pride in the Major's compliment: he smiled a little.

Burt said, "Okay, what do we do?"

The Major looked at Baraclough. "How many grenades have we got?"

"Two."

"That should be enough. We're going to set up an ambush a fly couldn't get through."

They went back down toward the horses. Burt said, "What do we use *him* for?" He meant Hanratty's corpse, belly-down across the saddle.

"Bait," the Major said, and mounted his horse.

Baraclough smiled.

6

At about three o'clock the sun came out. Baraclough had been squinting across the snow for hours and the added brightness was painful against his grainy eyes.

Up ahead the Major made a turn to the left and threaded the pines downhill. In places the storm had left deep drifts of feathery-loose snow in timber shadows where the day had not begun to melt it; the horses floundered through belly-deep, plunging, splashing up clouds of white powder.

"This will do." The Major dismounted just inside the edge of the forest.

The trees ended at the lip of a loose shale rockslide that covered a ten- or fifteen-acre slope, very steep, all the way to the creek at the bottom. The forest enclosed the rockslide on three sides and there was a thick line of aspens and sycamores along the opposite bank of the creek. Beyond that the ground flattened out, a scrub-covered plateau that stretched south at least half a mile to the foot of another pine-timbered mountain.

In the past two hours they had spotted tracks twice, both times to the east of them, both times heading north. Once they had established that much the Major had made up his mind and they had pushed directly north with all the speed they could get out of the horses, staying within the trees on west-facing slopes with a high ridge or two between them and the pursuit. It was the Major's aim to get at least a mile ahead of the cops and they had probably achieved that margin by now because the cops would be doing a good deal of backing and filling to scout side-canyons and discover ambushes.

It was a fair bet the cops would come down that slope beyond the brushy flat, sometime within the next half hour, and when they got that far they would have a clear view of this shale rockslide. That was what the Major wanted—a spot in plain sight.

"Roll him down," the Major said.

Eddie Burt helped Baraclough unstrap Hanratty's corpse and lift it off the horse. They carried it to the lip of the shale slide and laid Hanratty down between the trees. Hanratty's joints had stiffened up and his face had swollen and turned a very deep crimson color in post-mortem lividity because his head had been hanging down by the stirrup.

The Major was using his glasses and when he was done he passed them to Baraclough and Baraclough did a confirming sweep. "Nothing. But they'll be along."

"Most likely," the Major agreed, and said again, "Roll him down."

Baraclough got down on his knees behind Hanratty, as if the corpse were a barricade from which he intended to shoot. He hooked his hands under a shoulder and a buttock and heaved.

Hanratty was butt-heavy, hard to roll over, but Baraclough got the body over the lip of the slide and then it was rolling down the snow-carpeted rock like a chunky log. It made some noise, not much, and started a few loose bits of shale tumbling. The disturbance threw a cloud of snow into the air and the corpse half rolled, half slid down the mountainside, picking up a coating of white like a rolling snowball. Little avalanches of rock and snow were triggered by Hanratty's violent passage and the corpse left a deep rumpled groove in its wake, a gouged-out trench that a half-blind observer couldn't miss from across the valley.

The shale slide was so steep that there was no chance Hanratty would stop rolling and sliding before he hit bottom. He went right into the creek, clattering some rocks together, breaking up a thin rime of ice. The water was accustomed to avalanche debris; it made a path around the corpse and continued to flow.

Baraclough went back to his horse and they got mounted. The Major turned and they stayed inside the trees, making a circuit around the edge of the rockslide, keeping to cover all the way down to the creek. Horseshoes clattered on the rocks when they crossed the creek; they turned in the aspens and rode upstream.

The Major wanted to set it up himself. Baraclough gave him the grenade. He stayed on his horse and watched the Major walk over to the bank of the stream beside Hanratty and squat down on his heels.

The long tumble had ripped Hanratty's clothes and pulped his face pretty badly. The Major dragged the corpse closer to the bank and positioned the dead arms and legs with the body half in the water, half on the bank, as if Hanratty had fallen that way naturally. Face down: that was important, because when the cops found him they would want to know what he looked like. If you left him face up they might not disturb the body right away.

The Major took his time bracing the grenade under the dead man's breastplate, making certain the grenade was lodged firmly between corpse and rock. Then he pulled the pin from the grenade gingerly, using both hands, and removed his hands slowly and carefully. Now the corpse's weight held the grenade's handle down against its spring pressure and when the corpse was moved the handle would fly off and the grenade would explode.

The Major motioned to Baraclough and Burt to dismount. "We've got two spare horses now." Walker's and Hanratty's. "Let's turn them loose—it'll give our friends something else to worry about."

Horses were gregarious animals and it was not all that easy to persuade the two beasts to go away by themselves but after Baraclough had led them a hundred yards upstream and whipped them harshly across the flanks with his rifle butt they trotted away snorting and kept going out onto the scrub flats, heading south. He had removed the bridle bits and reins to keep them from snagging and he knew that if the horses weren't caught soon they would find their way back over the mountains to the ranch they had come from. That would help confuse the pursuit, but the important thing right now was that the three cops up there were likely to come in sight of this plateau at any moment now and they would spot the two horses right away. That was what the Major wanted.

Baraclough walked back to the creek and the Major said, "We'll post ourselves in the pines. Up there. When they come along they'll take their time and take pains not to expose themselves, but sooner or later they'll have a look at Hanratty. I want to be up there with a bead on them. If the grenade doesn't take them out we'll do it with rifles. All set? Let's go, then."

Baraclough let Burt go ahead of him, leading the pack animals. He stayed behind a few moments to look it over and it looked good. A lot of tracks coming in and out—that would whet the cops' interest and make them nervous. Hanratty's corpse, like an open honey jar, with the armed grenade under the breastbone. The creek exposed fully to enfilading fire from the pines above, along the edge of the rockslide. It was a fine ambush: but then the Major always set up fine ambushes. That was why the three of them were still alive after four tours of combat duty.

He went along after the others, forded the creek and rode up the steep pitch of the hillside. Tied his horse back in the trees with the others' and carried his rifle along to the edge of the rockslide.

The Major had made himself comfortable with his rifle balanced across a fallen log. Like a bench-rest shooter. The distance from here to Hanratty's corpse was no more than two hundred yards. It would be just about impossible to miss.

They waited no more than twenty minutes. Clouds drifted across the sun, their shadows riding quickly along the mountains. Out on the half-mile flat beyond the stream Baraclough could see the two riderless horses browsing their way indolently toward the mountain beyond. And then the Major, peering through his field glasses, said in his businesslike voice, "Here they come."

CHAPTER

1

"Damn it, something fell down that mountain," the FBI agent argued. "Suppose it was one of their pack horses. It got away from them and they let Walker's horse go too, they didn't have any more use for it. The two horses got together out here. It makes sense."

"Then where's the pack saddle?" Buck Stevens asked. He leaned over to pat one of the horses.

The two animals had trotted up amiably when Watchman had led the party out onto the flats. Watchman had taken a look at them and taken a harder look at their tracks, which led back toward the aspens at the foot of the shale slide, and that had drawn their attention to the long raw trench something had gouged out of the snow down the length of the slide.

The abandoned horses were a bay and a blue roan and they both had Lansford's brand on them. One of them had an empty rifle boot strapped to the saddle.

Vickers was going through the saddle pockets but he didn't come up with anything that looked like a clue. Watchman sat with his hands folded across the saddle horn, squinting toward the shale slide seven or eight hundred yards away.

Vickers got mounted in his ungainly way and fumbled for a cigarette. "I suppose the next step is to go in and see what it is. Whatever fell down that hill is probably still there."

Watchman, still thinking, did not reply. Buck Stevens whipped off his hat and chased the two riderless horses off to the south, driving them along like a cowboy with a lot of whooping and slapping of his hat against his thigh, until the two horses ran into the pines. Then Stevens trotted back to rejoin them. "They'd have tagged along otherwise. We can always pick them up on the way back for Walker and Mrs. Lansford." His face changed: "If we come back."

Vickers said, "Don't be ridiculous," and pulled the walkie-talkie out of his saddlebag and punched it up and talked into it, and listened, and said, "Still nothing."

Watchman wasn't surprised. Walkie-talkies didn't have much of a daytime range and the bulk of the mountains lay between here and Constable Cunningham.

They had had no contact with the outside world for more than twenty-four hours and Vickers was obviously restless about that. By now the case would be in all the headlines and on all the networks. Probably journalists had descended on San Miguel in battalions with sound trucks and camera crews. All that potential publicity and here the nominal commander of the chase was incommunicado in the wilderness. It made Watchman smile a little. Actually it probably wasn't the reporters so much as his own superiors who had Vickers worried: right now there was probably a good bit of apoplexy in Phoenix and Washington.

Vickers inquired drily, "Is there some compelling reason why we're just sitting here?"

"Could be."

Buck Stevens said, "We were getting ready to fix up an invitation for Hargit and his crowd. It looks like they may have beat us to it."

"Now I do recognize that," Vickers said. "I may learn slowly, but I do learn. And it may amaze you to know this but I've had a small bit of experience with criminal types in my time. Now I'd suggest we don't follow the horse tracks into those trees. It might well be a trap, as you say, but we can't very well sit here until we get boils on the off-chance of avoiding an ambush. The thing to do is swing to one side and get into those trees over there"—he pointed off to the left, then swung his arm to the right—"or over there. Come in from one side or the other and, if they're in there waiting for us, flank them."

During the FBI agent's pedantic sarcasms Watchman was looking and thinking. Stalking and being stalked in country like this required levels of sophistication considerably beyond what Vickers was willing to credit. A good deal of the maneuvering consisted of double and treble bluffs. At the single level you set up an ambush which you hoped your enemy wouldn't detect, you waited for him to walk into it, and you jumped him. At the double level you set out an obvious invitation, making it so obvious that your enemy would take pains to avoid it, because you expected him in avoiding it to fall into another trap you had set. At the treble level you set up an invitation so obvious that your enemy would recognize its clumsiness as a fraud and would come ahead and investigate it because he believed you didn't expect him to investigate it. You could go on working out reverse bluffs like this to infinite levels but in the end your only real guide was your ~~own~~ judgment of your enemy's level of sophistication—and *his* judgment of your judgment of it. It wasn't only Hargit's woodcraft that had to be taken into account; it was also Hargit's assessment of the intelligence of his pursuers. You would set a different kind of trap for a crafty man from the kind you would set for a fool. In a way it was exactly like the psychology of the game of poker; and Sam Watchman was a fair poker player.

Now Hargit had set out an obvious invitation. It had to be one of two things. A trap or a time killer: something calculated to draw the police into an ambush, or something calculated to keep them busy circling slowly around *because* they thought it was an ambush, to give Hargit plenty of time to get away while his pursuers fooled around in the woods here.

In two hours it would be sunset. Hargit probably felt his chances of escape would be far better after dark. Possibly they were, but the clouds were clearing off and there would be a three-quarter moon tonight.

Vickers was scowling at him. "Did you hear what I said?"

"Does it matter?" Watchman was cool because he was running out of patience with him. "We'll circle it. I want to find out if they're still in there."

"Circle it? How far out?"

Watchman made a sweep with his arm. It encompassed the aspens in front of them and the mountain above, with the shale slide at the center.

"Do you have any idea how long it will take us to make that circuit?" Vickers demanded.

"I'd say an hour and a half. Maybe two."

"And give them just that much more of a lead on us."

"You can go right on in straight up if you want to. I'm tired of arguing with you. Come on, Buck."

In the end, of course, Vickers came along.

2

It took almost the two full hours. They entered the aspens about a quarter mile upstream from the point where the long snow-trench ended at the creekbank; so far they had crossed no tracks except those of the two abandoned horses. They went up through the pines and over the crest of the ridge, and ten minutes down the back of it Watchman began to circle to the right. About half a mile along the back of the ridge they found the tracks of the seven horses where they had come in from the southwest and gone up to the top of the ridge above the shale slide. This was where they had come in; it remained to be seen where, or if, they had gone out.

Watchman continued along the backside of the ridge about two miles, keeping to the trees, and circled the end of it with his rifle across his saddle horn and all his senses keyed up atavistically. They rode in a spread-out single file, fifty feet apart, and Watchman was alert to the possibility of tripwires stretched across his path: God knew how many more grenades the fugitives were armed with.

They reached the creek at a point more than two miles below their original crossing. Watchman looked both ways with considerable care before he put his horse across and ran into the aspens. He didn't circle to the right; he went straight ahead through the fringe of sycamores and leafless aspens, angling up a little slope so that when he reached the edge of the trees he was on an elevation overlooking the scrubby flat they had crossed two hours ago. The sun threw long shadows across the flats and it was not hard to make out the dotted shadow-line of two groups of tracks emerging from the trees quite a distance to the south and crossing the flat. One set belonged to the abandoned horses and the other set was the tracks Watchman and Vickers and Stevens had left two hours earlier.

"It doesn't have to mean they're still in there," he said. "They may have seen what we were up to and decided to go around behind us and clear out. But they were still in there until recently, we know that much, and I wouldn't be surprised if they've stayed put and decided to wait us out."

"All right," Vickers said testily, "we've killed a couple of hours and most of the daylight we had left. What bright idea comes next?"

"We go in after them."

He rode slowly back to the creekbank and turned left to ride upstream, keening the forest, scouting for tracks. About a half mile downstream from the point where the object had rolled down the slide to the creek, Watchman dismounted. "One of us stays here—that's you, Buck. If I sing out bring the horses along fast. Vickers, we go on foot from here."

3

"If anybody starts shooting don't crawl. It just makes you a slow target instead of a fast one. Run like hell and get behind a tree. If we lose touch stay put. Don't move. *I'll* find you."

"You don't have to treat me like a novice Boy Scout."

Watchman shook his head and said, "Just give me room, then—don't crowd too close behind me," and moved away.

He stayed inside the trees some distance back from the creekbank, moving upstream parallel to it. The sun had gone beyond the ridge; shadows shifted and settled. The snow was soft and loose and his boots sank through the surface without sound. As long as he was traversing snow that had not been disturbed he was fairly confident there were no boobytraps and so he was able to move at a steady speed through the trees. At any point an unseen rifleman might open up on him but if you used that possibility as your basis for movement you would never move at all. The trees were without leaves down here and it was possible to see eighty or a hundred feet in most directions, even with the light fading, and he was willing to gamble that the range of his visibility was as great or greater than the effective range of any rifle in these trees: it only took one twig to deflect an aimed bullet.

He had glimpses of the stream off to his right and when he estimated he was at the right point he stopped and turned and began to move, much more slowly now, toward the stream. Vickers was too close behind him and he made a hand signal that slowed Vickers down and put ten yards' distance between them.

He had brought Vickers along rather than Stevens because he wanted Vickers where he could see him. Leave Vickers off by himself and he might start shooting at anything that moved and it might turn out to be yourself.

From forty feet inside the trees he caught his first glimpse of the body in the creek. He crouched down and moved forward a further ten feet and studied it.

The body lay on its stomach with its arms and legs asprawl, face buried in the creek. From the gray hair that floated out from it he surmised it was the one called Hanratty. Either that or a stranger who'd got in their way.

Vickers crawled up beside him. "It could be booby-trapped."

"Likely is."

"But we need to know who he is."

That was true: they needed to know how many guns there were against them.

Twilight ran red along the crest of the ridge above the shale slide. Watchman studied the lie of it. Thick pines growing close together surrounded the rockslide in a horseshoe the ends of which descended to the far bank of the creek. If Hargit and his men were waiting in ambush they could be anywhere along that fringe and still have a good field of fire across the creek. On the other hand they might be gone by now, counting on their pursuers to lie up in these woods for a while investigating, giving Hargit time to get clear.

The first thing to do was to find out which it was, and the second thing to do was to be ready to take advantage of whatever disclosures Hargit might be kind enough to make.

Watchman moved back a few yards and picked up one of the dead saplings the storm had blown down; they were all over the woods. He chose one that seemed long enough and hacked off branches with his sheath knife until he had it trimmed to his satisfaction. Dragged it past Vickers and laid it on the ground. He positioned himself behind the bole of a sycamore trunk and pushed the sapling out toward the creek-bank as if it were an oversized pool cue. It reached, just; he pushed the end into the corpse's armpit and let the sapling lie like that, where one good shove would overturn the corpse, but he didn't shove it yet. He left it there and slid back into the denser trees and said, "We can't spend half the night here, we seem to be agreed on that much. If they're not around here we need to know that, and if they are we'll want to draw their fire."

"You're asking for a volunteer."

"That's right," Watchman said evenly, and watched his face.

Vickers said, "Tell me what you've got in mind."

"Get behind that sycamore and get ready to roll him over. If there's a grenade under him you'll hear the handle click—drop flat behind the tree and cover your head. Now either he's booby-trapped or he's not. Either way I want you to make a little run after you've flipped him over. Run out into the open three or four paces as if you're going out to have a closer look at the corpse. Give them enough time to see you but not enough time to snug down their aim. Three or four steps, and then break right and dive into those trees on your belly. Then run back through the trees and hope they take a few shots at you."

"I see. And you'll be where?"

"Down there." Watchman pointed toward the lower end of the pine-forest horseshoe. "We'll be on horseback and if you can draw their fire I'll be able to spot their muzzle flashes. We can get close pretty fast on horseback, before they've had time to fade back into the timber, and we'll have a crack at them. How about it?"

Vickers thought about it, visibly. Watchman looked at the sky through the bare treetops. Dusk; a handful of stars already showing on a field of navy velvet. Moonrise in maybe half an hour. "All right, we'll try it," Vickers said.

"One other thing. I'll need to know if that's Hanratty. You'll get a look at him when you flip him over. If you're pretty sure it's Hanratty fire three quick shots as soon as you have time."

"Then what?"

"You'd better stay right here so I'll know where you are. I know you don't like that but if you come chasing along after us you're likely to get yourself shot at by both sides."

"It's not appetizing. What makes you so sure they've waited around all this time?"

"I couldn't put words to it. Maybe a feeling they need to get us off their backs—they don't want to waste any more time than they have to. They want to get it over with." It was a lame explanation but he didn't add to it. The subconscious sorts and files according to experienced intuitions; what came to the surface was mostly hunch. He was beginning to develop a feeling about the way Hargit did his thinking.

"We may as well try it," Vickers conceded. "How much lead time do you want?"

"What time do you have?"

"Eight minutes past six."

Watchman took off his glove to set his watch back from six-eleven. "Roll him over at six-forty."

"That long?"

"We'll have the moon by then."

"All right," Vickers said, and when Watchman turned away Vickers said in a softer voice, "Good luck, Trooper."

"Sure." Watchman waved a hand and kept moving.

CHAPTER

1

The last ribbon of twilight faded out of the sky behind Baraclough's right shoulder and Eddie Burt said in a distressed whisper, "What the fuck are the bastards doing?"

They had seen them—shadowy movements in the aspens down below. Once one of them had come tantalizingly close to Hanratty's body. But they had never offered a clear shot, they had never come out of the trees.

The Major said, "The sensible thing is to stay put. Stay here. Let them come to us—we'll hear their movements. I want this finished tonight."

Baraclough turned his head and looked down through the pines. The tracks they had deliberately left there were easy to see for a distance of at least two hundred feet, even in the dusk, but it was evident now that the pursuers weren't going to fall for that.

Burt said, "Christ, the damned finish line keeps moving, don't it? These ain't no regular hick cops, not the way they keep one think ahead of us."

The Major's jaw muscles stood out like cables. "I underestimated them. I accept the responsibility for that. But remember who we are, Sergeant. We're graduates of the finest guerrilla training academy in the world. They've given us a little trouble because we didn't anticipate their intelligence—I take the blame fully for that—but just remember they don't have a chance. Now let's get ourselves spread out and wait for them. No more talking."

"Yes, sir," Burt said, and moved away, fifty feet downhill through the pines, slithering on his belly like an eel.

Baraclough remained a moment before he moved away. "We're using up a lot of time here. Maybe they're not coming in after us at all. Maybe they know we're in here and they just figure to bottle us up until they get reinforcements."

"If that's the case we'll move out by dawn. But we'll have a try at them first. We can't move freely with them this close to us, you see that."

"I do. But I wouldn't mind moving out right now, Major."

"No," the Major said. "We'll wait. Get to your post now."

2

Baraclough burrowed into a snowdrift like a child digging himself into beach sand; he left nothing showing except his head and arms. Wrapped in waterproof boots and an oilskin rain slicker he had no worry about getting frostbitten; the cold was uncomfortable but he had always enjoyed discomfort.

He could see the Major and, just barely, Burt down below; they had always made it a practice to set up in such a way as to afford one another protective fire. The mechanics of it were cut and dried, old hat to them ~~all~~, but what troubled him was a sense that something was out of place. They had consistently misjudged the quality of the men who pursued them: no matter what they did, the pursuers always seemed to have got there just ahead of them—Burt had been right about that and it was hard to explain it to himself. But when he thought about it he saw the Major was right about waiting it out. Whoever the pursuers were, breaking out of here now wouldn't get rid of them. Other cops, maybe, but not these three. It was a hell of a handicap not knowing who they were, not knowing anything about them; but of course that wasn't altogether true. Baraclough did know several things about them, the main item of which was the fact that these three cops were good. Very good.

A searchlight caught him right in the face and he blinked in momentary panic before he realized it was the moon, rising past the peaks to the east. The temperature had dropped fast since the sun had gone and he saw the breath steam down from his face, white and hazy in the sudden moonlight.

3

Watchman had crossed the stream before the moon came up and posted himself on horseback in the lower fringe of pines about forty feet downstream from Buck Stevens. If Hargit's bunch was here ~~at all~~ it was most likely dug in somewhere along this flank of the horseshoe perimeter because only on this side would they have an easy back door to escape through. If they were here they were somewhere in the two-hundred-yard stretch of woods above him.

His first thought had been to pick a position with a good

field of fire and wait for Hargit to open up. The sound and spark-flash of gunfire would give away Hargit's position and give Watchman a target to shoot at. But then he had vetoed the idea. It would have been playing the game by Hargit's rules. To Hargit this was a military exercise and in military exercises the objective was to annihilate the enemy: keep shooting at one another until only the winners survived. But that was warfare, not police work, and it wasn't Watchman's job to indulge in pocket battles. The highway patrolman's oath said "apprehend and arrest"; it didn't say "kill."

He had discussed it with Stevens: "They'll be spread out a little and one of them's bound to be closer to us than the others. I want you to keep the other two pinned down while I take out the first one."

Stevens had given him a lot of arguments, some of them unarguably logical, but a crazy notion had lodged itself in Watchman's head and he had turned Stevens' objections aside. Now he removed his gloves and checked to see that the flap of his service-revolver holster was within easy reach but he didn't lift his rifle out of its scabbard; he removed his left foot from the stirrup and locked his fists down in tight handholds on the saddle and got ready to make his run.

4

The explosion took Eddie Burt unawares. He wasn't looking in that direction, which was a good thing because it didn't night-blind him. He picked it up in the corner of his vision— the flash came an instant before the noise. Instinctively he swung his rifle toward the creek and then in the darkness that followed the explosion he saw a man break out of the trees, running toward Hanratty's corpse. A spasm peeled Burt's lips back and he laid his cheek along the rifle stock and steadied the sights with the speed of long practice and squeezed his shot, but he saw just as he fired that the running man had dived off to the left. Burt worked the bolt, threw a fresh cartridge into the chamber, fired again at the moving shadow in the woods. Baraclough was firing and the Major's gun barked once, and Burt chambered a new round and sought his target.

5

When Vickers made his run and Hargit's bunch started shooting Watchman slammed the horse up into the trees, not caring about the noise because Hargit's men wouldn't hear anything for a little while after firing rifles close by their own ears.

He slipped his leg over the back of the saddle and hung there on one side of the horse with all his weight on a crook'd leg in one stirrup, fist locked around the saddle horn, and twigs and branches raked his shoulders and head with wicked stings. The noise had excited the horse and it rammed up through the pines on the dead run.

6

The target had disappeared and Eddie Burt turned his head to scan the shadows, suddenly afraid.

A rifle started talking in hard echoes down toward the creek, inside the pines somewhere, and the Major was up on one knee, rifle lifted, answering that fire. Burt could hear Bara-clough's rifle above him and he swung his ~~own~~ weapon toward the gun by the creek but then he caught a tail-of-the-eye movement imperfectly and wheeled.

It was a horse. Riderless, whipping erratically through the pines.

A decoy, Burt decided instantly. The stupid cops had driven the horse toward them to draw their fire. He wasn't going to fall for that one.

He held his fire and switched his attention back to the bottom of the hill. The rifle had moved down there; it spoke again, three times quickly—or was that another rifle? Proba-bly; it was too far to the right, the first man couldn't have moved that far in these few seconds. All right, two of them down there. Where was the third one? Burt waited for one of the rifles to speak again, to give him a target. He kept the running horse in the edge of his vision. It was beginning to lose momentum, starting to drift; it wandered forward on a tangent that would take it past him, behind him.

In the pines below him a rifle barked and Burt put the horse out of his mind, steadied his aim and squeezed a shot. The buttplate jarred his shoulder and he had the satisfaction of hearing a man's brief cry: he had scored a hit.

The riderless horse had turned and was bearing down on him. Burt chambered a shell and threw an irritated glance at the horse. If the damned animal got in his way he'd have to shoot it. Then the rifle by the creek opened up again: either there were two of them down there or he hadn't hit the guy very badly. He shouldered his weapon again and fired another one.

Then the horse was wheeling right past him and he looked up in time to see a shadow drop free of the stirrup—right on top of him.

7

The man was trying to work his rifle bolt but Watchman was too close. He dropped on the man and when the rifle went off its muzzle was up in the air somewhere, harmless.

The man had the body of a heavy-duty shock absorber and Watchman felt the muscles twist and tense under him when he rolled for purchase: the man was flexing his arm like an expert who'd had plenty of practice on bricks and two-inch pine boards and Watchman had no liking for that kind of contest. When the man stabbed at his eyes with spread rigid fingers Watchman whammed his fist against the man's plunging wrist to deflect it and let himself fall across the man with his forearm against the man's Adam's apple; he jammed two fingers into the man's mouth and clenched them down against the mandibular nerve under the tongue. His father had taught him that: it was an unbearably painful grip, it paralyzed the mouth and jaw so that the man couldn't bite his fingers, it made the man go limp with agony. On the reservation his father had subdued belligerent drunks effortlessly with it. Watchman lifted the service revolver in his free hand and showed it to the man and held it against the man's throat while he took his fingers out of the man's mouth and got his handcuffs.

It had taken only a few seconds. The horse was drifting on past him, screening him from the two men higher on the hill. He cuffed the man's hands together behind the back and gagged the man with his own scarf. The horse was still moving and someone a few yards uphill in the snow said, "Sergeant?"

"Yessir," Watchman whispered. His prisoner was Burt, then. He put Burt's hunting cap on his own head and pushed Burt into a drift of snow that had piled up against a tree trunk. When he came up on his knees he had Burt's rifle.

The racket of shooting had died away. The horse was going back into the woods at a frightened trot. When Watchman looked uphill he saw one man moving across his line of vision, threading the trees; he couldn't spot the second man. He flattened himself in the snow and brought the rifle up and when the man in the trees stopped to search the forest Watchman had a perfect target, range not more than thirty yards. He worked the action to load the breech and heard a voice somewhere above him to the left: "Steve? Where do you think you're going?"

It turned the man's head and that was when Watchman shot him. He aimed for the right shoulder and the spinning 180-grain plug of lead snapped the man's body around under its impact.

Watchman skittered to one side up against a tree but no one answered his fire. The tall man was sagging, cursing in an abrasive voice, and then the other one was going fast through the trees, running in deadly silence: Watchman had a glimpse and then the man was gone, absorbed into the night.

8

The one he had shot in the shoulder had slid down with his back to a tree until he was sitting on the snow. He still had his rifle, clumsily upheld in his left hand, and Watchman spoke to him from cover:

"You may as well drop that thing. I've got a bead on you."

The man thought about it for a while and then threw the rifle down with a grunt of disgust and Watchman approached him cautiously, alert to the threat from that third man who had faded into the timber. He heard soft hoofbeats start up in the snow somewhere to the right, and he stopped and waited while the sound diminished with distance. It could be a ruse. He stood by a pine, his shadow blending into the tree, and said, "Get up on your feet."

"I don't know if I can. I think you broke my shoulder."

"Then roll over on your belly and stick your arms out to the sides."

He could hear the grate of broken bone ends when the man moved, slowly, bracing himself on his left arm, lowering himself onto the snow. The left arm went out at a ninety-degree angle, cruciform; the right arm was buckled and Watchman made another sweep of the trees before he stepped forward and knelt down and patted the man for weapons. He extracted an automatic pistol and put it in his pocket and stood up. "On your feet now. You can make it. Which one are you, Hargit?"

The man sat up slowly and sneered. "Not fucking likely."

"Baraclough then."

"You know everything. You tell me."

"Come on. Up." He gave Baraclough a hand.

9

He collected Burt and prodded the two of them down the hill and let his call sing out so that Stevens wouldn't take a shot at them.

Stevens answered in a weak voice hoarsened by pain and Watchman hurried in alarm.

He found Stevens seeping blood into the snow from a hole in his hip. Stevens tried to grin but agony pulled his mouth awry. "Jesus. You took two of them alive."

"Roll over and pull your pants down."

"Now you're a God damn sex fiend."

The horse stood ground-hitched in the trees and Watchman went to the saddlebags to get the first-aid kit. When he taped thick gauze bandages on the two holes in Stevens' hip he said, "Feel like any bones are broken?"

"I can't feel much of anything down there."

"That's shock. It'll start to hurt after a while."

"Thanks heaps, *kemo sabe*."

Watchman was keeping one eye on the two prisoners. Baraclough sat droop-lidded, ready to pass out, but Burt's eyes were bright with venom.

Stevens said, "Sam, you take some pretty dumb chances. I suppose you learned that trick of riding the off-side of the horse from your old grandpappy Crazy Horse."

"Matter of fact I saw John Wayne do it in a movie once."

"One of those movies where the cavalry wipes out all the Inyuns, I'll bet." Stevens pulled his pants up and suppressed a groan. "I take it these two beauties are Baraclough and the Sergeant. Where's Hargit?"

"Gone."

"With the money?"

"I heard more than one horse moving."

"That makes him pretty rich all by himself."

Eddie Burt tried to say something through his gag.

Stevens zipped up his fly. "Those bastards shoot pretty damn good at night."

Watchman took the first-aid kit over to Baraclough. Little pulsating jets of blood spurted out of his shoulder; when Watchman cut the coat away the broken bone ends showed white. Baraclough, half-conscious, stared down at the wound with bleak bitterness. Watchman said, "It's vein blood, not artery."

"Now that's sensational." Baraclough's eyes lifted to his face. "You're a God damned Indian, aren't you. If the Major'd known that . . ."

"If the Major'd known that, what?"

"Nobody ever took us apart before. But he'll be back for us. He knows how good you are now and he'll take you next time. He's a better Indian than you are." Baraclough smiled with his teeth.

It reminded Watchman of something Keith Walker had said. *A better Indian than you are.*

"He'll be back," Baraclough said again.

"Don't count on it." Watchman dressed the wound as well as he could. While he was pasting the bandage over the sulfa powder Baraclough passed out.

He got Buck Stevens' handcuffs and trussed Baraclough's good hand to Eddie Burt's wrist. When he walked back to Stevens he said, "You're going to have to stay awake awhile, white man."

"Going somewhere?"

"Vickers."

"Oh yeah. Where'd he go?"

"I told him to stay put till we came after him."

"Okay. I'll watch them. They don't look too dangerous right now. How the hell did you do it, Sam?"

"Nothing to it. Genius. A teaspoon after meals and at bedtime."

"Conceited bastard."

"Buck."

"What?"

"Keep your eyes open and use your ears hard. Hargit may come back."

Stevens' face changed quickly. "Yeah. Hand me my rifle."

10

Not knowing where Hargit was made it difficult: he didn't want to sing out for Vickers and give himself away in the bargain. But if Vickers caught him creeping up Vickers would just as likely shoot him before making sure of his identity.

The thing to do was to make Vickers show himself first. He went up along the aspens on foot and kept close to the tree trunks, resenting the time this was taking; he didn't like leaving Stevens back there alone with Hargit loose in the woods.

If Vickers had done as he'd been told he would be somewhere around here. Watchman stopped and groped in the ground-snow for a rock. When he found one big enough he gave it a heave. It made a bit of a racket crashing through the twigs and when it landed in the stream it crashed through a film of ice.

If Vickers was here it would draw his attention. But there was no sign of movement.

Twenty paces further he repeated the performance with another rock but it didn't pull Vickers out of hiding. Watchman took a chance: he whispered Vickers' name, loudly enough to carry a good distance.

No answer. He scowled at the creek. The grenade had made a mess of Hanratty's body. Moonlight made a silver shine on the snow-blanketed shale slide. It was very cold now; ice was forming quickly on the surface of the creek. Probably going down below zero. He wasn't sure of the altitude here but it was at least seven thousand feet. The top layer of ground snow was freezing hard; his feet cracked through it when he moved.

He tried to put himself in Vickers' boots but it was hard to do, hard to figure how the man would think. Time was going by too fast and it would take too long to find Vickers' tracks and follow them. He didn't want to leave Buck alone that long. He stopped to concentrate his thinking.

Vickers wasn't here; so he'd gone somewhere. Where would he go? Then Watchman had it. He turned around and went back downstream through the aspens, angling to the right away from the stream, toward the little hill where they'd left Vickers' horse. That was where Vickers would go because that was where the walkie-talkie was.

11

The tracks showed that Vickers had stood around for a while, probably trying to get through to somebody on the walkie-talkie, and then had led the horse up toward the top of the hill, maybe hoping to get out of the dead spot and pick up a signal.

He found Vickers at the top with his ear against the walkie-talkie. Vickers had his rifle and looked quite alert; Watchman put himself against a tree and spoke his name.

Vickers came wheeling around with the rifle and Watchman said, "Take it easy. I'm coming in."

"All right. What's happened?"

"We took two of them. Hargit's gone with the money."

"Two of them, hey? Not bad, Trooper."

"You raise anybody?"

"I just heard Cunningham talking. I didn't want to answer because I didn't know who might be around here in earshot."

"You're learning. Come on."

Vickers was pleased to see the two prisoners. Watchman had a look at Buck Stevens and when Stevens grinned he said, "You'll be all right, Buck." Then he turned to Vickers:

"Hargit might hide the money somewhere and think about coming back for these two, but he knows Baraclough's been shot and he can't drag an injured man with him. I can't see him caring more about Burt than he cares about the money—I think he'll try to get down in the foothills by morning. There are a lot of places he can disappear into. If he gets that far we may lose him for good."

"Then you want us to go after him."

"Not us. Buck can't stay awake all night on guard with a hole in him. You'll have to do that—and keep alert because Hargit may come back. I doubt it, but it could happen."

"One against one? So far he's slipped you every time."

There was no point answering that. Vickers turned to stare past him at the prisoners. Baraclough had come to; he was looking on with a kind of self-disgusted bemusement. Burt's eyes glittered with steady anger. Without Hargit and the money the two of them weren't much of a consolation prize: that was probably what Vickers was thinking when he turned back to Watchman. "We've played it your way so far and you've done a good job. All right, try it. In the meantime I think I can get through on the walkie-talkie. I'll get helicopters up here first thing in the morning to pick up your partner and these two and the corpse up the stream there, and we'll try to get another chopper up to the top to collect Mrs. Lansford and Walker. I'll try to cordon the foothills north of here as well as I can, so that if Hargit gets down that far he may be driven back into your arms."

"Fine."

"Anything else?"

"You're doing all right so far," Watchman said.

"I'm beginning to learn my limitations." Vickers smiled with white teeth, his features looking firm and frank and clean and fully in command, but underneath there was an absence of center: he had never found his own core. He was playing up to Watchman now because he saw Watchman as his only chance for redemption and if Watchman succeeded he wanted Watchman on his good side afterward. And if Watchman failed it wouldn't have cost Vickers anything to cement relations beforehand. The rest was a lie: Vickers hadn't learned anything; he didn't have the capacity to learn. When this was over, if they nailed Hargit, Vickers was going to claim credit for the whole thing because he knew Watchman wouldn't dispute him: Watchman didn't care about glory.

It wasn't very fair. But Watchman had stopped expecting things to be fair when he was eight years old. If he nailed Hargit all he'd get out of it would be another citation. There wouldn't be any promotion in it for him; there was never going to be a promotion as long as the old-line hairbags cops had control of the HP. Vickers would come up smelling like roses with a new job as district director back East somewhere.

He'd already caught the man who'd killed Jasper, in a way at least: Hanratty was dead. Baraclough had killed the other cop and they had Baraclough too. The money was of no particular importance except to the men who stole it and the men from whom it had been stolen. Altogether, Watchman had very little to gain and a great deal to lose by going after Hargit, risking his neck when he didn't have to, taking the chance when there were plenty of cops and FBI agents down on the Utah side of the mountains who could take the blame for losing Hargit if he got through.

In the end it was a foolish thing that boosted him onto the saddle of Buck Stevens' horse and sent him up into the woods after Major Leo Hargit. It was the fact that two people had told him Hargit was a better Indian than he was.

Nobody was a better Indian than Sam Watchman. He didn't know why, but it was necessary to prove that.

CHAPTER

1

The temperature kept dropping sharply, well past midnigh.;
Leo Hargit had everything buttoned and belted and wrapped
around him but the cold was in his bones and he cursed it. It
was the one thing he had never had to fight before. All his
fighting had been in semitropics or along the barren slopes of
the warm montagnard country of the Indochinese Central
Highlands. Up here now it was probably ten or fifteen below;
he knew it wouldn't kill him but he couldn't stop cursing it.

He reached the end of this particular stretch of forest and
stopped to scan the open slope above him before he put the
horses out onto the packed snow and ran across the rocks into
the farther pines, where he drew rein and hipped around to
look back across the heaped-up mountains he had traveled.
The moon was about halfway down; there was a surprising
amount of light on the slopes, reflected back from the frozen
surface of the snow that covered them.

He had a faint sense of regret. Steve and the Sergeant had traveled a long way with him. But he had seen the way the bullet had smashed Steve's shoulder and he knew Steve wasn't going to survive a horseback ride out of these mountains. He'd be better off in a police chopper. Burt had been a good man, steadily loyal, but in warfare you had to be practical, you had to take your losses. The world was full of Eddie Burts, competent and reliable; it made no sense to risk sacrificing a Hargit for a Burt. The money on the two packhorses would be enough to hire a thousand Sergeant Burts.

In a way being alone made it easier. Easier to disappear, easier to fade into the traffic and escape. There would be men looking for him at the foot of the range but that didn't worry him. He would isolate one of them, kill the man and take the man's uniform. He'd had plenty of experience infiltrating enemy lines. The only danger came from the rear. There was no way to conceal the tracks his three horses left in the crusted snow. And now, waiting at his vantage point and watching his backtrail, he saw a slow-moving dot detach itself from the shadows two or three miles back and advance down the slope like a crawling ant. But from the haze of kicked-up snow that drifted around the moving figure Hargit knew he was being deceived by mountain distance; the rider was coming along at high speed across the open there.

He waited long enough to be sure there was only one rider and then he checked the packhorses' lead-ropes and turned into the forest, and began to cast around for a good ambush spot.

2

Quarter past two. Watchman stopped and looked out across the ascending boulder field. The tracks went straight up and into the trees beyond. A good place to get whipsawed. He turned right and circled the boulder patch and came back along the upper timberline until he intersected the tracks. He studied them long enough to see what had happened here. Hargit had stopped and the horses had milled a little. Watching the backtrail. One of the horses had dropped a pile of manure marshmallows and Watchman got down to touch it. Still green and a little warmer than the frozen ground: forty-five minutes old, perhaps, no more.

From here he looked back to see what Hargit had been able to see. He measured the distances with his eye and decided Hargit had watched him cross that saddle two and a half miles above this place. So Hargit knew how much of a lead he had and knew he was being followed by a solitary horseman.

When Watchman put his horse into the trees he knew Hargit would be setting up the ambush somewhere very near and very soon.

He began to think about how Hargit would set it up.

A grenade, tied to a tree with a tripwire running across the trail. A likely possibility: and so instead of riding in Hargit's tracks he rode parallel to them, a dozen feet to the right of them.

The thing about this snow was that nobody could hide tracks in it and so what Hargit had to do was tie up his horses and backtrack on foot, either using rocks for stepping stones or trying to walk in the horse tracks to conceal his ~~own~~ passage. Then set up the ambush in a place where it looked as if he had merely ridden on through.

Watchman had heard somewhere that in Vietnam the favorite mantrap was an elephant pit with pungi stakes, a big pit dug in the trail and covered over with a thin lattice of jungle twigs and vines, made to look like a regular part of the earth. When you trod on it the lattice gave way and you were plunged into the pit and impaled on the upthrust poisoned stakes. Well Hargit wasn't going to try that kind of thing; no time for all that digging. That was no help.

The tripwire idea was attractive but that had a weakness too: if the pursuer took the precaution Watchman was taking now, it would fail.

Of course Hargit could simply be waiting alongside the trail to shoot him. But Hargit's mind didn't seem to work that way. He always set a boobytrap first and then waited to see who walked into it. If the boobytrap didn't finish you the rifle would.

A grenade didn't make a positive trap, not against a man on horseback. The shrapnel might wound the man but the horse might absorb most of it and branches might deflect it too. A grenade was an intimate weapon designed for close quarters and indiscriminate mass targets; if you wanted to kill one man with a grenade you had to explode it very close to him. Hargit wouldn't just sit up in a tree somewhere and throw a grenade at him; too much chance he'd miss.

Stalking, Watchman moved slowly, constantly turning his head to catch sounds on the flats of his eardrums. A search for shadows: he keened every tree trunk before he passed. At frequent intervals he stopped the horse and listened to the night.

The thin coat of frozen snow treacherously concealed an underlayer of loose granulations and it was hard to spot pits and gullies in the forest floor; once or twice the horse went in stirrup-high and floundered for footing.

It was the old Mexican shell game: under which shell was the pea? And of what did the pea consist?

He was on a downslope now, so steep it was almost sheer. Hargit's horses had bucked the drifts hard, leaving great wallows. The track ran down to the sloping-off bottom and penetrated a district of ten-foot boulders and broken slabs of rock that stood upended and sometimes weirdly balanced on top of one another. From this elevation Watchman saw that the tracks went straight on through the boulder field and into the timber beyond.

The air was still now, but earlier winds had blown most of the rocks clear of snow. You could walk around in there, jumping from rock to rock, and not leave a trace.

If Hargit was waiting for him it was probably in there.

He stopped in the trees and considered the alternatives. The slopes on either side of the canyon, going past the sides of the boulder field, were too steep to travel. If you wanted to get across to the far side you had to go through, or over the tops of, the boulders. Either that or go all the way back over the mountain and go around. That might take three hours. No, this was the place. Maybe Hargit could see him right now. Three hundred yards, uphill, the moon going down behind the mountains; it would be a tricky rifle shot and Hargit would want to wait for a better one.

All right, assume he's in there. Now how do I get at him?

3

Come on, Hargit thought impatiently.

He could see by the length of time the horseman spent up there in the trees without moving that the horseman smelled the trap. That was expected. The man had already proved himself, whoever he was. He wasn't anybody's fool. Well that was all right too. There was no challenge in doing battle with fools.

He'll find a way in and I won't see him when he comes. That was all right too. Right now he guessed the man was waiting for moonglow to fade out of the sky. There were a few clouds but the starlight was sufficient on the snow and on the pale boulders. The cop would leave his horse up in the trees, or maybe send it scooting down here to distract Hargit's attention; the cop meanwhile would be slithering down inside the trees, keeping to cover, coming into the boulders on his belly.

No, you won't see him until he's on top of you.

He had wedged the grenade into a crevice at the foot of a boulder and tied the string to the pinloop. He had the end of the string tied around his arm. When he pulled it the grenade would go off. The grenade was about forty feet away and there was a rock for Hargit to hide behind when he pulled the string so he wouldn't get hit by flying shrapnel. He didn't expect to kill the cop with the grenade but the noise would distract the cop and that was when Hargit would put a bullet in him.

If only it wasn't so God damned cold. He was shivering in his clothes. His toes hurt with a bony kind of pain that was altogether different from the numbness he'd fought against when he was leading them through that hell of a blizzard. Then he'd been moving, making an active fight of it, and that was what he was best at.

None of them knew how much it had taken out of him, breaking trail in that storm. At the end of it he'd been drunk in his legs, shaking with fatigue, an incredibly deep drained ache in all his fibers.

This coldness wasn't the blasting fury of the blizzard. It was still, soundless, clear; there was no way to fight it. Fifteen or twenty below, he judged. His lips were cracked, his eyes felt painful. It was hard to breathe. He kept clenching and un-clenching his hands inside his gloves.

The horse came plunging down the hillside and he watched it come. Nobody on board.

He looked around in the trees for sign of movement and once he thought he saw something sliding between trees but he wasn't sure and he just waited. He had good cover here. He squatted in a groined joining of two ice-split boulders. They formed a kind of cave, a right-angle corner with a flat shelf of rock lying across the top. Nobody could creep up behind him. The cop had to come at him from the front. Either the cop would come in sight between the boulders in front of him or the cop would come over the top. Probably the former; the cop wouldn't expose himself on the skyline by climbing over the top. When the cop appeared, Hargit would yank the rope and the cop would hear the click of the grenade handle flying off; the cop would dive for cover and the grenade would explode and Hargit would know where the cop was but the cop wouldn't know where Hargit was. That would give him his shot at the cop.

Hargit squatted with one leg bent to run, and laid the rifle across his thigh. Carefully he bit into the fingertips of his right-hand glove and pulled his hand out of it, and put the glove in his pocket.

The steel haft and trigger of the rifle were very cold to the touch. He wrapped his hand around them, deliberately disregarding the icy pain. Positioned his index finger on the trigger and lifted the rifle, braced his left elbow on his bent knee and snugged the stock into the hollow of his shoulder. He was ready to swivel toward any point within the range of his vision.

He lifted his right arm until the rope tautened. That was good: one yank of his right arm and he'd pull the pin. He wouldn't even have to take his hand off the trigger.

He settled in to wait. His breath made a frosty film on the metal breechbolt of the rifle. The cold air sliced into the bare knuckles of his right hand and the steel conducted frigid chills into his bones but as soon as he'd shot the cop he'd rub his hand to warm it up and then he'd put his glove on again.

He heard the horse clattering around in the rocks and he steadied his aim and waited for the cop to come to him.

4

Watchman wormed into the boulders on his elbows with his rifle in an infantryman's carry across his forearms but when he got into the rocks he laid the rifle down and left it. If there was shooting in here it would be at close quarters and for that a pistol was more maneuverable. He stood up, flat against a boulder that towered above his head, and removed the service revolver from his holster and put the revolver in the pocket of his mackinaw. Then he removed his glove and put his hand on the grip of the revolver deep inside the sheepskin pocket.

He moved very slowly through the rocks. He did not crawl; he walked, bent over in a crouch, because he wanted his legs under him in case he had to jump for cover fast. Every turning in the maze of tumbled passages was a potential ambush and he stopped at every pace to study the new contours that his progress revealed. Several times he turned into blind clotures and had to retrace his steps. Once he climbed onto a handy shelf and put his head up cautiously to look around. He saw only the piled-up rocks in a jumbled panorama. His horse was moving around a few yards away; he saw its ears and the saddle horn go past a rockpile. He backed down and circled the boulder and moved on.

The shadows were deep and threatening. He moved very slowly and without sound. The pressure of time grated on the raw exposed ends of his nerves because there was always the chance Hargit wasn't in here at all, the chance that Hargit had kept riding and was halfway to the flats by now, but Hargit was never going to find a better spot for an ambush than this one and Watchman had to rely on his ~~own~~ judgment of Hargit's conceit.

The adrenalin pumping through his body made his hands shake. He took a step forward, easing around the jutting shoulder of a house-size rock, and that was when he heard the snick and clack of the grenade handle flying free.

He saw it spinning across the granite and he flung himself flat below the rock shelf.

The blast was ear-splitting. Shrapnel clanged off rock facets above his head and a chipped rock splinter fell hot against his calf.

He was still rolling, desperately spinning his head to catch sight of Hargit because Hargit had to be there somewhere drawing a bead on him; he tugged at the revolver in his pocket and it snagged, and he ripped the pocket wide open dragging the gun out, and now he saw Hargit in the dim shadows under a balanced-rock cave, the snow reflections pale against the graven face, the rifle muzzle black and steadying, and he knew he didn't have nearly enough time to bring his revolver around before Hargit killed him but he had to make the try.

The rifle bore was dead-aimed at him and he waited with his body braced for the bullet while his arm came up incredibly slowly with the revolver. And still Hargit wasn't shooting, Hargit's eyes went wide with alarm and terror and disbelief, and Watchman snapped a shot from the ground. It missed; the bullet whanged off the rocks; and the rifle stirred in Hargit's arms but did not fire, and Watchman lifted the revolver at arm's length and pulled the trigger and saw, vividly, the jump and puff of Hargit's coat as the flesh received the bullet.

The frenzied glitter of Hargit's eyes changed focus. He was buckling, the rifle dipping toward the ground, he folded up over the rifle and fell over on his side with his knees drawing up against his chest.

Watchman ran forward and kicked the rifle away. The Major's eyes brooded up toward him dully, not tracking properly, and slowly the Major's right hand fell to his side. The fingers were bluish in the bad light and Watchman understood then: the man had kept his hand wrapped around cold steel too long, the fingers had gone rigid in the subzero night It was something Watchman had known and Hargit had not known and now, crouching down beside the man, Watchman heard himself say, "I guess I'm a better Indian, Major."

He saw the puzzlement in Hargit's dying eyes. Hargit had no idea what he was talking about.

The reaction hit Watchman then and his jaws began to chatter like a pneumatic hammer.

CHAPTER

1

The FBI agent was counting the money. He packed it back into the duffel bags and sealed it with adhesive tape from the first-aid kit and initialed it under the figure he had written: "931,670." Watchman signed his initials in a crabbed hand below Vickers'.

They had laid out the two dead bodies—Hargit and Hanratty—and covered them with blankets and they were all waiting for the choppers. They had seen the first chopper go over already; it had waggled its rotors and kept climbing toward the summit to pick up Mrs. Lansford and Keith Walker. Now they heard the flut-flut-flut of another helicopter coming up from the flats and Vickers got to his feet and shaded his eyes in the morning sun to look for it. The sun made little clouds of steam rise from the ice surface on the brush flat.

Baraclough and Burt were still cuffed together and Buck

Stevens lay on a folded blanket with his hip bulky in bandages. Vickers turned to Watchman and said, "Thanks, Trooper. I guess you know what for."

"No need to keep books on it."

"I'm going to give you a hell of a write-up in my report." It was said with the expansiveness of a man who could afford to be generous: Vickers had a livid feather to stick in his cap.

"Don't bother with any purple prose," Watchman said.

"It may creep in. I owe you, Trooper. I wish I had your skills."

Sure you do. You took my buffalo and my land and naturally you want my skills too. It wasn't what Watchman said out loud because it would sound like what it was: a stray thought in the head of a man who had gone too long without sleep.

What he said was, "I'd appreciate it if you'd save some room in that report for Buck. For a rookie he carried a considerable load."

"Don't worry about it," Vickers said, and turned to wave at the descending chopper. It created waves of blown-up snow under its rotors as it settled and Vickers shouted against the din: "Next vacation I get I'm coming up here hunting season. I'd like to go out after big game with you if it suits you."

"Maybe," Watchman answered, knowing Vickers wouldn't do it, knowing Vickers knew it. He turned and walked over to Buck Stevens.

2

He carried Stevens to the chopper, although the back muscles of his legs almost gave way. When he set Stevens down on the litter pallet Stevens' grin made a broad streak across his tired young face. He glanced back at Vickers and jerked his head conspiratorially and when Watchman bent down close to hear his words Stevens said, "Say, who was that masked man anyway, *kemo sabe?*"

Watchman smiled a little. And then he said, "Don't call me that any more, Buck."

Stevens searched his face and after a while nodded with slow understanding. "All right, Sam."